What could be better than a match made in heaven? Four of them! Set in the not-too-distant past, these four romantic novellas sparkle with tender sentiment and timeless spiritual values. They'll sweep your heart and imagination back to classic springtimes when courtship was more formal, but the newfound gift of love was every bit as thrilling as it is today. Enjoy!

Set Sail My Heart by Colleen Coble launches you onto the high seas with Miranda Leyton, a mousy, unassuming nurse on a five-month voyage to Australia. Remarkably, both a brooding doctor and a dashing lord find her completely maddening—in more ways than one!

The Wonder of Spring by Carol Cox crackles with the risks of assumed identity gone awry. Charlene Markin has been using a pen name to sell her grandfather's Western adventures to a charming Baltimore publisher. Now he's coming out to meet "the author" and she's in *trouble!*

The Blessing Basket by Judith McCoy Miller follows the up-and-down fortunes of Sing Ho, a Chinese orphan stranded by the San Francisco earthquake of 1906. Sing Ho is eventually overwhelmed when God pours out more blessings than she can handle—*two* marriage prospects!

A Valentine for Prudence by Darlene Mindrup brings a mysterious secret admirer to the door of plain Prudence Hilliard, the girl who has always paled in her sister's shadow. Even Prudence is surprised by the miraculous transformation that begins in her heart.

Spring's Memory

Colleen Coble

Carol Cox

Judith McCoy Miller

Darlene Mindrup

BARBOUR
PUBLISHING, INC.
Uhrichsville, Ohio

Published by Barbour Publishing, Inc., P.O. Box 719, Uhrichsville, Ohio 44683 http://www.barbourbooks.com

 Member of the
Evangelical Christian
Publishers Association

Printed in the United States of America.

Spring's Memory

Set Sail My Heart

Colleen Coble

Chapter One

M iss Leyton, how many times must I remind you that Alexis is not to come dragging in looking like a street urchin?"

Miranda stopped on the back stairway and turned slowly. She had managed to sneak Alexis in the back doorway, and they'd almost made it up the back stairway undetected.

"I'm sorry, Mrs. Rathbun." Miranda gulped and continued speaking a bit louder. "I took her out to pick flowers to arrange for the hall table, and she fell in the pond."

Miranda tried to do her best with her headstrong student, but Alexis was used to having her own way. She'd totally ignored Miranda's warning to stay away from the pond, and now mud covered her new sprigged-cotton gown. Why didn't Mrs. Rathbun notice how much trouble Miranda kept Alexis *out* of?

"Well, get her cleaned up, then come to the library." Mrs. Rathbun, her outrage evident with every movement, turned and stalked toward the library.

Miranda sighed. What would she do if she lost her job? She marched Alexis up the staircase and rang the bell for the maid to prepare a hot bath for the little girl. If only she would hear from Nathan! On

May 8, it would be five years since her brother left for Australia. In all that time, she'd only received three missives from him, the last nearly eight months ago. Now it was 1875. The past five years had been lonely indeed.

Miranda hurriedly bathed Alexis, slicked down the tendrils of curls that had escaped her severe bun, and rushed to the library, filled with foreboding. Ten minutes later, she climbed the staircase again on trembling legs. What she'd feared most had happened. Mrs. Rathbun had dismissed her! What was she to do? Where could she go? The only money she had was the small amount she'd saved to help with the voyage to Australia. It was tied tightly in a handkerchief in her drawer, awaiting a letter from Nathan telling her to join him. Now Nathan would have no idea where to reach her. Mrs. Rathbun wanted her gone by the end of the week. Miranda blinked back despairing tears.

The only other day she'd felt such despair was five years ago when her parents were killed in a carriage accident. Their home in Sussex had been worth just enough to pay their debts, leaving Miranda and Nathan only a pittance. She'd insisted Nathan use what was left for his ticket to Australia. She'd been fortunate, too, very fortunate. A family acquaintance had arranged this post for her as governess to one-year-old Alexis, and she'd been here ever since. She was grateful, but she hated London. Hated the hustle and crowds, the dirt and the clouds of black soot from the factories. She longed for fresh air and solitude.

She closed the door to her room and sat down on her bed. There was no one she could turn to for help, no way to contact Nathan. Hot tears coursed down her cheeks. "Where do I turn, God?" she whispered. A timid knock came at the door. Miranda looked up.

"Miss Leyton? Here's yer supper."

"I'm not hungry, Annie," Miranda said. Her face flamed at the coaxing tone in Annie's voice. The news had evidently already spread to the servants.

"Ye has a letter, too, Miss Leyton. Me thinks it's from yer brother."

Miranda drew a quick breath, sprang to her feet, and swung the door open. "Oh, Annie, let me see!" She avoided the kitchen maid's sympathetic eyes as she took the thick packet from Annie with eager fingers and sat back down on the bed.

"I'll leave yer supper here on the stand, Miss Leyton." Annie set the tray down on the nightstand and left the room after a lingering look at Miranda.

Miranda drew the papers out with shaking fingers. Maybe there would at least be a return address. There was a thick sheaf of pound notes, a letter, and some kind of legal papers. Miranda glanced at the papers and the money, then laid them aside to read the letter. He wanted her to come now! The money was to pay for her passage. She read on eagerly:

Guard the papers above all else, my dear sister. I send them to you for safekeeping as unscrupulous men would seek to steal them. I have reason to

*believe they will bring us much wealth someday.
Tell no one you have them.*

He then gave her the address where he might be found when she arrived in Australia.

Miranda looked over the deed and the money. The deed didn't make much sense to her. But the money—nearly one hundred pounds! A veritable fortune to her in her present circumstances. Nathan must be doing very well for himself. She thought of the last time she'd seen her brother. He'd stood on the dock and chucked her under the chin as she struggled not to cry. "It won't be long," he'd promised her. But it had been. Five long years. An eternity.

She unpinned the watch on her dress and looked at the time. Only 4:00. If she hurried, she could get to the quay and back before dark. She caught up her shawl and reticule, stuffed the money and papers inside, and dashed down the steps to the street.

As she hurried along the London streets, a brisk spring breeze tugged wisps of hair loose and stung her cheeks. It was perhaps foolhardy to be going to the East India dock unescorted, but there was no one to go with her. Miranda gave a slight smile at the thought. She had her Lord, and He would protect her. He had seen her through every other trial of her life. She gave a little skip of joy at how He had arranged things this time. His timing was perfect.

The dock teemed with all kinds of men and animals. Some stevedores hauled cargo to the merchants waiting with wagons, while others loaded the holds of ships bound for the Americas, Australia, New Zealand, and the Orient. Miranda wrinkled her nose at the strong smell of tar and steam engines. She looked out toward the water and saw ships jammed so closely together their sails overlapped. Which one would carry her to her new home?

A very large, fierce-looking man nearly ran into her when she stopped and looked around for a ticketing agent. His scowl deepened when she looked up into his face. He was about thirty years old with dark hair that fell untidily over his forehead, great meaty arms that looked as though they could break her in two if he wanted, and piercing brown eyes that looked her over and dismissed her as of no importance.

"What's the matter with you, miss?" he barked. "You can't stop in the middle of the street without getting run over. Move out of the way."

Miranda scurried to the side with an apologetic smile that he ignored. He shouldered his valise and brushed past her. What a boorish man! She watched his broad back disappear into the throng, then turned her attention to the problem at hand.

❧

The gaslights at the Rathbun home had been lit to dispel the gloom by the time Miranda pulled the front door closed behind her and started toward her room.

"Where have you been?" Mrs. Rathbun's harsh voice stopped her at the bottom of the steps. "Alexis has been looking everywhere for you. I didn't expect you to go running off like this." She drew her shoulders straighter. "I've reconsidered your dismissal. Alexis is fond of you, and I don't want to upset her. I'll give you one more chance—at a reduced salary, of course." Her blue eyes dared Miranda to object to the cut in pay.

Miranda tried to quell the joy in her heart, but she smiled and it bubbled up anyway. "I'm sorry, Mrs. Rathbun, but I'm leaving tomorrow."

Miranda felt the heat rise in her cheeks with the excitement of just saying the words. God was so good! He had provided a way out for her.

"Leaving? That's impossible!" Her employer's mouth hung open in a decidedly unladylike way. "How could you possibly find another position so quickly?"

"My brother has sent for me to join him in Australia." Miranda dug in her reticule and produced her ticket. "I'm leaving on *Euterpe,* the Star of India, tomorrow morning at nine."

"After all I've done for you! How dare you repay me like this? What will Alexis say?"

"You dismissed me just a few hours ago," Miranda reminded her.

Mrs. Rathbun glared at her a moment, then stalked away without another word.

Relieved the interview was over, Miranda hurried to her room and packed her few belongings in a small trunk that had been her mother's. The trunk was the only possession of her mother's that Miranda had been able to save. There were very few items to pack. Miranda had only four dresses, all castoffs of Mrs. Rathbun's that Miranda had made over to fit her diminutive size. The dresses kept her neat enough as a nanny and would serve her well now as she went on to her new life. A faded quilt her mother had made, a warm wool coat, her only nightgown, a comb and mirror, a few books, and, of course, her Bible all went into the small trunk.

When she shut the lid, she felt as though she were closing the door on a chapter in her life. The next time she opened the trunk, she would be in strange surroundings with people she didn't know.

❧

The next morning when Miranda crept out of bed, she felt as though she hadn't slept at all. She'd been so afraid of oversleeping and missing her voyage that she'd barely closed her eyes all night. Hurriedly, she gathered her belongings and made her way out of the house. By the time she started up the gangplank to the *Euterpe,* her little watch showed 5:30.

She stopped at the top of the gangplank and looked around. The ship was smaller on deck than it had looked from the dock yesterday. A figurehead representing Euterpe, the ancient Greek muse of music, gazed out from the bow. The highly polished oak trimmings gleamed in the early morning sun beneath sails hanging loosely on their masts, awaiting the command to hoist yards.

Miranda looked around for someone to give her directions about where she was to go, but none of the bustling throng paid any attention to her. She saw a sailor with a friendly smile and started toward him when she felt a terrific shove from behind. She tried to keep her balance but went sprawling headlong onto the deck. The drawstring on her reticule opened, and its contents scattered on the deck beside her. Shaken, she rolled over and looked up into the scowling face of the same gruff man who'd scolded her yesterday.

"You again!" he said, frowning fiercely. "Do you always make a habit of standing in the middle of the walkway?"

Was he just going to stand there looking at her instead of helping her up? She felt a guilty flush on her cheeks. She *had* been gawking again.

A tall, blond-haired man knelt down and began to pick up her papers and stuff them back in her reticule. "Good grief, Phillip, don't just stand there. Help the lady up."

The burly man grunted, then offered Miranda his hand. "My pardon, miss," he said grudgingly. "But if you persist in standing in the way, you're going to get hurt."

The blond-haired man handed back her reticule. "Lord Geoffrey Brewster," he said, taking her hand and gallantly raising it to his lips.

"Thank you," Miranda stammered softly. She glanced around and saw a crowd beginning to gather. Her cheeks hot, she started to move away from both men. If there was one thing she disliked above all else, it was being the center of attention. "It was entirely my fault," she said to the blond man. "I'm sorry for standing in the way."

Mortified, she hurried away without waiting for his reply. She just wanted to hide in the bowels of the ship and hope that hateful man would forget all about her.

Chapter Two

Doctor Phillip Jackson watched the tiny slip of a girl as she found a sailor who pointed her toward a ladder that led down to the 'tween deck. He felt a vague irritation both with himself and with the young woman. What was she doing always gawking in the middle of the path? Typical female!

Phillip's disgust with persons of the opposite sex had started when Tamara, his fiancée of three years, had left him standing at the altar and run off with his best friend. That was ten years ago, but he'd vowed never to let another woman close. Many had tried. He'd been invited to coming-out parties by the fistful, and he was heartily sick of being looked over as husband material. He had some inheritance—enough that some young ladies were willing to overlook his boorish mannerisms—but he had no inclination to change his marital status.

He was in no danger here on board ship, though, and certainly not from that little nondescript person he'd just knocked over. She was a little too plump for his taste—and too short, too. Her mousy brown hair didn't appeal to him, either, but he had to admit she did have extraordinary blue eyes, thick-lashed and wide with innocence. He shook her features from his mind and went in search of his cabin. As surgeon superintendent, he would be too busy to worry about a young woman with her head in the clouds. He would be doing far more than just doctoring.

He looked up when he heard a shout coming from the hold. Someone screamed, then he heard a call for a doctor. He moved quickly down the steps and found a woman of about fifty lying on the floor at the bottom of the steps. Her leg stuck out at an odd angle, and he could see bone through the skin. He winced inwardly. It was a nasty break. The young woman he'd knocked down knelt on the other side.

"I'll take care of her," he told her brusquely. "I'm a doctor."

The young woman set her chin. "You need my help," she said. "I've set my brother's bones several times."

He stared at her, then nodded. Her calm demeanor indicated that she wouldn't fall apart with the job that had to be done, and having another woman around might help keep the patient calm. "Follow me." He motioned to a nearby sailor. "Help me get her to my infirmary."

He pointed to the young woman. "Come with me. But no vapors."

The young lady nodded and followed him without protest. He and the sailor carried the older woman to the small infirmary off the first-class saloon. They placed her on the small bed, and Phillip noted that she'd fainted from the pain. "Just as well. Hold her leg here."

She placed her small hands where he indicated.

They were not the hands of a lady unused to any toil. They were dainty but looked capable, and he saw a callous where a pen usually rested. He glanced at her face and noticed with approval that she looked calm and alert without any of the vapors the women he was familiar with would have displayed.

Within minutes, the injured woman's leg was set, and the young lady helped him wrap it securely. He sat down on a chair and wiped his brow and frowned as he looked around at his new environment. He'd known it would be close quarters, but he'd expected a bit more room than this. It couldn't be more than five feet by eight feet and had only four bunks, two fastened to the wall on his right and two on the wall to his left. A small wooden examination table bolted to the floor occupied the center of the room.

When he finished his perusal, he noticed the young woman walking slowly toward the steps leading to the lower hold. She must be in second class or steerage. He frowned. Who was she? She spoke well and carried herself with dignity and grace. He dismissed the question with a shake of his head. It was none of his business.

"Thank you," he called.

She turned and smiled at his grudging thanks. "You're welcome."

❧

People crowded the lower 'tween deck, and it seemed huge to Miranda. Large open spaces were bordered by several doorways that opened into makeshift cabins at the after end. Several men looked her over and grinned. Her face flaming, she picked her way through the throng to a woman of about thirty-five with a kind smile.

" 'Lo, love," the older woman smiled. "If yer looking for the unmarried lassies, ye found us. Me name is Lucy, and I'll be the chaperone for ye lassies." A tide of laughter rose from the men lounging against the far wall, and she frowned in their direction. "Take no notice of the men, and they'll not bother ye." She gestured to the room behind her. "This here's our cabin. Ye can bunk over there."

Miranda looked at the bunk where she pointed. Thank the good Lord she was short. The bunk was about five feet long and eighteen inches wide. She'd just barely fit. On the other wall, two larger bunks were bolted to the wall.

Lucy saw her look and shook her head. "The late-comers will have to take those, lassie. Those are for two to share."

Miranda nodded. She would much rather have her own bunk. She held out her hand to Lucy. "I'm Miranda Leyton. I'm pleased to meet you, Miss Lucy."

"La, it's just Lucy," the other woman said with a laugh. "No sense in bein' so formal here. We're going to be spending many hours together in the next five months. We'll likely know one another better than we'd like by the time this voyage is over."

Lucy left her to make up her bed and stow her few belongings. Miranda felt the floor roll beneath her feet and felt a rise of excitement. It didn't seem possible her life could change so dramatically in just one day. She had just finished stowing her belongings when another woman entered the small cabin.

Her round, rosy-cheeked face peeked out from a mass of blond ringlets, and she smiled at Miranda. "Cor, but me dogs hurt," she said with a wide grin. "That last two miles near did me in." She sat down on the bunk across the room from Miranda and bent over her very pregnant belly to take off her shoes. "Me name's Mary," she said. "Mary Morgan."

"Miranda Leyton." Miranda couldn't take her eyes off her colorful companion. This was the cabin for the unmarried women. Should she tell her? She was surely married, wasn't she?

"Um, are you sure you're in the right place? I think the cabin for the married folks is a little farther down."

Mary laughed. "Oh, ya mean me babe? Me man left last fall, and I ain't seen him since. 'Course we never was wed legal. There ain't nothing for me in England any-more, so I took the last of the money he left and bought a ticket fer Australia. Some man will take me and me bairn over there." She said the words matter-of-factly, without a trace of self pity.

Miranda knew she should be shocked and have no-thing more to do with the young woman. But she'd seen too much heartache herself in the past few years, been snubbed and ridiculed herself, and knew she couldn't do it to someone else. Perhaps she would have the opportu-nity to tell Mary about Jesus.

She had helped Mary stow her things and settle

21

into the wider bunk when Lucy opened the door and peeked in.

"Miranda, there's a gentleman out here looking for ye. He didn't know your name, but it has to be ye he's describing." Lucy's eyes were bright with curiosity.

Miranda patted her hair down and picked up her reticule. She thought fleetingly of the tall blond gentleman who'd helped her up on the deck, but pushed the thought away. He wouldn't bother with the likes of her. She opened the door and faced the grumpy doctor, although he wasn't scowling at the moment. He gazed around at the groups of people with a thoughtful look on his face. She had to admit he wasn't bad-looking without a frown on his face. But he *was* still very large.

He looked toward the door to her cabin and his gaze locked with hers for a moment before she looked away. He straightened up and bowed slightly. "Miss, forgive me for intruding. I wondered if I might ask your assistance once again."

Miranda smiled at his obvious discomfort. She could tell he didn't usually ask anyone for anything. He seemed to be a man who was used to giving orders. He must really be in a bind of some kind. He'd made no secret of his obvious dislike of women. Or was it just her?

"I'll certainly help if I can," Miranda said.

He seemed to suddenly remember his manners. "Allow me to introduce myself. I'm Dr. Phillip Jackson."

"Miranda Leyton." Miranda held out her small hand. He took it briefly in his own, and Miranda was surprised at its warmth. He seemed so cold and gruff.

"I need someone to help out in the infirmary," he said abruptly. "You seem to be comfortable around sick people. I couldn't pay much, but it would keep you busy on the trip."

Miranda considered his request quietly. She would like to have something to occupy her time, and she really would like to help that poor woman. She'd hated to walk away and leave her in the care of a man, even though the doctor seemed very competent. If *she* were injured, she'd want another woman to help her. She nodded in agreement, and the doctor looked relieved.

"When do you want me to start?"

"Right now, if you could."

"All right. Let me tell the chaperone." Miranda quickly told Lucy she would be helping out in first class, then followed the doctor up the steps.

Chapter Three

The first-class section gleamed with the light bouncing off the highly polished wooden floors and walls and off the brilliant brass fixtures. A large dining saloon furnished with a mirror-smooth oak table and chairs occupied the center of the hold, and various cabins opened off from it. Dr. Jackson led Miranda to the infirmary beside his cabin and left her to offer what comfort she could to their patient, Dora McDonald. Miranda fetched a bedpan and helped her use it, then sponged her down with cool water.

While Mrs. McDonald napped, Miranda went topside and watched the tugs pull the ship down the Thames. She wanted to sing with the joy of leaving London behind.

"Mind if I join you?"

Miranda turned to see Lord Geoffrey Brewster's smiling face. She felt her own face flame at the warm look in his eyes. "Pl–please do."

Lord Brewster leaned against the railing and looked out over the water. "Beautiful, isn't it? I've always loved to sail out into the wind." He took a deep breath. "There's nothing like the smell of the sea—all briny and rich with life." He turned and looked down at Miranda. "Are you heading for Australia or New Zealand?"

Why would he care? In Miranda's experience, rich lords didn't care what the common folk did. But encouraged by the admiring light in his eyes, she told him about going out to join her brother.

"Have you heard from him much since he left?" The question seemed casual enough, but his intense blue eyes told Miranda that he really cared about the answer.

"Just three times. Yesterday I got the letter telling me to come join him. He's worked so hard. He says—" She broke off suddenly. She shouldn't say too much about Nathan. He'd told her to tell no one about the deed to the land.

"He says what?"

"That Australia is a wonderful place," Miranda said lamely. "It's been lovely talking to you, but I really must get back to my patient."

"I hope to run into you again, Miss Leyton," Lord Brewster said. "Please, call me Geoffrey. May I call you Miranda?"

"Of course." She knew her cheeks were pink, and she turned to go. As she neared the ladder to the first-class hold, she saw Dr. Jackson glowering at her. She sighed. What now?

❧

Phillip felt a stab of jealousy when he saw Miranda talking to Geoffrey. Didn't she know what a bounder he was? A shaft of irritation followed the jealousy. What was wrong with him? The girl wasn't even his type. He preferred the tall, willowy, blond type—like Tamara. He scowled at the thought of his erstwhile fiancée. He didn't like remembering what a fool she'd made of him.

"I'm not paying you to flirt with the passengers." He scowled at the look of hurt that crossed Miranda's gentle face when she heard his words. "Never mind," he said abruptly. "Of course, you need to get some air occasionally. I didn't intend for you to stay cooped up in the infirmary all day. But Mrs. McDonald is awake and asking for you."

"Is she in pain?" Miranda hurried to match his long stride.

"Just grouchy." He smiled slightly. "I'm a bachelor and not used to dealing with fractious women."

❧

Miranda was amazed at the difference a smile made on his face. He looked much more approachable. She stifled a smile. Maybe she was feeling more charitable because of the warm glow the encounter with Geoffrey had brought. Her thoughts whirled as she followed the doctor to the infirmary. Geoffrey had actually seemed interested in *her*, in what her life was like and who she was. It was a new experience for Miranda.

When she was fifteen, she'd thought she would marry Gerald Manchester, the young man who lived in the farm next to her father's. But when her parents were killed and the bank took all their possessions, Gerald soon found another young lady to squire around to the dances. The realization that the only man who had found her interesting only wanted her money still stung.

Miranda tended to Mrs. McDonald, then went back to her cabin to get her Bible. She thought she might study a bit while her patient slept. Mary and Lucy both waved to her from across the room where they were talking with some other women. She waved back, then ducked into her cabin. When she reached the bed, she noticed her Bible no longer lay on her pillow where she'd left it. She frowned, then opened her chest to get her pen. Her things were just slightly out of kilter there, too. Who had looked through her things? Mary? Lucy? She felt a shaft of betrayal. Why would they go through her possessions? She didn't have anything worth stealing.

Her eyes grew wide when she remembered the deed. Where was it? Her reticule! She quickly pulled out the deed to make sure it was still there. She'd never forgive herself if something happened to Nathan's deed. But who would know she had it? She frowned, tucked the deed back into her reticule, and picked up her Bible. Perhaps she was jumping to conclusions. Likely, Mary or Lucy had looked through her things out of curiosity. But just in case, she resolved to keep her reticule on her person at all times.

The next few weeks passed in a blur. The doctor kept her busy helping him. Miranda was amazed at the variety of his duties. He organized races and concerts on deck to keep the emigrants busy, made sure the passengers aired their bedding, supervised laundry days, and conducted lifeboat drills. Miranda wanted to do something to help her fellow emigrants, so she asked Lucy if she might lead a Bible study for anyone who was interested. Eight ladies were eager to join her. Mary drank in the Word of God eagerly and began to blossom spiritually even as the baby blossomed in her belly.

They studied 1 John. When Miranda read chapter one, she saw Mary's eyes get bigger and bigger. "If we say that we have no sin, we deceive ourselves, and the truth is not in us. If we confess our sins, he is faithful and just to forgive us our sins, and to cleanse us from all unrighteousness. If we say that we have not sinned, we make him a liar, and his word is not in us."

Mary stared at Miranda a moment as though trying to peer deep into her soul. "That book is wrong. You ain't never sinned, have you, Miranda?"

Miranda looked gently into Mary's eyes, then laid her hand on her arm. "Many times, Mary. More than I want to count. But God in His wonderful grace has always forgiven me."

Mary's eyes grew wider. "Then what hope does someone like me have of gettin' in heaven?" Around her the other ladies began to nod and murmur.

Miranda smiled. She never tired of telling about God's grace and mercy. "By Jesus only. He paid the penalty for our sin on the cross. When God looks at a Christian, all He sees is that the penalty was paid in full. All we have to do is accept Jesus' free gift of salvation. He doesn't put degrees on sin like we tend to do. In God's eyes, all sins are equal." They discussed the passage a bit more, and by the time the evening was over, Mary and two other ladies had asked Jesus to save them.

Miranda also began to teach a few of the children

how to read. She had twelve children eager to learn, and they kept the boredom at bay after supper before they trooped off to bed. After her self-imposed duties, she slipped away onto the deck as often as she could. She loved to hear the waves lapping against the ship and the sound of the wind in the sails. The sky stretched out endlessly until it met the blue of the ocean and became one with it. How wonderful that the God who created this vast, teeming ocean loved her enough to send His Son to die for her!

One evening she climbed the steps to the poop deck after Bible study. The stars and moon cast glimmers of light over the water. They were nearing the equator, and she took a deep breath of sultry air and leaned against the railing.

"Miss Leyton."

She turned and saw Dr. Jackson step out of the shadows on the other side of the deck. "Doctor, you startled me." They were still so formal. He'd never invited her to call him Phillip, though that's how she thought of him.

"You're out a bit late." He walked to where she stood. "Don't you ever rest?"

Miranda smiled and turned back to the glimmering sea. "I just can't get enough of this, Doctor. I sometimes wish I'd been born a man so I could be a sailor and spend all my days right here." She loved to listen to the sails fluttering and snapping in the wind above her head.

He leaned against the railing and glanced over at her. She wondered what he was thinking. He had just started to say something when a scream sounded behind them.

A sailor lay writhing on the deck where he'd fallen from the mizzenmast. Phillip was beside him in a flash with Miranda close behind him.

The man moaned. "There, son, calm down." Phillip put a calming hand on the sailor's arm. "Miss Leyton, would you fetch my bag?"

Miranda jumped to her feet and ran down the steps to the infirmary. But by the time she returned with the doctor's bag, it was too late.

"Yea, though I walk through the valley of the shadow of death, I will fear no evil: for thou art with me." Phillip closed the man's eyes and straightened up. He stared into Miranda's eyes, then touched her shoulder gently. "He's gone."

Miranda slumped back on her heels. Tears filled her eyes. She had no idea if the sailor had known of God's grace. Only God knew the destiny of this man.

Phillip helped her to her feet and she slowly began to walk back to her cabin.

"Miss Leyton."

She stopped and looked back.

"Thank you." His dark eyes probed her blue ones.

She raised an eyebrow. "I didn't do anything."

"You cared."

Tears filled Miranda's eyes again, and she nodded. "I must go," she choked out. "It's already past curfew." She turned and ran down the steps.

Chapter Four

Miranda bolted down her breakfast and almost ran to the steps leading up to the poop deck. Several people had become seasick in the night, and the hold reeked of vomit and human sweat. The seas had been stormy as they'd rounded the dreaded Horn of South America. It could have been worse, much worse. They'd all been glad when they left the rocky, frozen shores behind them. The air was still cold, but the sunshine warmed her face.

Geoffrey leaned against the railing at the stern of the ship and looked up as she approached. "Miss Leyton—Miranda! How good to see you. You've been avoiding me." The last was said with a reproachful frown.

Miranda laughed. "Not at all. I've just been busy with my duties." In truth, she never knew quite what to say to him. He had sought her out at every opportunity over the past three months, and she couldn't understand what he saw in her.

Geoffrey shook his head. "I must have a talk with Phillip. He needs to allow you more time off."

"I'm just grateful for the job," Miranda said. Geoffrey had to be the most good-looking man she'd ever met.

When he looked at her with those blue eyes, he made her feel beautiful and special. She forced her gaze away and looked out over the sea. A school of dolphins splashed and frolicked just ahead, and she laughed and pointed them out to Geoffrey.

"I'd rather look at you," he said. His intense blue eyes never left her face.

Miranda couldn't help the tide of heat that crept up her cheeks. She didn't know how to handle him, what to say. She wasn't good at repartee—she'd never had the opportunity to practice that art. She laughed a bit uneasily.

Geoffrey caught her hand. "I want to spend more time with you," he whispered. "You're like no one I've ever met." He raised her hand and pressed his lips against her palm.

Shivers ran down Miranda's spine, and she hastily pulled her hand away. She didn't know if she wanted to stay or run. How could he say such things when he really didn't know her? She was no beauty. She knew that and accepted it.

She felt a sense of relief when a sailor hailed her from over by the ladder to the hold and told her the doctor needed her. She said a hasty good-bye to Geoffrey and practically ran down to the infirmary.

"I'll look for you later," Geoffrey called.

She knew her cheeks were red by the way Phillip raised his eyebrows when she came into the infirmary.

"You didn't need to run," he said mildly.

Miranda put cool hands to her hot cheeks. "Mahoney said you needed me."

"Your friend Mary has started her labor. We have plenty of time, but I thought you'd want to be with her."

"Oh, yes!" Miranda's heart pounded with excitement. The baby was coming! "Where is she?"

"In your cabin. I thought it best if she stayed in familiar surroundings. Childbirth is stressful enough without being up here. I'm going down now to check on her." He picked up his bag and started toward the door with Miranda close on his heels.

Mary looked up as they came into the cabin. " 'Lo, love. Me bairn has decided to make her appearance."

Miranda sat down beside her and took her hand. "Much pain yet?"

Mary shook her head. "Just a twinge or two."

The women waited quietly while Phillip examined Mary. He smiled, then straightened up. "So far, so good, Mary. It will be awhile, though. Perhaps you'd like Miranda to stay and keep you company?" In the grip of a contraction, Mary nodded. The doctor motioned for Miranda to follow him to the doorway. "Keep an eye on her and call me if things start happening."

Miranda thanked him and turned back to her friend. Mary asked her to read from the Bible. As a newborn babe in Christ, Mary took advantage of every opportunity to learn more about what the Bible said.

After two chapters, she looked up at Miranda with tears in her eyes. "I ain't afeard no more, lovey. I want to thank you for showing me about God. Before I met you I was scared all the time." She gripped Miranda's hand

and pulled her close. "I'm gonna name me bairn after you and the doctor. Philippa Miranda Morgan. Sounds good, don't it?"

Miranda chuckled. "What if it's a boy?"

Mary shook her head. "It be a girl. I know."

Tears clogged Miranda's throat, and she couldn't speak for a moment. "I'd be honored for your baby to have my name."

"And I ain't going to live like I did no more. My little Philippa is going to be proud of her ma."

Miranda smoothed Mary's sweat-soaked hair back from her forehead. "She will be. I'm very proud of you, Mary. You have a lot of courage."

Mary grimaced as another contraction gripped her. She lay panting for a moment, then shook her head.

"Would you like a drink of water?"

"Aye, that I would." She pushed herself up on one elbow and sipped from the tin cup Miranda held to her lips, then fell back against the straw mattress.

"Try to rest," Miranda said. "I'll be right here."

When Mary closed her eyes, Miranda settled into her chair and opened her Bible. The long day and night passed slowly. Mary tried to sleep between contractions. Just before dawn, Miranda decided it was time to go for the doctor. She asked Lucy to keep an eye on Mary and went to get Phillip. He was just coming down the steps, so she stepped outside and waited for him.

"How's she doing?"

Miranda noticed the dark circles under his eyes. For just a moment, she wanted to smooth his untidy hair back from his eyes. Her cheeks turning red at the thought, she turned away quickly. "I was just about to come get you. You don't look like you've slept tonight."

Phillip shook his head. "Several of the crew had dysentery. Got any coffee?"

Miranda shook her head, and wisps of hair fell out of her neat roll. She pushed her hair away from her face impatiently. "I could go to the galley and get you some."

"I'll get it later." He followed her inside the cabin.

While he examined Mary, Miranda hurried up the stairs to the upper hold and found the cook in the galley preparing breakfast. The place smelled like burnt bacon and years of grease. The heat hit her like a fist. The cook grunted when she asked for a cup of coffee, but pointed to the pot on the cookstove. She wrinkled her nose at the strong smell, then poured a mugful and hurried back to her cabin.

She wondered at her own temerity in disobeying the doctor. But she wanted to see him smile at her one time. He smiled at passengers and chatted with other men on the deck. Why did he act as though she might steal his wallet if he turned his back on her for an instant? And why did she care if he smiled or not?

≈

Philip scowled at the mug of coffee she handed him. "I told you I'd get it. I don't need to be waited on." Didn't she realize by now that he hated to be coddled? He'd had enough of the fake concern women show to get a man. He wasn't about to be sucked into that trap again.

"It was no bother." Miranda pushed the hair away

from her face again and turned to smooth Mary's forehead with gentle hands.

Philip scowled again. He couldn't help a niggling bit of admiration for her. Every time he turned around, she was doing something for someone else. Between teaching children, helping with patients, and listening to the problems of various passengers, when did she have time for herself? But no one was as perfect as she seemed to be. She had some flaws hidden somewhere. With time, they'd come out. He'd thought Tamara was perfect, too.

He took a gulp of coffee and gave an audible gasp. It was strong! What did the cook brew it with—acid?

Miranda caught his eye and smiled. "I thought you were tough enough to take it," she said sweetly.

Phillip stared at her for an instant, and then he couldn't help himself. He threw back his head and laughed. Miranda opened her blue eyes wide with astonishment, then joined him. Her clear, sparkling laughter caught him off guard. Why had he thought her unattractive? He eyed her furtively and quickly turned back to Mary. Well, even if she was a bit attractive, he still wasn't interested. No way.

Mary moaned and Phillip leaned over her. "It won't be long now," he told her. He motioned for Miranda to join him at the bunk. An hour later, all three of them were covered in perspiration as a tiny body slipped out into Miranda's waiting arms.

Miranda blew in the baby girl's face gently, then began to rub the tiny arms and chest.

Phillip looked up sharply at the silence. "Let me have

her." He flipped her upside down and patted gently on her back. The baby gave a gasp and then another.

"Thank God."

"Amen," Phillip said. He looked at Miranda and smiled again.

"I didn't know you had such a way with babies." Miranda took the baby as Phillip turned back to Mary.

"There's a lot of things you don't know about me," Phillip said. Now why did he say that? He didn't intend to *let* her know much about him. He cleared his throat gruffly. "You'd better get her cleaned up and let her mama see her."

Chapter Five

Miranda hummed as she bathed Mary's baby. The past three weeks had sped by and they'd all grown to love the mite. Little Phillipa Miranda Morgan. Mary had insisted on naming the baby after the doctor and Miranda. When told about it, he had smiled one of those rare smiles that softened his gruffness and made him seem almost human. Miranda still didn't know why she liked to see him smile. Even though she couldn't say they were friends or that she even liked him, she had to admit an increasing respect for him.

He always had time for his patients. When Mr. Pettigrew went on and on about his gout, the doctor listened patiently. When the children played ball and nearly ran him over racing up and down the deck, he played with them for a few minutes before lecturing them gently on the fine points of manners. One of the children brought him a wounded albatross which he bandaged up. He wasn't outspoken about his faith but quietly lived it.

His main flaw was just that he seemed to freeze up and get gruff around women. Especially attractive women. Delia Lambert, a black-haired beauty in first class who seemed to want every man's undivided attention, had gone out of her way to speak to him. He froze her out after the second conversation. Adelaide Burton had also tried to catch his eye, but he'd disdainfully ignored her. The whole thing puzzled Miranda. Why did he freeze up around her? She wasn't a beauty like Delia or Adelaide. He seemed fine around married or older women.

She pushed the puzzle out of her head, dressed Phillipa, kissed her, and tucked her into her crib made from a crate and padded with Miranda's old quilt. The baby's thumb was corked in her mouth, and her delicate, blue-veined eyelids quickly closed. Mary also slept soundly, so Miranda decided to go up on deck.

The sun shone brightly, and perspiration beaded on her forehead almost immediately. She walked up to the forecastle and looked ahead to the far horizon. The sea blazed as blue as the sky overhead, and the salt spray hit her in the face occasionally. It was a good day to be alive. She'd been told it wouldn't last, though. Mahoney said a storm was coming.

"I've been hoping to see you."

Miranda looked up to see Geoffrey coming toward her. The warm look in his blue eyes made her heart speed up. She had to admit she'd hoped to see him, too.

He took her elbow and guided her to the wooden bench in the center of the poop deck. "I asked Phillip where you've been. He said one of the women had given birth. But I've missed you." He gently stroked the curve of her cheek.

Miranda did not know how to respond. He was certainly a very attractive man. But why did he keep seeking *her* out? Delia made no secret of the fact that she found Geoffrey attractive. Did she dare hope that a man like Geoffrey would be genuinely interested in her?

He answered her unspoken question. "I wondered if you would like to come to a party here on deck with me tomorrow night."

"A party?" The idea sounded appealing.

"The passengers are a bit bored, so Delia suggested a party. We'll have that motley orchestra play and just enjoy ourselves." He leaned forward, and his breath grazed her cheek. "Do say you'll come," he said with a coaxing smile. "I really want to get to know you better."

"All right." She felt breathless. They talked a few more minutes, then Geoffrey left her to go work on plans for the party. Miranda felt dazed when he left her alone. Geoffrey was interested in her! It didn't seem possible. She wanted to fling back her head and laugh out loud, to whirl around the deck and shout at the top of her lungs. Was this fever she felt love?

"What are you so happy about?" Phillip's gruff voice interrupted her thoughts.

"Ju—just enjoying the day," she said. She felt so foolish to be caught daydreaming. Especially by Phillip! She could feel her face flame hotly. She felt his eyes on her face and turned away.

"The sun must be hot. You look warm."

Was that amusement in his voice? She stole a glance at him and saw his wide smile. Her face flamed again, and she turned away. He wouldn't be smiling if he knew why she'd been daydreaming. For some reason he seemed to dislike Geoffrey.

Later that afternoon, Miranda looked over her sad choice of dresses and reluctantly laid out her best church dress. It was a plain gown of serviceable brown wool with a simple collar. She had worn it only for special occasions at church, since it was the best thing she owned. Her brother used to call her a brown wren when she wore it. He'd bought it for her to celebrate her new job just before he left for Australia. He tried to talk her into a flashier blue dress, and now she wished she'd listened to him.

Lettie Stanton, who bunked with Missy Gleeson on the other side of the cabin, had been a lady's maid until her mistress caught her sneaking out to meet her boyfriend. She helped Miranda sweep her hair up into a swirl of curls on top of her head.

"Cor, but ya look lovely, Miss Miranda," Lettie said. "I'm a wishing I could go. Robert said he smelled cake when he was topside a wee bit ago."

Miranda felt a pang of guilt at the wistfulness in Lettie's voice. The first-class food was far superior to the paltry fare in second class and steerage. "I'll bring you back a piece if there is any." She caught up her wrap and climbed the ladder to the deck. She looked around for Geoffrey and was beginning to wish she'd never agreed to come when she saw him coming toward her. He smiled tenderly when he saw her, and her pulse raced.

"How lovely you look," he said. "I like your hair like that." He touched a recalcitrant curl against her cheek, then guided her toward a group standing back by the mizzenmast.

Miranda knew most of the first-class passengers because of working with the doctor, but she'd never spoken with them except for short conversations about their health. Delia, clad in a beautiful yellow gown that showed off her lovely shoulders, looked up from her conversation with Phillip. Miranda felt a sharp thrust of some emotion as Delia tossed her head and laid her gloved hand on his arm. Was it jealousy? Surely not. Why would she be jealous of Delia and Phillip?

Geoffrey struck up a conversation with Mr. Pettigrew, and Miranda looked desperately around for someone who would talk to her. She saw the McDonalds on the other side of the mizzenmast and stepped toward them. Mr. McDonald had carried his wife topside, and she sat in a chair with her leg propped out in front of her. Even after nearly four months, the leg still didn't flex well, and steps were hard for her to manage. Miranda stepped over and knelt down beside her. "It's good to see you out and about," she told her.

Mrs. McDonald smiled. "My gracious, don't you look pretty, Miranda dear. Isn't it lovely to be out in the fresh air?" She gestured to her husband. "Wally about killed himself carrying me up the ladder, but he made it somehow." She winked. "Now if he can just get me down without breaking my other leg!"

Miranda laughed, and Phillip and Geoffrey both turned at the sound. Geoffrey came to her side at once. "I'm sorry. I had some business to discuss and didn't mean to ignore you."

"I was just chatting with Mrs. McDonald." She felt the eyes of both men on her and flushed uncomfortably. She sensed an unspoken hostility between the two men and didn't quite know how to respond. Before she had time to think of something to say, Delia strolled over to their small group and slid her hand into the crook of Geoffrey's elbow.

"Geoffrey, dear," Delia crooned. "Mama's looking for you. She had a question about that property you mentioned in Queensland. Do you have a moment to explain it to her?"

Geoffrey looked awkwardly at Miranda. "I'll be right back," he whispered. "It's business."

Phillip stared at his retreating back then turned back to Miranda. "I told you to stay away from that bounder! Don't you have any sense?"

Anger and surprise kept Miranda speechless for a moment. How dare he tell her what to do? She drew herself up to her full five feet and glared at him. "I'll have you know that I can take care of myself," she said through gritted teeth. "I've been on my own for five years and have made it just fine without any help from you!"

"That's debatable," he shot back. "And the way you're going on, you'll be stranded in the streets of Sydney with a baby in your belly and Geoffrey nowhere in sight."

Miranda gasped, then felt the telltale flush upon her cheeks. Tears of hurt and outrage came to her eyes, and she whirled to go. Phillip grabbed her arm.

He muttered something, but she was too upset to

hear what it was. She wrenched her arm out of his grasp.

"What?"

"I said I'm sorry," he muttered a bit louder. "I know you better than that."

She was too busy fighting tears to respond. She just shook her head and turned her back to him.

He grasped her shoulders and turned her around to face him. "I said I'm sorry."

He tilted her chin up, but she refused to look in his eyes. She didn't want him to see the tears, but one escaped and rolled down her cheek.

He touched it with his fingertip. "I didn't mean to make you cry."

Miranda thought his voice sounded pained, and she dared a glance up into his face. He did indeed look penitent.

"Forgiven?"

She sniffed and shook her head, but he smiled anyway. "You know you can't stay mad." He took her arm and guided her back toward the group. "Have your fun tonight," he said. "But before you get involved with Geoffrey, take a good hard look at the type of man he is. I don't think he's the kind of man God would have you love."

As the evening wore on, she found herself thinking about what Phillip had said. Were her feelings so obvious? And was it love she felt for Geoffrey or just infatuation because he was the first man who'd really shown an interest in her? It was something she would have to think and pray about.

Chapter Six

The pitching of the ship awoke Miranda, and she lay in the dark listening to the sounds around her. The waves slapped against the iron hull with a dull bong, reminding her of a great bell sounding. A child wailed, and a mother's soft voice shushed it gently. In the bunk under hers, Miranda heard Mary's even breathing and the occasional snuffle of tiny Phillippa.

She rolled over onto her other side and stared at the dark ceiling. She had so much to consider. What was it she really felt for Geoffrey? Phillip didn't trust him, that much was obvious. But did she? She didn't know him well enough to judge. All she knew of him was that he was gentlemanly and seemed interested in her and her family. She would give him the benefit of the doubt. If he wanted to spend time with her, she would go along with it and see what she thought of his true character. She would try to discover if he was a God-fearing man and just how he felt about spiritual matters. That meant more to Miranda than good looks or wealth.

She felt too agitated to go back to sleep so she decided to go up on deck and watch the sunrise. She quietly slipped out of bed and pulled on a wool dress. The chill in the air made her gasp. She felt in the dark for her shawl, then tiptoed out of the cabin and climbed the steps to the deck. The sea was choppy, and she heard the canvas sails flap like some great bird above her head. The tang of the salt air stirred her senses, and she smiled. It felt good to be alive.

A distant glow in the east heralded the dawn. She sat down on the bench near the bow of the ship. The stiff breeze made her nose run a bit, and she reached for her reticule. It wasn't there. Then she remembered. She'd left it below. She considered going back for it because Nathan's papers were in it but decided against it. She didn't want to awaken Mary. Besides, her things hadn't been disturbed more than that one time. She sent up a quick prayer that the Lord would protect her belongings and then settled back to enjoy the show.

"Mind if I join you?"

A bulky shadow moved toward her, and she shifted over on the bench to make room for Phillip.

"Gawking as usual, I see," he said with a grin. "At least you're not in the middle of the walkway." He sat down beside her. "Couldn't sleep? You seem to have that trouble a lot. Something bothering you?" The doctor eased his large frame onto the bench and looked at her curiously.

"The pitching of the ship woke me," Miranda said. She wasn't about to confess her vaporish imaginings to him. He would look at her with those penetrating eyes and say something that would make her feel even more foolish. She already felt that he looked at her as someone barely out of the schoolroom.

"You know, I've never told you what a good job you're doing with the patients."

Surprised, Miranda looked away from the lightening sky and into his face. "Me?"

He grinned. "Much as it pains me to admit it of a woman, you've done a first-class job. In my experience, women are usually out to please themselves and see what they can get out of a man, but you seem more interested in what you can give to others. Why is that?"

Miranda didn't know how to respond. "Why do you say that about women? It's just not true."

Phillip gave a snort of disgust. "You should go to a few of the society balls like I have and see the women circling like vultures to try to trap the man with the most money. They don't give a fellow with short pockets a glance. I had a good friend who was engaged to a woman like that. Another friend tried to tell him what she was really like, but he wouldn't listen. Until she dumped him for someone with deeper pockets." He scowled at the advancing sunrise and stood abruptly.

Miranda followed him to the railing and touched his arm gently. "Was it you?" For a moment, she didn't think he would answer her. Then his head nodded almost imperceptibly.

"I'm sorry, but you mustn't let it color your view of life and all women in general," Miranda said softly. "Men haven't treated me all that well, you know. I know I'm not beautiful, but that doesn't mean I don't have feelings the same as other women. It still hurts to feel rejected and unloved. But I've had the Lord to cling to. I know you're a believer. You must let go of the bitterness and anger, Dr. Jackson. It will hurt you much more than your fickle fiancée ever did."

He was silent for several long moments. "You're a good woman, Miranda," he said finally. "And I don't say that lightly." He smiled down at her. "And you shouldn't put yourself down like that. Obviously, Geoffrey finds you attractive." He cleared his throat gruffly. "And I think you're beautiful." He strode abruptly toward the hold without giving Miranda a chance to respond.

Miranda swallowed hard. Did he actually say he thought she was beautiful? She blinked back tears. No one had ever told her she was beautiful. Not even her doting mother. She made her way back to her cabin with a lighter heart.

She entered the cabin, and Mary looked up with anxious eyes. "Cor, there ye are, love. Somethin's wrong with Phillippa. She won't hardly open her eyes, and she looks funny."

Miranda hurried to look at the baby. Phillippa's pasty color and lethargic movements alarmed her. "I'll go get the doctor," she said. She ran to the ladder and climbed up to the first-class deck. Delia saw her come through the saloon on the way to the infirmary.

"I'd like to speak to you a moment, Miss Leyton," she said with an imperious toss of her head.

"Not now," Miranda said. "I must fetch the doctor."

"Surely it can wait. It's only for someone in steerage, obviously." She grasped Miranda's arm and started to pull her toward her cabin. "In private, please."

Miranda wrenched her arm out Delia's grasp. "No! I must find the doctor. It's urgent!"

"Well, I never!"

Delia stared after her with narrowed eyes, but Miranda didn't care. Some sixth sense told her there was no time to waste. She charged into the infirmary, shouting for the doctor. He grabbed his bag and followed her before she even finished her explanation.

By the time they were back in Miranda's cabin, Phillippa was blue. The doctor took her and laid her on the upper bunk. He moved her arms and legs gently, then picked her up and gently shook her. Miranda stood cradling Mary in her arms. She could feel her friend shiver with terror and found it hard to stay calm herself.

The tiny chest finally began to rise and fall, and Phillip stood back with a sigh of relief. "I want her in the infirmary for a few days with round-the-clock observation. I've seen this kind of thing before. Usually, we aren't so lucky. The little one just seems to forget to breathe, and by the time we realize it, it's too late."

Mary wrung her hands. "Oh, doctor, ye can't let anythin' happen to me Phillippa! She's all I got." She burst into torrents of tears and grasped his arm. "Please, ye gotta save her!"

He put his arm around Mary and patted her on the back. "Now, Mary, you must be calm for Phillippa's sake. I'll do everything I can. Why don't you get her things and come up to the infirmary with them? Miss Leyton and I will go on ahead with the baby and get her settled."

Mary swallowed and rubbed her eyes with the back of her hand. Miranda handed her a handkerchief and gave her a quick hug. "I'm praying already, Mary. You must pray, too."

Mary nodded. "I be praying for all I be worth." She gave an audible gulp. "Ye go with the doctor now and take care of my baby girl. I'll be along shortly."

Miranda gave her friend a final pat and followed Phillip up the ladder. She felt a rush of relief at the empty dining saloon. She didn't want to face Delia again right now. Little Philippa was all that was important. Mary would never be able to bear up under the loss of her baby. Miranda sent another fervent prayer heavenward. *Please, God, don't take this precious one now. Let us enjoy her here on this earth. Let her grow up and bring joy to her mother's heart.*

"Make up some kind of bed for her, would you, Miranda?" Phillip's gruff voice interrupted her thoughts.

She found two blankets and padded the bunk attached to the wall with them. A wooden lip went around the bunk, so she didn't think Philippa could fall out. The doctor laid the baby down on her side.

"You watch her for now and I'll go check on the sailors with dysentery." He touched her shoulder briefly, then ducked out of the short doorway and disappeared.

Miranda pulled a chair up beside the sleeping infant. She leaned forward and traced the smooth curve of the baby's cheek. Her skin was so soft, like goose down. Fear gripped Miranda's heart. She had a terrible feeling of dread as she watched Philippa's chest rise and fall. *Breathe, little one, breathe.*

Chapter Seven

Harried, Phillip hurried through the ship toward the hold where the crew members slept. The baby seemed fine now. He'd stopped in to check on her just as she woke and made everyone aware that she wanted to eat. When he left, Mary was preparing to nurse her.

Through it all, that faithful little mouse, Miranda, never left the infirmary. He had tried to get her to go back to her cabin and get some rest while Mary sat with the baby, but she'd refused. She did agree to lie down on a spare bunk in the infirmary for a bit, but when he came back in around midnight, she was still awake. The circles under her eyes had darkened, but Phillip thought she looked lovely.

He groaned softly. Had he really told her that he thought she was beautiful? What was wrong with him? He didn't want to get tangled up with any woman ever again, even if she were as sweet and kind as an angel. He couldn't get her big blue eyes out of his head. He grinned. Maybe he should check his own pulse. He surely must be sick.

When he got back to the infirmary, Miranda looked up and smiled. She looked tired, and Phillip checked his pocket watch. Two o'clock. Mary snored softly on the spare cot. "You've got to get some rest," he told Miranda firmly.

"I will," Miranda's voice was nearly inaudible.

Phillip looked at her closely. "What is it? Has something happened?"

She shook her head but bit her trembling lower lip. "Not really." She hesitated, then gulped back a noise that sounded like it wanted to be a sob. "I just have a terrible feeling about little Phillippa. When I pray, it's as though God isn't listening."

He put a hand on her shoulder, and she covered it with her own small hand. "You know better than that, Miss Leyton. God is always listening."

She nodded. "I know. But what if He says no?"

He knelt beside her chair and tipped her chin up so their eyes met. "If He does, we'll have to deal with it then. Don't borrow trouble before it comes."

Miranda sighed and nodded. She looked so young and fragile, Phillip longed to draw her into his arms and kiss away the pain in her eyes. He stood abruptly. He must be daft.

He turned away and bent over the baby. She opened blue eyes and looked up at him with a soft, unfocused stare. She seemed fine, but Phillip knew Miranda could very well be right. When a baby stopped breathing once, it was likely to happen again. He touched her tiny hand, and she grasped his finger with a firm clasp.

"That's right, little one," he murmured through a lump in his throat. "You hold on tight to life."

"There's no sense in keeping her in the infirmary." Phillip straightened up. "She seems fine now, and you can watch her just as well in your cabin. Maybe you can all rest a bit better in your own room."

Mary had just awakened and heard his words. She clambered out of the bunk with rumpled skirts and a relieved smile. "Lovey, you've saved my baby girl!" she told Phillip.

He held up a cautionary hand. "She won't be out of the woods for several months, Mary. You must watch her closely. It could happen again."

Mary's smile faded, and she nodded soberly. "Aye, doctor. I be watching her every minute." She bent over her daughter and, lifting her out of the bunk, snuggled her close and spoke softly to her. Miranda followed her out of the infirmary and down the ladder. Phillip watched her lagging steps. She was becoming way too important to him. Way too important.

༄

Mary insisted Miranda get some rest while she sat beside Philippa the rest of the night. Miranda was too tired to argue. She climbed into her bunk and fell asleep as soon as she pulled her thin quilt over her. Even the bong of the water against the hull didn't keep her awake.

When she awoke, it was light, and she could hear people moving about the deck. She heard Lucy's loud voice berating one of the men out by the galley. It must be quite late. She looked over at Mary and saw she was fast asleep.

"Oh, no." Her heart in her throat, she swung her

legs out of the bunk and, nearly tripping over her skirts, rushed to the baby's makeshift crib.

Philippa's tiny fingers were wrapped around her mother's index finger. They were blue, and so was her little face. Miranda knew there was no use in calling Phillip. God had come in the night and taken their little angel. God *had* been saying no when she prayed.

Tears welled up in Miranda's eyes. "Oh, Philippa," she said softly. How could they all stand it? The infant had crept into all their lives. She wanted to gather the baby to her breast and kiss her one last time, but she knew that right belonged to Mary. She touched Mary's shoulder, and Mary came instantly awake.

"The baby," she said and bent to look at her daughter. As soon as she touched her tiny cold hand, a wail burst from her lips. "I've killed her, I've killed her!" She pulled the little body into her arms, and Philippa's head bobbed lifelessly. Mary screamed again, a drawn-out sound of hopelessness. "How could I be sleepin' when my baby needed me?" She turned anguished eyes to Miranda and held out Philippa's body. "Do something," she begged.

Her eyes streaming with tears, Miranda took the baby and gently blew into her mouth, more to appease Mary than because of any real hope for reviving Philippa. After a few moments, she shook her head. "She's with the Lord now, Mary. I'm so sorry. I loved her, too." Miranda tried to swallow the tears in her throat and nearly choked. She laid Philippa down in her crib and put her arms around Mary.

Mary's shoulders shook with the violence of her sobs. "She be all I had, Miranda," she said. "All I had."

Miranda hugged her closer. "Shush now, Mary," she murmured against her ear. "You have me and you have Jesus. He'll see us through this. We can't always know His ways or understand His purposes. But Philippa is in a beautiful place even now. More beautiful than we can even imagine. No hunger, no cold. She has loving arms to hold her. We'll see her again someday." Where was Phillip? She longed for his strong, confident presence.

Finally Phillip's deep voice boomed outside the door. "It's me, ladies. May I come in?"

"Oh, Dr. Jackson," Miranda said. "We need you."

Phillip pushed open the door and moved quickly inside. He glanced at the baby. "Dear God, no." He pushed past them and bent over Philippa's tiny body. It seemed like a long time before he straightened up, but Miranda knew it was only moments.

He turned around slowly, grief on his own face. "I'm so sorry, Mary," he said. "I was afraid of this."

"I killed her, doctor," Mary sobbed. "I be sleeping when she quit breathing again."

Phillip's face hardened. "Don't even think that, Mary. Even if you'd been awake, there was likely nothing you could have done. We were lucky last time that she began to breathe on her own again." His face softened, and he patted her shoulder. "You need to rest." He rummaged in his bag and fished out his sleeping powder. "Miranda, would you fetch me some water?"

Miranda hurriedly poured him a glass from the

pitcher under the porthole, and he mixed some powder with it.

"You take this, Mary." He handed her the glass, and she took it with a listless hand.

"I don't ever want to wake up, doctor," she said. "I just want to go to heaven with my baby." She lifted the glass and drank down the potion in one long gulp as though she really thought the sleeping powder would give her the oblivion she craved.

Tears flooded Miranda's eyes, and she choked back a sob. She'd felt that way when her parents were killed and knew the despair Mary felt.

Phillip put his arm around Mary and led her toward the bunk. "I know this is a terrible blow. Just rest now. We'll talk later." When Mary closed her eyes, he turned and picked up the baby gently and motioned for Miranda to follow him.

They told the other emigrants what had happened, and Lucy promised to look after Mary and let them know when she awoke. Phillip left Miranda in the infirmary with the baby and went to find the captain to request a funeral. He came back grim-faced. "The captain said we must have the funeral this afternoon. It looks like a storm may be brewing by tonight, and we'll have to stay in the hold if it does."

Miranda sucked in her breath. "A storm? How bad?"

Phillip shrugged. "No way of knowing. But the captain didn't seem unduly concerned. He just said we would need to have the funeral first. Would you put Philippa in some clean clothes while I go check some other patients?"

There was nothing suitable in the infirmary, so Miranda decided to see if any of the emigrants would donate something.

Mrs. McDonald stopped her outside the infirmary. "My dear, I just heard about the wee one. I have a little white dress I was taking to my granddaughter, but I can have another made." She held out a snowy white gown lavished with lace and satin. "Please, let the little one be buried in it."

Miranda took the gown. It was as soft as silk beneath her hands and exquisitely made. "Oh, Mrs. McDonald, are you sure? This is lovely."

"Yes, yes, my dear." She wiped her eyes gently. "I lost a little one of my own many years ago. Please give the mother my condolences."

"I will. Thank you so much." She watched Mrs. McDonald hobble back to her first-class cabin. It still sometimes amazed her how the Lord always provided for His children. Mrs. McDonald was His instrument today.

Chapter Eight

Dark clouds hung over the edge of the world as the crew and some of the passengers met on deck with Mary, Miranda, and Phillip for the funeral. The air was still but held a threatening promise in the crisp air. The approaching storm would soon be upon them, but at the moment, the sails hung limply above their heads.

Geoffrey stood beside Delia and smiled encouragingly at Miranda. Miranda looked away quickly when Delia saw the exchanged smiles and frowned. The last thing she wanted to think about today was how she felt about Geoffrey. Mary needed her. The young mother clung to Miranda's left arm for support. Her eyes were filled with pain and seemed to focus on some far point in the horizon.

Captain Thomas Phillips stood with his assembled crew near the bow of the ship. The Reverend Masters opened his Bible and cleared his throat. Miranda's thoughts drifted. She knew she should be paying attention, but she couldn't seem to corral her thoughts. They tumbled around like thistle in the wind. She wanted to comfort Mary but didn't know the right words to say.

"And now, Lord, as we commit the body of this child into the deep, we ask that You comfort her mother with the knowledge that someday this small body will rise in the resurrection. Amen."

The air felt eerie, and the sky in the distance roiled with blackish-green color. The little band played "Amazing Grace" as Philippa's tiny body went over the side and dropped into the sea with hardly a ripple.

"Noooo!" Mary screamed suddenly. She threw herself toward the poop deck railing.

Time seemed to slow for Miranda. She saw her friend swing her legs over the railing before anyone could react. She reached out a hand to stop her, but the next moment, she heard a splash. She raced to the railing and saw Mary's head bobbing in the waves. Miranda didn't stop to think. She had to save Mary. She swung her leg over and started to go after her, but strong arms pushed her back. Phillip dove into the waves.

She struggled to follow Phillip into the sea but Geoffrey held onto her. "There's nothing you can do," he said.

"Lower the lifeboat and be quick about it!" Captain Phillips shouted.

Crew members raced to the railing and quickly lowered the lifeboat. Two seamen clambered down the rope ladder into the boat. They bent their backs into the oars and rowed out to Phillip's bobbing head. Miranda couldn't see Mary. Phillip kept diving under the waves, but each time he came up, he still didn't have her.

"Don't watch," Geoffrey said. "They'll find her." He tried to lead her away from the railing, but Miranda wrenched herself free from his grasp.

She ran to starboard and saw Phillip's head drifting farther and farther away from the ship. In a flash of understanding, she realized *this* was love. Not the way she felt about Geoffrey. She'd simply been flattered by Geoffrey's attention. He was handsome and a lord, but it was Phillip she loved. Phillip with his gruff voice and heavy brows. Phillip with his gentle, caring hands. Phillip with his piercing eyes that saw into her soul. How could she have been so blind? How could she bear it if something happened to him?

Scarcely breathing, she watched Phillip's head go beneath the waves again. This time the wait was an eternity. Suddenly, one of the seamen dove into the water and, moments later, had Phillip by the hair. He dragged him to the side of the lifeboat, and the other seaman pulled him out of the waves. Phillip lay motionless in the bottom of the boat. Was he dead? From her vantage point, Miranda couldn't tell if he moved. The seamen looked around for Mary, but there was no sign of her.

"Come aboard!" Captain Phillips shouted. "The waves are increasing, and we don't have much time!"

The sailors waved their arms in response to their captain's command and began to row toward the ship. Mary was drowned? Tears welled up in Miranda's eyes, and a sob escaped her throat. Was Phillip dead as well? If not for him, she would be at the bottom of the sea with Mary and Philippa. Her knuckles white, she gripped the poop deck railing and leaned over to watch as the men brought the boat alongside the ship. Several sailors heaved to on ropes to bring the boat up. She watched Phillip's face for any sign of movement, but he lay still in the bottom of the boat.

The sailors lifted him onto the poop deck. She dropped to her knees beside him and cradled his face with her hands. "Dear God, please don't take him too," she whispered. His skin felt icy and clammy from the sea, but she saw a pulse beat in his throat. "Thank You, God."

The captain ordered two of the men to carry Phillip to the infirmary. Miranda followed at once. She glanced back and saw Geoffrey staring after her with a mixture of rage and jealousy on his face. *He knows.* She turned back to Phillip. It didn't matter. Nothing mattered but tending to Phillip.

When they got to the infirmary, she had the men put him in a bunk. A bit of color began to come back to his face when she threw a warm blanket over him. She told the men to take off his wet clothes while she went to his cabin for dry ones. As she carried his clothing back to the infirmary, she ran her fingers over the rough cloth of his trousers. What would it be like to be the wife of a man like Phillip? To wash his clothes and care for his needs? To see him smile when he came home from the end of a long day?

She shook herself out of her revery. She would never know. Phillip had shown no indication he felt anything beyond a general admiration of her abilities. He'd told her she was beautiful, but there had been no emotion in his face when he said it. He might as well have told her that her hair was brown.

When she got back to the infirmary, she gave his clothing to Flannery and told him to help the doctor dress. Moments later, Miranda heard Phillip bellow.

"I can dress myself! I'm not an invalid. And tell that Miss Leyton I don't want her hovering over me like I'm one of her patients."

After a few more growls and barks, Flannery opened the door with a wry grin and stepped outside. "He said—"

"I know what he said," Miranda interrupted. "Is he dressed?"

"Yes, miss."

"Fine. You can go back to your duties." Miranda squared her shoulders and opened the door.

Phillip didn't look at her as she came in. He sat on the edge of the bunk, buttoning his shirt. A gash still leaked blood on his forehead, and several alarming bruises already darkened the skin of his right cheekbone.

"Don't start with me," he said when he saw her pick up bandages and ointment. "I'm fine."

Miranda advanced to the bunk and poked him in the chest with her finger. "Right now, I'm the doctor. I'll say when you get up and what you do. I'll decide when you're ready for duty again." Every time she said "I'll," she poked him in the chest.

His eyes widened, and he burst into laughter. "Oh,

is that right? And just who do you think you are, Miss Leyton, to be telling me what to do?"

Miranda's smile died. "I'm the one whose life you saved today. I thank you for that, Dr. Jackson. It was a brave thing you did—jumping into the sea like that."

Phillip sobered instantly. "Mary?"

Miranda shook her head. "No one could find her."

Phillip was silent for several long moments. "She wanted to be with Philippa. Perhaps God in His wisdom chose to give her the desire of her heart."

Miranda swallowed hard and suddenly found herself sobbing against Phillip's chest. He held her close, and she could smell the salty tang of his skin. She clutched his shirt with her fists and burrowed deeper into his arms. She wished she never had to leave the sanctuary of his embrace. What a marvelous thing marriage to a man like this would be. Remembering that state would never be for her, she pulled away and fished for her handkerchief. "I'm sorry," she muttered.

"Don't be." He smiled crookedly. "I didn't mind. Of course, now I have to change my shirt again."

Miranda sniffled and forced a watery smile. Time seemed to stand still. Phillip stared into her eyes. She couldn't read the expression on his face. She didn't have enough experience with men to know what he was thinking. She wished desperately that he would kiss her, but he released her arms and stood up.

"Well, Miss Leyton, with your permission, I'll go tend to my patients."

"Not until I bandage the wound on your forehead,"

Miranda said firmly.

Phillip sighed but gave in to her demand. All the while Miranda cleaned and wrapped the cuts, she was conscious of his eyes on her. Her fingers felt clumsy, and the bandaging took much longer than it should have. When he strode out of the infirmary to check on his patients, she felt bereft. She'd better get used to being without him. When they reached Australia—probably sometime next week—she'd likely never see him again.

Chapter Nine

The ship pitched and rolled. Phillip found it hard to keep his footing as he checked on the sick sailors. The ship shuddered suddenly and he fell to the floor of the 'tween deck. He heard men shouting topside and struggled to his feet. The ship rolled again and he staggered.

The storm had arrived. The wind howled around the porthole above his head, and he found it hard to keep to his feet. He made his way to the first-class deck of the ship and found clusters of passengers huddled in groups. He heard women crying and men praying aloud for deliverance.

He spotted Miranda with Delia, Geoffrey, and Mr. and Mrs. McDonald against the hull on the port side of the ship. Her gaze caught and held his. He wanted to go to her and take her in his arms again. He shook himself mentally. There was no room for a woman in his life. Why did he have to keep reminding himself of that fact? But those moments when he'd held her had seemed so right. Her head had just come to his chest and she fit in his arms as though she'd been made for that spot.

Someone screamed as water poured into the hold

from above. "Don't panic!" The ship pitched and yawed with the violence of the waves crashing against it. Time and again, the ship tossed them to the deck as it crested the mountainous waves, paused, and slid down into the depths again. Most of the passengers gave up trying to stay on their feet and simply stayed on the floor and braced themselves against the bulkhead or the hull.

Mrs. McDonald fell against the table, and a gash on her head gushed blood. Dragging his bag with him, Phillip crawled over to her and took out some bandages.

She smiled at him gratefully. "Always right there when we need you, aren't you, Doctor?"

He smiled at her. "I *am* the doctor," he reminded her.

She saw him look over at Miranda. "She's a lovely girl, is our Miranda," she said. "The man who takes her to wife will be a lucky fellow."

"I'm not looking for a wife," he told her. He avoided her eyes, afraid of what she might read in his own.

"More's the pity. I think you need her."

Startled, he looked up from his bandaging. "Need her?"

Mrs. McDonald nodded. "You have a hole in your life, Doctor. I've seen it. You don't want anyone to get too close. What you don't realize is that without pain, there is no real life. Without the chance of hurt, no real pleasure exists. Without someone like Miranda who will love you in spite of yourself, you'll drift through life never having really lived. Why do you think God gave us marriage and that special love for another human being?"

Phillip shrugged, intrigued in spite of himself. "I've

never really thought about it."

"Only as we learn to love do we grow more like our Savior. In marriage, we learn what it is to give uncon-ditional love, to forgive and be forgiven, to hurt and allow someone to bind our wounds, to step outside our-selves and put someone else's desires before our own." She wagged a finger at him. "I know I'm a meddling old woman, but I can see what's right in front of my nose."

She leaned forward and whispered gently. "You *need* Miranda, Doctor. Don't be too proud to admit it." She leaned back against the bulkhead and closed her eyes.

Phillip stared at her for a moment before moving on to the next patient. He would think about what she said when he had time.

Miranda didn't know when she'd been more tired. The stress of the day had sapped her strength. The storm raged around her, but she was almost too tired to be afraid. Whenever the terror seized her by the throat, though, she recalled the words of David in Psalm 32: *For this shall every one that is godly pray unto thee in a time when thou mayest be found: surely in the floods of great waters they shall not come nigh unto him. Thou art my hid-ing place; thou shalt preserve me from trouble; thou shalt compass me about with songs of deliverance.*

As the storm intensified and she sat praying silently, Geoffrey slid over closer to her. "How can you be so calm?" he burst out. "We're probably all going to die out here in this storm."

"Because God is in control." The words popped out

before she had time to think, and she felt the heat of a blush warm her cheeks. It was one thing to talk about her faith to other women or to hurting steerage passengers, but to speak of such things to a lord was another thing altogether.

"Do you really believe that?" Geoffrey shook his head. "What about what happened to Mary and her baby? Was God in control of that, too?" He gave a derisive laugh. "I prefer to believe in things I can see and touch."

"Can you see and touch the wind?" Miranda asked. She wasn't sure where the words were coming from. "How about the sunshine? You can't touch it, but you can feel its warmth. That's the way it is with God. We see manifestations of His love and His care for us everywhere. Sometimes He allows things we don't understand, like Mary and Philippa, but He always has a plan and a purpose for everything He allows. And if He chooses for this ship to be destroyed, and you or me to be saved and no one else, or for us to die and others to be saved, that's what will happen."

Geoffrey shook his head. "You go ahead and believe that if it makes you feel better. But as for me, I'll stick with the tangible."

Miranda fell silent. There was nothing more she could say. Several hours later the storm finally subsided. She looked over at Geoffrey, but he didn't look her way. Would he even remember the words she said? She got to her feet and found she could stand without being thrown to the deck. She looked around for Phillip, but he was tending some cuts and bruises, so she climbed down the ladder to the 'tween deck.

Miranda couldn't see a thing. There were few windows middeck, and no moon shone in the dark night. The storm had been too violent for anyone to dare light a candle or lantern. She'd light a lantern and see who needed help. She picked up the lantern and began to tend to the injured emigrants. She sang hymns as she bandaged cuts and scrapes and soothed distraught women and children. Gradually everyone calmed down. By the time Phillip climbed down the ladder, most of the injured had been attended to.

He stood for a moment, listening to her sing. "You have a beautiful voice." He cleared his throat gruffly and looked away. "Do you have anyone you think I should see?"

"Several. Lucy has a badly sprained arm, and a man against the starboard hull has a cut I think you should look at." She felt suddenly shy in his presence. Her feelings were still too new for her to feel the old camaraderie she used to feel as they worked side by side. "I'll be in my cabin with Lucy when you're done with the redheaded fellow over there." She pointed to the man against the starboard hull with a cut on his forehead that still streamed blood.

She watched Phillip cross the hold, then gave a tiny sigh and went to her cabin. Lucy was sleeping, so she began to put away the things that lay strewn across the floor. Only when she was almost finished did she realize that she hadn't seen her reticule. Her heart seemed to stop. It had to be here! It just had to be. She went around the tiny cabin, searching in every crevice and corner. She checked all the chests, under the mattresses, everywhere she could think of.

She went to Lucy's bunk and shook her gently. Lucy opened her eyes groggily. "Have you been in here the whole time?" she asked her.

"Yes," Lucy sat up with an effort. "Except for when that nice Dr. Jackson come down and said you needed your reticule. I found it for him and took it out to him."

Miranda stared at her. Phillip took her reticule? She hadn't asked him to fetch it for her, had she? She shook her head in puzzlement. No, of course she hadn't. She must get it back. It had all her money, but more importantly, it held Nathan's deed. Why would Phillip take her things? Her throat tight, she went to find Phillip.

Chapter Ten

Miranda looked around the hold but couldn't see Phillip anywhere. She felt violated and betrayed. She'd never had anything stolen before, and to have someone she respected and loved take something of hers in such an odd way baffled and hurt her more than she ever would have imagined.

Perhaps he'd gone back to the saloon. She gathered her skirts and managed to climb the ladder in spite of the pitching ship. She peeked into the infirmary, but it was deserted. She thought about going to his cabin, but she shrank at the idea. Was he even now looking through her personal things and laughing at her miserable stash of funds?

Miranda bit her lip and forced back the tears. What should she do? Who could she turn to? The captain? He seemed such an austere, controlled man. He would look at her with those pale blue eyes, and she would feel small and insignificant. But she had no choice.

She turned to go the captain's quarters when she caught sight of Phillip's familiar untidy head of dark hair. Sudden anger quickened her step, and she hurried to catch him. He looked surprised when she caught his arm.

If she hadn't been so upset, she would have been ashamed of her forwardness. "What have you done with it?"

Phillip knit his heavy brows together in puzzlement. "What are you talking about?"

"Don't pretend you don't know what I'm talking about! Lucy told me you came and took my reticule. She said you told her I asked you to come get it."

Phillip stared down at her for a long moment. "I don't know what you're talking about. I didn't take your reticule. When would I have had time? I've been tending to patients."

Miranda was suddenly furious. Angrier than she had ever been before in her life. How dare he lie to her? She hated lies. Before she realized what she was doing, she raised her hand and slapped him hard across the face. Her hand left a red imprint on his cheek.

"Have you gone mad?" he asked slowly, his eyes wide with disbelief. He took hold of her shoulders and shook her a bit. "Listen to me. I did not take your reticule. Lucy was mistaken. Use your head. I've been treating patients. You saw me."

Slowly, the anger faded. Phillip was right. She'd sat right over there in that corner and watched him tending to cuts and bumps during and after the storm. Lucy had just awoken. Could she have been dreaming? She suddenly saw the red imprint of her hand stark against his cheek. Had she really done that? Horror filled her. She didn't even step on bugs. Where had that anger come from? Tears filled her eyes.

"I'm so sorry," she whispered. She whirled and ran

for the ladder. She heard Phillip shout her name, but she didn't turn. She was filled with humiliation. What must he think of her? How could she ever face him again?

Ignoring the stares, she ran across the hold and into her cabin. No one was inside, not even Lucy, and she thanked God for a few quiet moments. She threw herself across her bunk and burst into sobs. She loved him, yet she'd slapped him like a fishwife! Even if he had stolen her reticule, she'd been raised better than to behave that way. She sat up and wiped her face. How could she apologize? What must he think of her now?

Lucy opened the door and hurried inside. "I'm sorry, Miranda," she burst out. "I shouldn't have done it. But he gave me five pounds, and I needed the money." She held out the crumpled notes with a shaking hand. "It weren't the nice doctor what took your reticule. Lord Geoffrey had me pinch it for him."

Geoffrey. What would Geoffrey want with her reticule? "Did he say what he wanted with it?" Was this another lie? Nothing made any sense.

Lucy shook her head. "Just that you had something that belonged to him."

Miranda sighed. She didn't understand. But right now she had to find Phillip and apologize. She climbed the ladder on trembling legs.

❧

Scowling, Phillip cleaned his instruments in the metal basin then sat down in the chair to rest while they airdried. Miranda was a puzzle. Just when he thought he knew her, she did something so totally out of character.

Meek, gentle Miranda had actually slapped him! How could she believe he would steal from her, from anyone?

He felt anger but an even greater sense of hurt. Why should he care what she thought of him? Yet he had to admit, he *did* care. Very much. He'd thought he'd seen admiration in her eyes a few times. Was he mistaken? Did she really think so little of him that she immediately suspected him of being a common thief?

He looked up at a timid knock on the door. Her face white, Miranda stood there. "What do you want? What have I done now? Stolen from someone else? Have you called the captain to report a criminal in our midst?"

"I'm sorry." Miranda's voice was nearly inaudible. "I talked to Lucy. She said it was Lord Geoffrey who took my reticule, not you."

Phillip snorted. That idea was nearly as preposterous as the thought that he would steal. "Geoffrey has plenty of money. He has no need of yours." The girl was mad. Perhaps he didn't know her at all.

Miranda shook her head firmly. "Lucy was very adamant about it. Lord Geoffrey paid her to steal it for him. He told her I had something that belonged to him."

"Like what? Your heart?" Phillip couldn't believe the jealous words had come from his lips. He scowled to cover his discomfiture.

"I don't know, unless—" She broke off.

"What?" Phillip couldn't imagine what she could have that would be valuable enough to drive a man of Geoffrey's stature to resort to theft.

She drew a deep breath. "I'm so sorry for the way I

doubted you, Dr. Jackson. I know you would never do something like this. But I had some very valuable papers in my reticule. My brother sent me the deed to some land in Queensland and told me to take care of it for him. That it would be safer with me. Now I've lost it, and I don't know what to do."

"Queensland, you say." Phillip stroked his chin. "They've recently discovered gold in Queensland." He thought a moment and suddenly remembered a conversation he'd overheard. "Perhaps Lucy was telling the truth after all."

"What do you mean?"

"I heard Geoffrey tell Delia that he would be unbelievably wealthy soon. That he would soon be getting the deed to a vastly rich goldfield in Queensland." The scoundrel! He had known Geoffrey was not a man of honor, but to steal from Miranda put him beyond the pale.

"Bu—but how would he know I had the deed?" Miranda frowned in puzzlement.

"I don't know, but he obviously found out somehow. Has he ever held your reticule for you?"

Miranda shook her head. "I've tried to keep it close to me." She paused. "Wait, I just remembered something. When I first boarded the ship, I dropped my reticule and everything spilled out. Geoffrey picked everything up for me."

Phillip nodded. "I remember that. You were gawking in the middle of the path as usual." He chuckled at her look of embarrassment. "Well, we just have to get it back."

"How?" Miranda's voice was filled with despair.

He grinned wickedly. "I used to be pretty good at breaking into my brother's room to look for his stash of candy. I think I can remember how it's done."

Miranda bit her lip then shook her head slowly. "I don't want to do that. I hate sneaking and deceit. Let's pray about it first. He's not going anywhere soon. We're still several days from Australia."

"I could beat his head in for you," Phillip offered, "so long as you don't make me fix it." He wanted to do or say something that would erase that hopeless look from her face.

A tiny smile played around her mouth. "I believe you would." She laid a soft hand against his cheek. "Your poor face. Can you ever forgive me?"

"You could kiss it like my mother used to do." As soon as the words were out, Phillip berated himself. First, she accused him of being a thief, now she would think he was lecherous. But before he could apologize, Miranda leaned forward and placed soft, gentle lips against his cheek. He could smell the clean scent of her hair and skin. Without realizing what he was doing, he pulled her down onto his lap and buried his face in that sweet-smelling hair. She felt so soft and pliant in his arms. He bent his head and his lips found hers. His arms tightened around her as she gave herself over to his kiss.

After a few moments, Miranda drew back, her face pink. "I think maybe that's enough penance." She got up from his lap and straightened her skirt. "I'd better not take up any more of your time. I'll let you know what I decide."

Before he could say anything else, she had left. Was that all it was for her? Penance? Those few moments had taken his breath away, had threatened his very concept of what he wanted in life. Did she feel anything for him beyond friendship? Did he even want her to? Was he ready for that kind of complication?

Chapter Eleven

T hree days later, Miranda still burned with humiliation over the way she'd thrown herself at Phillip. First, she slapped him, then she wantonly kissed him. She fervently thanked the Lord she'd had enough sense left to leave before she confessed her feelings to him. What he would make of that she didn't want to hear.

The memory of his strong arms around her, his breath upon her face, and the feel of his lips on hers made her tremble. She firmly pushed the seductive memory away. She had to decide what to do about reclaiming her property from that rogue Geoffrey. Land would be in sight soon. She had to do something.

She went up onto the poop deck. The night was pitch-black. Clouds still looked down threateningly and blocked any light from stars or moon. The choppy sea slapped against the side of the ship, and it was still a bit hard to hold her balance. She made her way to the bow of the ship. The blackness of the night, the sea, and the sky wrapped around her. But God was here and knew the dilemma she faced. What should she do? How should she handle this?

She sighed and prayed for wisdom. She wanted more than anything to be the right kind of witness to others about God. *Use this situation. Help me know what You would have me do.* She leaned on the railing and let the sea air tug tendrils of her fine hair loose from its pins. As she stood there, a peace came over her. She must talk to Geoffrey directly, she suddenly realized. No sneaking around like he did. A straight, face-to-face confrontation. The very thing she hated. She was much more apt to just sweep things under the rug than to deal with them head-on. But she had no choice.

Miranda squared her shoulders. There was no time like the present. She would find him, ask him to step out on the deck for a moment, and talk to him privately. She turned to go and saw a shadow on the starboard side of the poop deck. Geoffrey! God had sent him to her.

Geoffrey looked up. "Miranda, I didn't know you were here. I haven't seen you for a few days." He looked away from her steady eyes. "We'll be to Australia soon. Will you be glad?"

"I'll be glad to see my brother again. That is, if I don't have to admit I've lost his possessions." Miranda kept her voice steady and her eyes on Geoffrey's face. Would he betray himself?

Geoffrey didn't ask what she meant. "I rather hate to see us dock. I will miss you."

His voice sounded so sincere. Did he have no morals or ethics? Miranda raised herself to her full five feet. "I want you to give me back my reticule with my brother's deed," she said firmly.

Geoffrey was silent a moment. "You know I can't do that," he said almost gently. "I won't insult you by pretending I don't know what you're talking about. I'm sure Lucy told you she gave it to me." He smiled, and even in the dark, Miranda felt the charm. "But there's nothing you can do, my dear. I would deny it, of course, if you were to go to the captain. Who do you think he would believe? The man whose father owns a half interest in his ship or a woman who is seeking revenge?"

"Revenge?" What was he talking about?

"I would have to tell him how you threw yourself at me and how you shrieked you'd get back at me when I was not interested in your charms."

Geoffrey's voice was so persuasive, she almost could believe his story herself. When she remembered how flattered she'd been at his attentions, her cheeks heated up. Had he been after the deed from the very beginning? Humiliation flooded her. Of course, he had. Why would he be interested in her? She wasn't beautiful or rich or charming.

"Dr. Jackson will tell him the truth." She heartened at the thought of her ally. "He overheard what you told Delia." Too late she realized she should not have revealed her plan. She could feel Geoffrey's sudden stillness.

"I don't suppose you'd consider marrying me and asking your brother for half interest in the goldfield as a wedding gift?" He correctly read her silence. "I didn't think so. Well, my dear, there seems to be just one solution."

Before Miranda could say another word, he grasped her arm and began to force her toward the railing. "I'm afraid you're going to be so despondent over my rejection that you will throw yourself into the sea. I, of course, will tell the captain how I tried to save you, but to no avail." Grimly, he pushed her upper body over the railing and sought to seize her legs to heave her into the sea.

The sea spray dashed against her cheeks, and Miranda fought desperately. Closer and closer the sea came. She hung on to the railing with all her might and kicked out at Geoffrey. She could feel her grip slipping. Soon she would be in the cold water with the waves bearing her down to the bottom of the sea. She turned her head and bit at his arm, but he just laughed. A high, excited sound of enjoyment. He really was quite mad.

There was a roaring in her head, and when the grip on her arm suddenly loosened, she realized the sound wasn't just in her head. It was Phillip. A large shadow had engulfed Geoffrey and was shaking him like a terrier shakes a rat.

"You filthy scoundrel!" Phillip shook him again then dropped him to the deck. "I should throw you into the sea yourself!"

Geoffrey lay on the deck for a moment, then sat up and shook himself and got to his feet. "You'll pay for this, Jackson! My father will see to it."

Phillip's tone left no doubt that Geoffrey's threat didn't concern him. "Your father won't have anything to do with you when he finds out you're in prison. Now hand over Miranda's property."

Geoffrey laughed and turned to go. Phillip seized him again and held his hands behind his back. "Miranda, search him."

She hesitated, then gingerly began to go through his pockets. In his right breast pocket she found Nathan's deed. She gave a glad cry. "It's here!"

"Now take out the amount of money you had. He's probably thrown your reticule into the sea by now."

She reluctantly counted out four pound notes from the wad of money in his pocket. It somehow felt like theft to be taking his money, but she knew she had to recover the money as well. She had to have something to live on until she could find Nathan.

Geoffrey regarded them both bitterly. "That deed belongs to me! At least half of it does."

Phillip frowned. "Not unless your name is Nathan Leyton."

"Listen to me! I was in partnership with Nathan. I needed to go home to take care of some other business and sold my share out to Nathan. That was before we knew for sure there was gold there. When I heard about the strike, I decided to go find Nathan and see if he would sell me back my half of the land. When Miss Leyton dropped her reticule and I saw the deed, I realized this was my chance to recoup my share."

"Sounds to me like you sold it fair and square." Phillip's voice was uncompromising.

But Miranda interrupted. "I'll talk to my brother, Lord Geoffrey. If you feel you've been wronged, I'm sure my brother will want to be fair."

Both men looked at her in astonishment. Why did they look so surprised? Not everyone felt that money was the most important thing in the world. Right and fair play, ethics and morality all meant more to her than money. And she thought Nathan would feel the same.

"Now if you'll excuse me, I'm very tired." She was, too. Tired of hiding her feelings. Tired of realizing no one could love her for herself alone. Tired of knowing that Phillip just admired her nursing ability. Nathan's property was safe and sound, but what about her heart? It would never be the same again after being in Phillip's arms.

Chapter Twelve

The lights of Melbourne glimmered in the dark of the predawn morning. Miranda didn't think she'd ever seen a lovelier sight. She'd avoided Phillip as much as she could the last two days, and soon she could begin to try to put that heartache behind her. Somehow. She knew she would never marry, never have a man to hold and love and care for, never bear children. Phillip had filled her heart too completely to hope there could ever be anyone else.

But there could be joy in serving her brother, in living her life to the best of her ability for God. She could love another mother's child, could cook and clean for Nathan, could simply go on with life until God called her home. It was all the future held for her. She faced that fact squarely. She was small and plain and insignificant to everyone but God. And she thanked Him every day that He loved her for who she was. These past four months on board the *Euterpe* had taught her she was strong enough to endure anything if she had the Lord on her side. The *Star of India* had shown her the true Star of Hope.

As soon as the boat docked, she hurried down the

gangplank and arranged for a boy to bring her trunk to her brother's address. The streets of Melbourne were crowded with miners, hawkers shouting their wares, and drovers taking their crates to customers. She hired a carriage to take her to the address Nathan had given her. Her heart pounded when she stopped outside the two-story clapboard with gray siding and green shutters.

A plump, cheerful-faced woman answered the door. "Sure, he's here, me darlin'. You look all done in. Come in for a spot of tea while I fetch him and tell him he has a lady to see him." She led Miranda into a parlor with lovely matched furniture and a beautiful oriental rug in the center of the floor. "I won't be but a minute," she told Miranda.

A few minutes later, Nathan stepped into the room. He stared at Miranda as though he couldn't believe his eyes. He opened and closed his mouth several times before he found his voice. "Miranda?" he asked. "Miranda, is that really you?"

In the instant before she flew into her brother's arms, she noticed his new handlebar mustache and the new lines on his weathered face. But it was her own dear Nathan.

Several hours later, after all the explanations had been made and they'd had time to laugh and cry together, Nathan suggested they go out to dinner to celebrate their reunion. As her brother escorted her to the carriage, Miranda looked out across the bay and saw the *Euterpe* anchored offshore. Where was Phillip? Did he even look for her to say good-bye before he left the ship, or did he leave without giving her another thought?

❧

Phillip strode along the quay, searching the faces of every person he passed. Confound the woman, anyway! Why would she leave without a word? He'd been aware that she'd been avoiding him for the last two days. He had just assumed she'd needed time to sort out her feelings after that kiss they'd shared in the infirmary. She'd responded to him. That couldn't be all penance for accusing him unjustly.

When he'd come upon Geoffrey attempting to throw her overboard, he'd been overwhelmed with panic and fear of losing her. In that instant, he'd realized he loved her. He loved everything about her. Her direct blue-eyed gaze, her upturned nose, and full lips. That soft brown hair that escaped the confines of her pins so easily. The soft roundness of her and the way she barely came to his chest. Why had he ever thought her plain the first time they met? He must have been blind and daft.

Where are you, Miranda? He had to find her. *Help me, Lord. You know where she is. Keep her safe until I come. This is a rough town. Help her find her brother.* Where should he look? He decided to start with the boardinghouses.

After hours of searching, Phillip was near despair. How would he ever find her? There were hundreds of boardinghouses in Melbourne. Maybe she'd already left for Queensland. There was one more house on this street. He would try there before giving up for the day. A plump lady with a smile on her face and in her eyes answered the door. Yes, Nathan Leyton lived here, and yes, his sister had arrived, but they were out to dinner, the landlady told him. She didn't know where they'd gone, but they should be home soon and he could wait in the parlor.

Phillip paced for what seemed like an eternity. When he thought of telling Miranda how he felt, his palms grew sweaty. What if she didn't love him? He shook his head. He couldn't think like that or he would never find the courage to tell her. *Just remember the way she kissed you,* he told himself.

≈

Miranda felt as though she wouldn't be hungry for a week as they left the restaurant. She wanted to walk home, but Nathan refused to hear of it. Fog had rolled over the streets and covered the muck and mire with a lacy curtain of white, and while pretty, it was just too dangerous. He'd been mugged only last week, he told her. Fortunately, he hadn't been hurt, and the thugs got away with only his pocket watch and a few coins.

She held Nathan's hand and tried not to think about Phillip. If she tried long enough, surely it would get easier as the days went by. Nathan had asked her why she seemed so sad tonight at the restaurant, but she hadn't told him. The pain was too fierce to talk about.

"Huh, Mrs. Drexel must have company," Nathan said. "The parlor lights are on."

When they opened the door, a pink-cheeked Mrs. Drexel came hurrying toward them. "There's a distinguished gentleman waiting to see you, Miss Leyton.

I've put him in the parlor, but he's very impatient."

Miranda caught her breath, and her heart pounded. Could it be Phillip? Surely not. He would have no idea where she was. She tried to quell the sudden hope in her heart. It was too ridiculous to be true.

Nathan looked at her with a grin. "I wondered if a man were the reason behind the sadness in your eyes, little sister. Am I going to lose you just when I've found you again?"

Miranda smoothed back her hair and straightened her skirts. She didn't know what to say. She suddenly felt tongue-tied and awkward. "I–I don't know who it could be," she said.

"It's a Dr. Jackson," Mrs. Drexel said with a twitter. "And a fine figure of a man he is, too."

It *was* Phillip. Miranda felt the blood drain from her face. Her heart leaped in her breast. She looked at Nathan uncertainly.

"Go on, you ninny. Go see what your Dr. Jackson has to say." Nathan gave her a little shove.

Miranda approached the parlor doors on trembling legs. She put out a shaking hand and slid the door open. Phillip's sturdy form stood by the window with his back to the door. A wave of love swept over her at the sight of his familiar burly frame. He turned at the sound of the door opening. They stood facing one another for several long moments. Miranda just wanted to look at him. It had seemed so long since she'd looked into his eyes. Was it only days ago he'd held her and kissed her?

"You left without saying good-bye." Phillip's voice was accusatory.

"I—I didn't know you would care to say good-bye." Her voice trembled, and she cleared her throat. "I left you a note in the infirmary."

"Ah, yes, the note. That polite little missive telling me how *grateful* you were for all I'd done for you." He gave an exasperated sigh. "I don't want your gratitude."

"Why are you here?" Miranda clasped her shaking hands together. "If you don't want my gratitude, what do you want?" She found it hard to think past the pounding in her heart.

In two steps, Phillip stood before her. He gripped her shoulders with his big hands and stared down into her eyes. The look in his eyes mesmerized her. Was that *tenderness* she saw?

"I about went out of my mind when you left without a word. There was so much I wanted to say to you."

He cupped her cheek with his hand and rubbed his thumb over her lower lip. Miranda thought surely he could hear her heart beating. She closed her eyes and leaned her cheek further into his palm.

"Look at me, Miranda." His deep voice was husky and compelling.

She opened her eyes and gazed up into his dear face. His hair fell untidily over his forehead as usual. His cravat was crooked and he needed a shave, but Miranda thought she'd never seen a more handsome man. He just needed a woman to take care of him.

"Do you think you could ever love me, my dear?"

Miranda heard the unsteadiness and fear in his voice and smiled. He wasn't so cocky and self-assured, after all. "I already do, Dr. Jackson," she said softly.

Phillip's face lit up, and he swept her into his arms. As his lips found hers, he whispered, "Don't you think it's time you called me Phillip?"

Colleen Coble

Colleen and her husband, David, raised two great kids, David Jr., and Kara, and they are now knee-deep in paint and wallpaper chips as they restore a Victorian home in Wabash, Indiana. Colleen became a Christian after a bad car accident in 1980 when all her grandmother's prayers finally took root. She is very active at her church where she sings and helps her husband with a Sunday school class. She writes inspirational romance because she believes that the only happily-ever-after is with God at the center. She now works as a church secretary but would like to eventually pursue her writing full-time.

The Wonder of Spring

Carol Cox

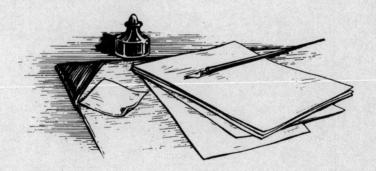

Prologue

1877, Northern Arizona Territory

Charlene Matkin gently set her basket of eggs on the counter of Foster's General Store and laid her list alongside it. Abel Foster glanced at the eggs, then the list of supplies. Charlene swallowed nervously. "If the eggs won't bring me enough to get everything on the list," she said, "just give me the items with a star next to them."

Abel nodded, his usually solemn face breaking into one of its rare smiles. "I reckon it'll do. Looks like it'll come out pretty even to me." Charlene smiled in return, trying to hide her relief. She and her grandfather might be scraping by, but she wasn't about to advertise the fact.

She accepted the wrapped bundle from Abel and turned to leave, but his voice stopped her. "Whoa, I almost forgot. You have a letter here, young lady."

Taking the proffered letter from his hands, she looked at the handwriting. It wasn't familiar. Mystified, Charlene carried her parcel and letter out to the wagon and glanced around to make sure no one was watching, then examined the envelope more closely. The return address bore the imprint of a newspaper in Baltimore. With her heart beating like a trip-hammer, Charlene carefully slit open the envelope and withdrew the single sheet of paper.

My dear Miss Matkin,

Thank you for sending your story, "Echoes of the Canyon." If you are not aware of it already, let me assure you that you have a great gift with words. Nick Rogers's adventures make a stirring tale, indeed. I am eager to publish your story.

Readers, unfortunately, do not take well to adventure stories written by a woman. If I may suggest it, you might wish to assume a pen name, as other women writers have done. This is unfair, I agree, but it is a fact, and I would hate to deprive the world of your stories because of a groundless prejudice. I await your decision.

Yours sincerely,
Howard Emerson

Charlene tried to still the trembling of her hands long enough to read the letter again, word by lovely word. Was it really possible that the story she had penned and submitted on a whim was good enough to be published? She gathered up the reins and clucked to the horses, anxious to get home and share the news with her grandfather.

The front door swung open when she pulled the horses to a halt, and Charlene barely gave herself enough time to set the brake before she vaulted from the wagon seat and sprang up the porch steps to throw herself into her grandfather's arms. Jed Matkin's eyes widened in surprise a split second before he wrapped one lean arm around his granddaughter and returned her hug with gusto.

"What's the occasion?" he asked, rocking a little on his good leg.

With a cry of dismay that he might fall over, Charlene steadied her grandfather, and then straightened, helping him to one of the rocking chairs on the neatly swept porch. While Jed propped his crutch against the wall, Charlene settled herself in the rocker opposite him.

"I didn't mean to bowl you over like that," she apologized, but nothing could dim the excitement shining in her eyes. "I've been holding it in all the way home, and I'm just about to burst." She drew a deep breath and reached out to clasp his left hand in both of her own.

"You remember the story I wrote about your early years out here before you married Grandma?"

"The one you sent off to that newspaper feller? Sure, I do. It was a plumb good story, if I do say so myself. Only problem I could see was that made-up character."

"Nick Rogers?" Charlene's brows drew together in a frown of confusion. "But, Grandpa, he's based on you. What's wrong with him?"

Jed Matkin twitched his nose and stared off at a spot over Charlene's head. "You didn't make him nearly good-looking enough," he pronounced solemnly. One eyelid lowered in a roguish wink just as Charlene caught the joke and sputtered with laughter. "All right," Jed said, "enough of my foolishness. What's your news, honey?"

The glow returned to Charlene's face. "I got a letter from the owner today. He wants to print my story,

Grandpa." She paused once more, fighting to hold back happy tears, and added in a wondering whisper, "He says I'm a good writer."

"Well, of course you are!" Jed roared, using both arms to envelop her in a bear hug. "I could have told you that. The man would have to be a fool not to see it— good to know he isn't." He pulled back and gave Charlene a resounding kiss on the forehead. "So when does this momentous event take place?"

"I guess it depends on me," Charlene said, sobering a little. "He wants to know if I'll agree to use a pen name, a male one, so the readers will accept the stories. I thought about it all the way home, and I'm just not sure. Do you think it seems dishonest?"

"Hmm. Now that is a poser." Jed leaned back and pursed his lips in thought while Charlene waited expectantly. "It doesn't seem right not to have that fine story printed. Seems to me that what you need is a way to give the public what they want, but still be able to live with yourself. Is that it?"

Charlene nodded anxiously. "That's right." She frowned again. "But is there any way to do that?"

Jed narrowed his eyes to slits and stroked his upper lip with a forefinger. A slow smile tilted the corners of his mouth, deepening the lines around his faded blue eyes. He moved his lips silently, then nodded in satisfaction. "That'll do it," he announced.

"What?" Charlene leaned forward, almost tipping off the chair in her eagerness. "What is it?"

Her grandfather grinned smugly. "Do you remember

what I used to call you when you were, oh, maybe five or six years old?" Charlene stared blankly, trying to recall. "Your grandmother hated it," he reminded her, chuckling. "Said it wasn't fit for a young lady."

Charlene frowned with the effort to remember, then her brow cleared as the memory returned. Her lips parted in a delighted smile. "Oh, Grandpa," she breathed, "do you really think it'll work?" At his nod, she leaped to her feet, gave him another quick squeeze, and hurried to unload the supplies, put the wagon and horses away, and begin preparations for supper.

After the meal, Jed made a show of setting the oil lamp and Charlene's writing materials on the table before her. "You set right here while I clean up the dishes," he said in response to her questioning look. "You need to write back to that newspaper feller right away, and it won't hurt me a bit to do some work around here."

When she opened her mouth to protest, he went on. "Go on and do what I tell you. It'll be good for me. After all the years I spent tramping these mountains, having to sit around and nurse this bum leg of mine makes me feel worse than useless. At least this way, I'll be doing something to help out. Besides," he added with a wink, "that story you wrote up was mine in the first place, so we'll just call it a joint effort."

Charlene watched him collect one dish at a time in one hand, then use the other to grasp his crutch and hobble to the washbasin. She ached to scoop the lot up in an armload and get it over with quickly, but she knew her grandfather would be mortally offended if she did so.

After her grandmother passed away, Charlene's parents had invited Jed to come live with them, an offer he reluctantly accepted with the stipulation that he would be a contributing member of the family. So it came as a tremendous shock when he outlived both his son and daughter-in-law and he and Charlene were left to care for each other. They had become a close-knit team, and Jed gallantly devoted himself to being parent, advisor, and friend to his granddaughter.

Then came the accident that crippled him. For a man who had spent his life roaming the mountains, taming the harsh wilderness, Charlene knew it galled him to watch her carry out the heavy work on their place and to know the money from the eggs her hens produced was now their major source of income. If he was willing to offer to help out with housework, there was no way she was going to tear away the remaining shreds of his dignity.

Wincing only slightly at the ominous rattle of crockery, Charlene selected a piece of writing paper and picked up her pen.

Dear Mr. Emerson,

I received your letter today, and am happy you wish to publish my story. Your suggestion to use a pen name to protect my identity caused me some concern at first, but I believe I have come up with a solution that will satisfy us both.

Thank you for your kind words of encouragement. Writing brings me much pleasure, and I am

*glad you think it may give pleasure to others, as
well.*

Yours truly,

Truly? Charlene chewed on the end of her pen for a
moment before continuing. Yes, it was true; the name
was hers.

She poised her pen and signed the letter with a
flourish:

Charlie Matkin

Chapter One

O ne year later.
    Nick Rogers stood on the mountain's summit and watched the rosy fingers of the sunset intertwine with the dazzling golden bands painted across the darkening sky. Nearby, the trickle of a stream formed by the melting snows fashioned a song of praise to the Creator as its icy current splashed along to bring new spring life to the valley below.

Charlene penned the final words to her latest manuscript and signed "Charlie Matkin" underneath, marveling at how natural the signature now seemed. She rested her chin in one hand and stared at the view beyond the window, lost in thought.

So much had happened in the last year. So much had changed! A year ago, she never would have guessed the letter of acceptance from Mr. Emerson and the subsequent printing of "Echoes of the Canyon" would be followed by a deluge of letters from readers eager for more stories of Nick Rogers and the West.

Raised from childhood on a steady diet of stories of Jed's younger days, she had a rich fund of her grandfather's tales available to weave into one Nick Rogers adventure after another. Readers clamored for more, and a delighted Howard Emerson begged her to oblige. It never ceased to amaze Charlene that she could entertain so many others through a pastime that brought her such joy.

Not to mention an income! As if seeing her story in print for the first time hadn't been thrill enough, an envelope from Mr. Emerson arrived soon after, containing not only a congratulatory letter, but a bank draft. His request for another Nick Rogers story, and then another, made Charlene feel she was living out some lovely fairy tale.

As the demand for Charlie Matkin's stories increased, so did the amount of the bank drafts, and for the first time since Jed's accident, they found themselves able to afford more than the bare necessities. Charlene had worried that Jed might feel resentful about her status as breadwinner, but he cheerfully reminded her that there would be no stories without his recollections. To his way of thinking, it was indeed a joint venture to which he could contribute.

Charlene tapped the end of her pen against her front teeth and sighed. The story she had just finished was her best to date; she knew she had grown as a writer over the last twelve months. Jed was happier than he had been in years, feeling he was once again helping to provide for their family. Everything was nearly as perfect as it could be. Except. . .

Why haven't I heard from Mr. Emerson? A worried frown creased Charlene's brow, and she rubbed her forehead impatiently. Two months had passed since she received her last correspondence from him. Two full months—when the time between his earlier missives had been measured in mere weeks. Granted, there had been delays before, but never one this long. And like it or not, Charlene was growing anxious.

Take it easy, she cautioned herself. *Remember, you haven't been to town for a while. There's every chance a letter will be waiting when you go in to post your story today.* She sure hoped so. She and Jed were down to an almost empty cupboard. It was possible, she knew from experience, to subsist on meager fare, but she would hate to have to return to that kind of bare existence. Not only would it mean squeezing every penny, but she didn't want anything to dim the new sparkle in her grandfather's eyes.

With a sigh of resignation, she addressed an envelope to Mr. Emerson, sealed the manuscript inside it, and prepared to go to town. She eased the wagon along cautiously at first. The ground, saturated by the spring runoffs, had been too soggy to drive on for the past two weeks. Today, Charlene was pleased to see that although the wagon wheels made deep depressions in the road, they didn't sink in enough to bog the wagon down.

If the letter and draft are there today, she mused, *I should be able to stock up on supplies.* She made a mental list of the things she needed, adding in a few special items she knew Jed would like. With the horses plodding comfortably along the familiar path, her attention was free to wander, taking in the new shoots of grass mingling with early-blooming wildflowers. The flat, rounded leaves of the aspen trees quivered in the light breeze, seeming to wave a cheery greeting.

Charlene's spirits lifted, as they always did at this time of year. Spring was her favorite season—a time of renewal and hope. *Lord, You provided for us this time last year, far and away beyond anything I expected. Help me to trust You to do it again.*

She tied the team in the shade of a pine at one side of the general store and made her way inside, making an effort to project an air of confidence. If the letter was there, well and good. If not, she'd rather exist on what she could forage from her cellar, even though her supplies were very low after the long winter, than let people know how tight their finances were. She knew her grandfather would feel the same.

"Good morning, Mr. Foster," she said with a bright smile. "I have something to mail." She pushed her manuscript across the counter to him.

"I'll make sure it goes out on the next stage." He accepted the postage price from her and added the parcel to the stack of outgoing mail. "By the way," he said as an afterthought, "you have some letters waiting. I figured you'd be in as soon as the ground dried out enough to travel."

Charlene accepted two envelopes, willing her hands not to tremble. Seeing that Mr. Foster was busy restocking his shelves and there were no other customers in the store, she withdrew into a far corner and examined her mail.

Both envelopes were addressed to C. Matkin. Both bore Baltimore postmarks. One had an unfamiliar return address, but to her vast relief, the other was inscribed with the familiar name of Howard Emerson.

She tore at it with eager hands, ripping it wide open in her haste. An oblong piece of paper fluttered to the floor, and she bent to retrieve it. Hallelujah, there was the bank draft! A quick glance showed her the amount covered all the stories from the last two months, and she murmured a prayer of thanks. Once she cashed the draft, she'd make a sizeable dent in Abel Foster's inventory. Her attention now turned to the letter in her hand.

My dear Charlie,

You must have been wondering at my long silence. I apologize for this, and for any inconvenience caused you by the delay of payment for your stories. Their popularity continues unabated. Readers constantly flood us with praise for Nick Rogers's adventures and pleas for many more. I feel confident that you can look forward to a long and successful relationship with this paper.

I tell you this because I have some news to share. My delay in writing was caused by recurring bouts of illness. I have been in a doctor's care for many weeks now, and he holds out little hope for complete recuperation unless I make some changes. I am sorry to say my ill health has forced me to sell the paper. I plan to retire to a small community near the area where I grew up, and trust that freedom from the pressures of business will hasten my recovery.

Charlene's fingers shook so hard she could barely see the quivering letters on the page. Concern for Mr. Emerson's health merged with fears for her own future. *Would* the new owner continue to use her stories? Even if he did, what would become of Charlie Matkin once the new owner discovered that Charlie was really Charlene? She smoothed the letter out on a shelf before her and continued to read.

> *I want to reassure you that Matthew Benson, the new owner, is fully aware of your contribution to the success of this paper, and has every intention of continuing to publish your stories at the rate we are currently paying you. I can recommend him to you as an honorable man with sound business sense and solid character. In closing, I also want you to know that he knows you only as "Charlie" and that your secret remains safe with me.*
>
> > *Your friend,*
> > *Howard Emerson*

Charlene's head swam as she tried to grasp the new situation. She had felt the very foundation of her income rock beneath her, but if she read Mr. Emerson's meaning correctly, it seemed all was safe, at least for the moment. The new owner thought she was a man.

With a shaky breath, she drew the letter from the second envelope and glanced at the signature. Matthew Benson! Unable to decide whether she should feel a sense of foreboding or relief, Charlene read on.

Dear Mr. Matkin, it began,

 I hope that one day I may call you Charlie, as Mr. Emerson does. I hasten to assure you that the change in ownership of this paper will in no way alter your status here. Your stories have played an important part in making the paper the success it is, and we look forward to a long and fruitful association.

 Your descriptions of the beautiful land you live in have filled me with the desire to see the scenes from your stories firsthand—so much so that I have made arrangements to travel to northern Arizona as soon as possible. If all goes well, I should arrive there on the seventeenth or eighteenth of this month. I look forward to making your acquaintance in person and meeting the author who has so stirred my imagination.

      Sincerely yours,
      Matthew Benson

It was a dream, Charlene decided. It *had* to be a dream for a day to take her from near-penniless status to financial well-being, from concern for a friend's health to hope for his recovery, from anxiety over the sale of the paper to relief at a secure future. To go from there to the dread of her identity being discovered and losing that security could have no basis in reality. None.

She would close her eyes and count to three. When she opened them, she was sure she'd find herself tucked safely in her own snug bed. She squeezed her eyes shut.

One. . .two. . .three. . .

"You all right, Charlene?" She opened her eyes to find Abel Foster staring at her with concern. "You look a mite peaked there." She reassured him that she was okay and began to gather her papers together. Apparently, this dream wouldn't be so easy to shake off. Over Mr. Foster's shoulder, she caught sight of the store calendar, each day neatly marked off with an *X* until it reached the current date, the eighteenth.

The eighteenth! She fumbled through the papers, drawing out the letter from Matthew Benson and scanning it with a rising sense of panic. If his journey went according to plan, he could arrive that very day!

Her mind in a whirl, Charlene made her own plans as she stuffed the papers carelessly into the pocket of her dress. First, she would cash the bank draft and stock up on supplies. Then if the worst happened, and Mr. Benson did arrive only to sever the paper's relationship with her, he wouldn't be able to take back the payment she had received. She and Jed would have something to live on for a time until they figured out what to do next.

The stamping of hooves and the creak of heavy wheels broke into her thoughts, and she realized the stage was just pulling in. Hurrying to the doorway, she peered out cautiously and watched the passengers disembark.

A worn-looking woman and two children were handed down first. *Good,* thought Charlene, *no Matthew Benson there.* Her relief grew when a buckskin-clad man stepped down and stretched mightily. She had turned back into the store with a renewed sense of hope when she heard a baritone voice call, "Can anyone direct me to the Matkin residence?"

Breathlessly, Charlene flattened herself against the doorjamb and eased her head just beyond its edge. She watched a broad-shouldered man emerge from the stagecoach. His rugged physique in no way fit her notion of what a newspaper editor should look like, but who else could possibly be looking for her? Or rather, for the nonexistent Charlie Matkin?

Her dream had just turned into a nightmare.

Chapter Two

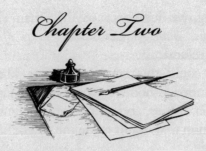

Charlene backed away from the door, trying not to make a sound. She continued moving past the counter, along the table containing bolts of calico, toward the back door, all the while straining to see anyone who might come in the front.

"They live about four miles out of town." A man's booming voice answered the newcomer's question. "But I could have sworn I saw Miss Matkin around here just a few minutes ago. Let's go check in the store. Hey, Abel!" he called out.

The shuffle of boots entering the store drowned out the tiny squeak the back door made as Charlene let herself out and eased it shut again. Sidling along the back of the building, she slipped quietly around the corner and sprinted for the wagon.

She reached it unseen and gave herself a moment to recover before she climbed into the seat, released the brake, and clucked to the horses. Holding them to a sedate walk, she made her way along the alley until she reached the edge of town, then urged them into a fast trot.

"I can't believe I just skulked out of town like that!" she muttered. "Why should I have to go hightailing off like a fugitive just because that man showed up?" *Because that man represents your source of income,* she admitted reluctantly.

How could this have happened? There she had been, stranded at home by the weather, happily churning out her stories, and all the while, plans were being set in motion that might cause the end of her newfound prosperity.

❧

"What can I do, Grandpa?" She paced past Jed's chair to the living room window and back again, wringing her hands. "I can't lie to him, but if he finds out I'm a woman, they might never print another one of my stories."

Jed shifted his bad leg to a more comfortable position, then settled back in his chair to think. Moments later, a smile creased his face. "I don't think you have any reason to worry," he said. "Remember who you're named for? Me—Jedediah *Charles* Matkin. Just introduce me to him that way, and don't say anything more than that." He chuckled. "After all, they *are* my stories."

Charlene turned this solution over in her mind while she scurried around, trying to ready the house for their visitor. Would it work? More importantly, was it right? *We won't really be lying,* she reasoned, *just letting him draw his own conclusions.* It would only be for a short while, surely no more than the time it took for him to sit and visit a bit. After that, he'd be safely back in Baltimore, and she could continue writing and sending Charlie's stories as before.

Grabbing a dust rag, she flicked it over the furniture

while calculating the time it would take him to hire a buggy and find the way to their place. *Maybe he'll get lost and it'll slow him down a bit.* Her conscience tingled a warning at her uncharitable attitude.

All right, she thought, offering a compromise, *he said he was interested in seeing the area. Maybe he'll take his time enjoying the sights along the road. I really don't wish him any harm—I just want time to be ready before he gets here.* She stood with her hands on her hips, surveying the tidy room. Twitching a curtain into place and straightening a picture frame, she decided the house was as ready as she could make it.

Now, what to do about refreshments? Her hands flew to her cheeks in dismay as she remembered she hadn't had time to cash the bank draft and replenish their scanty provisions. Scrabbling through the cupboards, she found flour, molasses, enough ingredients for a molasses cake. Perfect. She had it mixed and in the oven in minutes. Setting the coffeepot on the stove, she nodded approval and went down a mental checklist. The house was neat and food was in the making—it was enough to welcome Mr. Benson, but not enough to encourage him to make his visit a lengthy one.

She had begun to relax, patting her hair into place, when she noticed the flour caked on her hands. Looking down, she saw the white dust streaked across her dress. *Of all the times to forget to wear an apron!* she thought in disgust, and fled to her room to wash up.

It took only a moment to bathe her flushed face and slip into a clean dress. Her hair had escaped from its pins during her mad rush to get ready, and loose strands now hung untidily about her face. Pulling the pins out in haste, she yanked a brush through her ash-blond strands, wincing as it caught in the tangles. With her hair now caught back neatly, Charlene pressed her hands against her warm cheeks and tried to breathe normally.

Please don't let him stay for supper, she prayed. No sooner had the words formed in her mind than she heard the rattle of buggy wheels outside, followed by a knock on the door. It was the moment of truth—or something close to it.

Jed was waiting in his usual chair when she nervously entered the living room and cast him a despairing glance. His nod of approval and reassuring wink did little to calm her jitters. Resting one hand on the door latch, she took a deep breath and swung the door open.

The man standing before her was indeed the stranger she had seen dismounting from the stage. His shoulders were just as broad as Charlene remembered, his build just as rugged. She hadn't noticed his hair, though. Russet waves with glints of gold framed a strong, square face. Full lips parted to reveal even, white teeth.

Her gaze traveled upward and she found herself staring into the deepest, warmest brown eyes she had ever seen. Flecks of gold echoing the glints in his hair shone from pools of melted chocolate, and Charlene felt drawn into their depths.

She didn't realize she'd been staring until that breathtaking smile faltered and he asked, a trifle hesitantly, "This *is* the Matkin residence, isn't it?"

Jed spoke up from across the room. "Of course it is. Come on in, young feller."

Charlene blinked and stood back to admit their guest. "I'm terribly sorry." She had to force the words out. "You must be—" Her mind went blank and she cast about, frantically trying to recall the name on the letter.

"Matthew Benson." He turned his hat in his hands, apparently confused by her greeting. His eyes widened and he added, "You *did* get my letter, didn't you?"

Appalled by her own rudeness, Charlene answered, even more flustered than before. "Oh yes. Your letter. It came. Yes, indeed."

Matthew Benson shifted from one foot to the other, as if uncertain of his welcome. "I hope I'm not imposing."

"Not a bit," Jed called out in a cordial tone. "We're happy to have you here."

Charlene smoothed her skirt with shaking hands and recovered enough to cross the room and stand at Jed's side. "This is my grandfather." She wet her lips nervously. "Jedediah Charles Matkin." She looked at Jed, seeking his approval, and was heartened by the confident gleam in his eyes.

"Mr. Matkin." Matthew leaned over Jed's chair and pumped his hand eagerly. "I can't tell you how much I have enjoyed your stories. I've been one of your most devoted readers, even before the paper changed hands."

Jed nodded acknowledgment of the compliment and Matthew beamed. Charlene noted the way Matthew's eyes crinkled at the corners when he smiled, and she wondered at the fluttering in her stomach.

"Your stories," Matthew continued, "are more than just entertainment. They have stirred my imagination and created a burning desire to see the people and settings you've brought to life. I am truly honored to meet you, sir."

Jed had the grace to look somewhat embarrassed. "You're a younger feller than I expected," he said, in what Charlene thought was an obvious attempt to change the subject. "I'm surprised you'd own a big city newspaper at your age."

Matthew's neck grew red at the implied praise. "I guess it would seem a little surprising," he murmured, "although twenty-eight isn't really all that young."

He shifted back to his original topic. "As I understand it, the stories are all based on your actual experiences. Is that right, Charlie?" This time the wave of red washed clear up to his hairline. "May I call you Charlie?" he asked tentatively. "That's how Howard Emerson always referred to you, and I'm afraid I picked up the habit. I don't mean to be presumptuous. . ." His voice trailed off.

"No offense taken." Jed waved his hand graciously. "But why don't you call me Jed? I'm more used to that. Charlie is more what I guess you'd call a pen name." He gave Charlene a quick wink she hoped Matthew didn't see.

"Thank you—Jed. I can't tell you how happy I am to be here." He seemed to run out of accolades at that point, and the three of them maintained their positions in silence—Jed looking relaxed and confident in his chair,

Charlene standing next to him, hands folded across her skirt, and Matthew looking like a little boy who'd just been given a whole jar of cookies.

Charlene began to relax a bit, heartily approving of Matthew's apparent lack of anything more to add. It was evident that he had said what he'd come to say, and would soon take his leave to begin his tour of the West. Surely it was safe to offer refreshments at this point to speed the process along and hospitably hasten his departure.

"Would you care for some molasses cake and coffee?" she asked almost cheerfully. "It should be about ready now."

Matthew glanced at Charlene, ready to answer, but his reply caught in his throat. She'd seemed so solemn when she opened the door, but now a smile lit her face, transforming it. Sunlight streaming through the window behind her played upon the strands of hair that curled in wisps about her face, turning them into a golden halo. He opened and closed his mouth, aware that he was supposed to be saying something, but was unable to remember what it was.

Jed cleared his throat. "My granddaughter, Charlene," he said dryly.

Charlene ducked her head and flushed a rosy pink, obviously embarrassed by his scrutiny. Matthew could have kicked himself for being such a dolt.

"I'd love some cake," he said, determined to make amends. He sniffed appreciatively at the aroma wafting from the oven.

Light with relief at the prospect of ending this meeting with her secret still undiscovered, Charlene served portions of molasses cake with a lavish hand. Both Jed and Matthew did her baking justice, washing down the generous servings with mugs of hot coffee.

"Miss Matkin," Matthew said, "that was the most delicious cake I've had in ages." Charlene, happier with each second that ticked by, smiled and nodded her thanks.

"Call her Charlene," Jed put in, chuckling when Matthew gave him a startled glance. "We're not near as formal here as you folks are back east," he went on to explain.

"I—uh, I see," Matthew said. "Then let me give you my compliments again. . .Charlene." He turned the warmth of his brown eyes on her again, and her stomach did flip-flops. Confused at her reaction, she rose and began clearing the table, reminding herself that her ordeal was nearly over.

It hadn't been as hard as she feared. Neither she nor her grandfather had actually given Jed credit for the Charlie Matkin stories. She could breathe a lot easier, knowing they hadn't come right out and lied to Matthew —Mr. Benson, she corrected herself, determined to keep things on a professional level, in spite of his dazzling good looks. Although they hadn't been totally forthright, either. But she couldn't think about that now.

How much longer would he stay—five minutes? Ten? Surely no more than fifteen. Lost in speculation, she finished tidying the kitchen, content to know that within half an hour, at the most, life would return to normal. She poured herself another mug of coffee and leaned back against the kitchen counter, listening idly for Matthew Benson to take his leave.

"I don't think you give yourself enough credit," he was saying. "You have an amazing gift for evoking a sense of atmosphere that I have seen in few other writers."

Charlene allowed herself a moment of complacency, enjoying the compliment. Even if it was misdirected. She closed her eyes and lifted the mug to her lips for another satisfying sip.

"In fact," Matthew went on diffidently, "what I'd really like to do is make an extended stay right in this area and visit the scenes of the stories I've read."

Charlene choked, spraying a fine mist of coffee over her dress. Matthew jumped and started to come to her aid, but she waved him away, gasping, and wet a cloth to try to dab away the stain before it set.

Matthew seated himself again with his back to her, and Charlene tried to catch Jed's attention. As enamored as Matthew appeared to be with everything he had seen so far, it shouldn't take much for Jed to suggest other interesting—and distant—places for him to visit. It would be simple, really.

Jed beamed at Matthew. "Now that's a fine idea, if ever I heard one." He gave the younger man an approving nod. Charlene stared at her grandfather in astonishment, unwilling to believe what her ears had just heard. She renewed her efforts to attract his notice, shaking her head vehemently while mouthing "No!" and waving her arms back and forth.

"Charlene," Jed called, cheerfully ignoring her frantic signals, "how about another cup of coffee?" Wrapping a towel around the handle of the coffeepot, she carried it to the table, still making faces at her grandfather until she came within Matthew's range of vision.

"Can you recommend a place to stay?" Matthew asked as she began to replenish Jed's coffee. "Is there a good boardinghouse nearby?"

"Why don't you stay right here?" Jed offered. Charlene gasped, flinched, and sloshed coffee onto the table. Then she hurried, in a daze, to fetch a towel and wipe up the spill while her mind formed a lengthy list of arguments to Jed's blithe invitation.

She looked at her grandfather closely. Could he be getting senile? Up to now, she'd always thought his faculties were in remarkably good shape, but the events of this afternoon led her to wonder. What else could explain his behavior?

"You feeling all right?" he asked her solicitously. "You seem to be a little off plumb today." Charlene merely glared at him in response and stalked back to the kitchen where she leaned against the door frame and watched them.

"I wouldn't want to impose. . ." Charlene could hear the eagerness in Matthew's voice. Jed waved an affable hand, signifying that his company would be no trouble at all. "If you're sure," Matthew went on, "then I accept." His voice throbbed with excitement. "You don't know how thrilling it will be to stay with my favorite author. I just hope my presence here won't interfere with your writing."

It was Jed's turn to sputter, and Charlene looked on with satisfaction. He hadn't minded putting her in a tight spot with his invitation; it was about time he reaped some of what he had sown.

"I, uh, don't think it'll be a problem," Jed finally managed to say. "The, um, the writing can be done while you're out sightseeing." Charlene brightened a trifle. She had forgotten about Matthew's wish to explore the area. That should take him out of the house for long periods of time, hopefully long enough for her to keep up with her writing schedule.

"Speaking of that. . ." Matthew paused, as if uncertain how to continue. "I want to visit the settings of as many of your stories as I can. I had hoped to persuade you to guide me to them, but. . ." He glanced doubtfully at Jed's bad leg.

Jed came to his rescue without missing a beat. "My wandering days are over, that's true. But there's no reason young Charlene here can't show you around. She knows this area and the story locations as well as I do."

Charlene covered her face with her hands. What kind of madness had seized him this day? While she followed the conversation, she had been trying to decide how to rearrange her schedule so she would be able to write while they had company—*this* company!—and now Jed was setting things up so she'd have to spend precious time away from her writing while showing Matthew around. It had to be madness, she decided.

There was no other explanation for it.

She heard a chair scoot on the floor and she lowered her hands to find Matthew swiveling about to face her. "Miss—Charlene, would you do me the honor of acting as my guide?"

"Of course," Jed mused, as if he were thinking out loud, "with me laid up like this, she does have an awful lot of chores to do. . ."

"I'll be glad to help with those!" Matthew volunteered. He looked back at Charlene, those melting brown eyes full of hope. *You can't win,* she told herself. *You might as well do it with as much good grace as you can muster and get it over with. The sooner he sees everything, the sooner he'll go home.* She nodded, and the two men smiled at each other, happy to have struck a deal.

Matthew soon set off for town to collect his luggage. Charlene waited until the buggy drew away from the house, then wheeled about to confront her grandfather.

"How am I supposed to get any writing done with him under the same roof?" she demanded, hands on her hips. "It's bad enough wondering if he'll learn my secret, but now I'll fall behind on my stories. Why on earth did you invite him to stay here?"

"Don't you worry." Instead of looking the least bit remorseful, Jed's eyes sparkled with a mischievous gleam. "I know what I'm doing. I'll have that boy so busy that you'll have time to show him places and do all your writing, too. You can almost look at it as a little vacation," he added generously. Charlene rolled her eyes and went to take out her frustration on the defenseless bedding in the spare bedroom.

A city-bred gentleman like Matthew Benson is probably used to several courses of fancy food at each meal, she thought resentfully, punching a pillow into submission, foods she couldn't even pronounce, much less prepare. Well, he was out of luck! Without the supplies she intended to purchase earlier, they were down to basic fare. *Very* basic. She could imagine how that would compare with what he was used to.

As she considered the situation, a thoughtful smile curved her lips. If he wanted to see the way Charlie Matkin lived, that's what he would get. If he didn't like it, he could just up and leave. It could be the very thing to aid in his hasty departure. She wouldn't be guilty of doing anything overt to drive him away, and he couldn't hold it against her if he wasn't up to coping with frontier life.

Her smile broadened. Before she knew it, he would get tired of roughing it and head back east so she could continue writing in happy anonymity, and that was exactly what she wanted.

So why did she feel a quick stab of disappointment and see a vision of melting brown eyes?

Chapter Three

C harlene rose early the next morning in a thoroughly disgruntled mood. Far from turning up his nose at the simple meal she prepared the night before, Matthew had attacked it with gusto, savoring every morsel. When he had eaten everything on his plate except the blue-and-white pattern, he leaned back in his chair, the picture of contentment.

"That was wonderful." He sighed blissfully. "Much better than the restaurant food back home." He beamed at both Charlene and Jed. "Maybe the simple life is just what I need."

So much for Charlene's brilliant plan.

Disappointment kept her tossing in her bed far into the night before she found the solace of sleep. The new day, bright with the promise of spring, brought her no joy. It looked like she would have to put up with Matthew Benson's presence for an indefinite time.

Grumbling, she pulled on a plain blue dress and hastily whisked the brush through her hair, tying it back at the nape of her neck with a deep blue ribbon that matched her eyes. She stumbled to the kitchen to start the fire in the stove and knead the sourdough sponge she had set out to rise the night before. With the coffeepot in place, she made her way back to her room and plopped down wearily at the desk she had moved from the living room during Matthew's absence the day before.

With one hand supporting her head, she tried to focus tired eyes on the paper before her in the pool of light from her oil lamp and began outlining the next Nick Rogers adventure.

This one would be the story of the time Jed—Nick Rogers—curled up one night in a cave, to be awakened hours later by a grizzly bear who considered the cave hers. Only by making a perilous leap from the mouth of the cave to a crumbling ledge below had he managed to avoid being mauled or killed. It was an engrossing tale, and Charlene was soon deeply involved in the story line.

Loud, repeated *thunks* jarred her back to reality, and she recognized the sound as the ring of an axe on wood. Parting her curtains, she gazed out to find Matthew, clad in a very uncitylike plaid flannel shirt, splitting stove wood. Charlene resumed her seat, pleasantly surprised that she would have enough wood for the day with no effort on her part.

When the sound of the axe continued far longer than Charlene would have taken to split a day's supply, she ventured to the window again with an inward grin, wondering if he was finding it more of a challenge than he'd thought. Her eyes widened in amazement when she saw the amount of wood he'd managed to split. Where did a newspaper man learn to do that? It surely wasn't a skill she would have expected from a deskbound editor.

Resting her cheek on her palm, she leaned against the windowsill and watched in the gathering light as he set up another thick chunk of wood. With his hands spread apart on the handle, he expertly swung the axe up, whirled it around his head, and brought it down again with a loud *whack*. The axe blade struck the edge of the wood precisely in the center and it fell apart, split neatly in half.

Charlene made a face. It would have taken her at least two strokes, maybe three, to split a chunk that size.

Matthew set one half upright and swung the axe again. This time Charlene watched, not the axe, but the broad back muscles rippling under the fabric of his shirt. He worked with an economy of motion, like one accustomed to hard labor.

Grandpa must have looked like that in his younger days, she mused. *In fact,* she thought, resting both arms on the sill as she straightened up and sharpened her gaze, *I could almost be looking at Nick Rogers.*

The thought brought a wistful smile to her face. In addition to being modeled after her grandfather, Nick Rogers had one facet even Jed didn't know about—he was a compilation of every attribute Charlene thought desirable in a man.

At twenty-four, she had long ago given up hope of attracting the notice of any of the young men in the area. Women her age were already married, and usually had a passel of youngsters. Charlene had her home and Jed.

Not that I'm complaining, she reminded herself. The loss of her parents had brought her and Jed together in a special way, and she couldn't imagine life without him —feisty, ornery character that he was. But love, at least in the romantic sense, had passed Charlene by.

She could understand the lack of suitors whenever she looked in the mirror. She was plain compared to the young ladies in town. She didn't have money for the latest fashions. Other women might have time to primp before a looking glass, but Charlene had to work.

Her hair was usually caught back quickly with a ribbon, with the ends curling freely around her shoulders. Even then, instead of staying decorously in place, wayward strands crept out from the ribbon's confines during the day, until by late afternoon she generally had a cloud of loose strands swirling about her face. Hardly the picture of an attractive woman!

Nor did she know how to simper and flirt like other girls. She was just Charlene, prosaic and plain, except when it came to her writing. There she was able to let loose her flights of fancy, spinning wonderful tales of derring-do. That was when she felt the most real. She saved her romantic daydreams for Nick Rogers.

And there he stood before her, wielding his axe like a lumberjack.

Then he turned his head, revealing a face that was not Nick Rogers's at all, but that of Matthew Benson, the man who had come along to complicate her life. Disgusted with her wayward imagination, she went back to her desk and resumed writing.

By the time Matthew came in the kitchen door carrying a hefty armload of wood, Charlene had made a good start on her story, pulled two steaming loaves of bread from the oven, and set the table with coffee, bread, butter, and wild raspberry jam. She'd even had time to gather some early wildflowers to put in her mother's blue vase as a centerpiece.

She looked at the table with satisfaction and a touch of wonder. Splitting the day's wood was a routine part of her morning. She'd never before realized just how much time it actually took up. With Matthew taking over that chore, and by getting up earlier than usual, she had already made a surprising amount of progress that day.

Jed came out of his room in time to watch Matthew tumble a load of wood into the woodbox. "Not a bad morning's work for a city feller, eh, Charlene?" He chuckled, and Matthew beamed at his approval. Charlene agreed grudgingly, trying to ignore the guilt she felt about taking Matthew's willing help when she wasn't being completely truthful with him.

He looked even more handsome than the day before. With a good night's sleep, he had shed the signs of fatigue following his long journey, and this morning he looked invigorated and ready for the day.

This morning as they gathered for breakfast, she noted the way he bowed his head, completely at ease as he waited for Jed to ask the blessing.

She studied him as she moved to the kitchen and back, bringing the men more coffee. *It might be nice to have him here under other circumstances,* she thought. *As a neighbor perhaps, someone who was going to stay close by.*

There was no denying he was handy around the

place. Goodness, he must have split nearly the whole woodpile; she wouldn't have to do that chore again for a good while. And he certainly looked natural in that setting, leaning back contentedly in his chair visiting with Jed.

He brushed a hand at his ear, as if shooing away an irritating fly. Charlene stifled a giggle. A wave of his rust-colored hair curled forward, the ends barely touching his ear and apparently tickling it. She felt a sudden longing to reach out and tuck the wave back into place, and brought herself up short with a start.

Pressing her hands against her cheeks, she closed her eyes and shook her head. Maybe she had been spending too much time in the realm of fiction. It was time to move back to the real world and leave Nick Rogers in her stories, where he belonged. She sat down briskly and finished her last few bites of bread.

Matthew wiped his mouth with his napkin. "Is there anything else I can do for you, Miss Matkin?" Jed cleared his throat, and Matthew grinned sheepishly. "I mean— Charlene?"

"You've done a great deal already," she replied, fighting down the surge of pleasure she felt at the sound of her name on his lips. "I'll be ready to go as soon as I wash the dishes and straighten up a bit."

❧

Matthew watched her cheeks grow pink when he said her name. *Like the blush on a rose,* he thought. And her eyes were the deep blue of his mother's delphiniums back home.

What about her hair? He tried to think of some comparison that would go along with his fanciful garden theme. Ripe wheat? Maybe. No, more like corn silk. He liked the way the tiny wisps pulled free, forming soft tendrils around her face.

"Let me dry the dishes," he offered, wanting to study the effect more closely. He won out over her objections by pointing out that it would save them time, and soon found himself with a dish towel in his hand, wiping the dishes Charlene handed him, while Jed supervised.

Uneasy at first about working with Matthew in such close quarters, Charlene found to her surprise that it felt curiously natural to be sharing a chore with him, with Jed providing a running commentary while they worked. *Better get used to being close to him,* she told herself. *There isn't much room on that wagon seat.*

"You're pretty handy at splitting wood for a city feller," Jed commented.

"I've done a good bit of camping," Matthew explained. "I like being outdoors and roughing it. In fact," he said, wiping a cup and setting it down with care, "my family has a summer home in the country that I use as a retreat whenever I feel the need to get away from the city. I spend quite a bit of time there."

Charlene started at the mention of his family, and wondered for the first time if that included a wife. But she hadn't seen a wedding band on his hand. She mentally shook herself. *As if it's any of your concern! Get hold of yourself!* she scolded. With the dishes done, she soon had the house put in order and went to her room to get ready for Matthew's first tour.

The dress she'd put on earlier was serviceable enough, she decided, not something that would easily be ruined by a long drive in the wagon. She turned to the mirror to pat her hair into place and sighed in exasperation when she saw the unruly strands curling around her forehead. Loose already, and the day hardly begun! She shrugged and left them as they were. No point in tying them back when they'd be pulled loose again by the spring breeze as soon as she went outside.

A glance at the sun's position outside her window showed her it was much earlier than she'd expected to leave, and with her writing and housework caught up, too. Maybe she'd better make the most of this arrangement while it lasted. It might not be so bad, after all.

When she emerged from her room, she found Matthew had changed into a gray broadcloth shirt and had already hitched up the horses. She shook her head, marveling at the way she continually had to reassess her perception of the man. He certainly wasn't the helpless city slicker she'd expected.

After he had helped her into the seat and was climbing in himself, she asked him, "What do you want to see?" She forced the words out with difficulty, finding herself unaccountably shy now that they were going to be alone for the first time. Panic rose up in her, and she fought to keep it down. What would they talk about? Would she be able to keep from revealing her secret without her grandfather around to lend a hand?

"I'd like to start with a general survey of the area,"

Matthew said, apparently oblivious to her consternation. "Get the lay of the land, so to speak. When I'm better oriented, we'll start looking at specific locations, if that's all right with you."

Charlene nodded and waved good-bye to Jed, who sat on the front porch with an infuriatingly smug smile on his face. All right for him; he didn't have to spend the day watching every word he uttered! She guided the team in a meandering loop that took them through alpine meadows and forests, along craggy precipices and across rippling streams. Matthew stared in rapt wonder and breathed deeply of the tangy, pine-scented air, as if taking in every detail.

He peppered Charlene with questions, which she answered readily, identifying Ponderosa pines and aspens and the different kinds of grasses and shrubs. When she drew his attention to a red-tailed hawk gliding silently over an open glade, his eyes lit up with an excitement that tugged at Charlene's heart.

Passing along the edge of a clearing, she pulled the horses to a gentle stop. "Look," she said softly, pointing across the broad meadow. "Just coming past that clump of oaks. Do you see him?"

Matthew strained his eyes, searching for movement. Then his breath caught in his throat. A bull elk strode out of the trees into full view, carrying his rack of antlers with majestic dignity. Charlene leaned close. "It's late for him to still have his antlers," she whispered. "I guess he waited, just for you."

Before she moved away, Matthew caught the full

effect of her dazzling blue eyes, sparkling now with delight at being able to share the sight of the elk with him. He smiled back at her and suddenly, seeming as skittish as a forest creature, she pulled away, clucked to the horses, and they moved on.

Matthew closed his eyes and tried to regain his equilibrium. The scents, the sights, the sounds, and the unnerving presence of this girl all combined into a heady mixture that threatened to overwhelm his senses.

Charlene turned the team to the south, and Matthew realized they were heading into town. "I hope you don't mind," she said. "I need to pick up some supplies."

"Not at all," he replied. "I forgot to make arrangements to have someone come out and collect the buggy I rented, so I can take care of that while you shop."

He strode off down the street and Charlene headed into the general store.

"I have quite a bit to get this time." She handed the bank draft and her list to Mr. Foster with a smile. He pursed his lips in a soundless whistle at the number of items she had listed, then set to work retrieving them.

Charlene whiled away her time fingering bolts of fabric and wondering whether she could afford a new spring dress. *If not*, she reflected, *it doesn't matter.* They would have supplies aplenty for a good while to come, and that was the important thing. A new dress wasn't a necessity. It wasn't as though she wanted to impress anyone. *Oh, don't you?* sang a little voice in her head.

No, I don't, she retorted, putting the interfering voice firmly in its place.

Matthew chose that moment to enter the store. He stopped just inside the door and peered around, his dark eyes lighting up with pleasure when he spotted her. To her chagrin, Charlene caught herself reaching up to smooth her hair. She yanked her arms down to her sides and walked to the counter, trying to look completely relaxed and at ease. *I am* not *trying to impress anyone,* she repeated.

Matthew moved next to her, and Abel Foster quirked up one eyebrow when he saw them standing together. "Found the Matkinses all right, did you?" he asked, tallying up Charlene's purchases.

"This is Mr. Benson," she said, wishing she could control the flush she felt staining her cheeks. "He's visiting Grandpa and me for a while."

Abel nodded as though the information was of little interest, but Charlene was sure she caught a speculative glance from under his lowered eyelids.

Matthew waved off Abel's offer to help load the wagon and carried several heavy armloads outside. Charlene was supervising his placement of the items in the wagon when a voice behind her made her jump.

"Why, Charlene Matkin! Good to see you out and about again."

She whirled to find Brother Jenkins, the local preacher, beaming at her. "Hello," she replied warmly, genuinely pleased to see the man. "It has been a while, hasn't it? I think the roads have been worse than usual this spring. Now they've dried out, I'll be back in church again."

"I'll look forward to seeing you." Brother Jenkins picked up a sack of flour and swung it effortlessly onto the wagon bed. "How's that ornery old grandfather of yours?"

Charlene laughed. "He's doing well, thanks. I know he'd like to get out more, but he doesn't let it get him down." She introduced Matthew, and the two men shook hands.

"Good to meet you," said the pastor. "I hope to see you both in church." Charlene shot a sidelong glance at Matthew, wondering what appeal their little country church would hold for someone who had undoubtedly heard many well-trained ministers. To her delight, he seemed buoyed up by the prospect of attending.

"I look forward to it," he said with enthusiasm. It gave Charlene food for thought long after Brother Jenkins had waved a cheery good-bye and they had started for home.

❧

Supper that evening was more elaborate than the night before, and Charlene breathed a prayer of gratitude for their replenished larder. When the meal was over, Matthew helped dry the dishes as though it were a matter of routine before he settled in front of the hearth with Jed, barely noticing when Charlene said a quiet good night and slipped off to her room.

Matthew stretched his legs out toward the fire and heaved a sigh of sheer contentment, letting his eyelids droop nearly closed. The weather had been pleasant earlier, but now there was a distinct chill in the air, and he welcomed the warmth of the dancing flames. Matthew glanced at Jed, who stared at the flickering points of light as if watching scenes of his early years.

"When I first saw these mountains," said the older man, confirming Matthew's thought, "it seemed like there was only me and God out here. I helped open the way for others to come. And I did it willingly, but it will never be the same. Never again."

"I envy you, seeing it in that pristine state," Matthew told him, without moving his gaze from the fire. "You were able to witness something only a very few people have. What I treasure, though, is sharing a small part of that experience through your stories. Thousands of readers like me will have at least some idea of what it was like because we've traveled through it with Nick Rogers, seen it with his eyes."

Matthew turned his head lazily toward his companion. "You're quite a man, Jed. Not many men who helped conquer the West would have the desire or the ability to share it so well."

Jed shuffled his feet, apparently lost in thought, and Matthew wondered if he'd heard a word of his praise for Jed's stories.

"I came out here hardly more than a youngster," Jed reminisced. "But a man has to grow up and catch on quick out here, or he doesn't survive. I trapped beaver, fox, and marmot all through these mountains. Sometimes I'd go for months without seeing a living soul."

"Didn't you ever get lonely?" Matthew asked softly, not wanting to break the other man's concentration.

"Lonely?" Jed shook his head. "I came out here to get away from people. Back where I came from, a body didn't have any elbow room, and it seemed like folks were so busy pushing each other aside to get what they wanted, they didn't have time to be decent to one another anymore. Out here, a man has room to walk, room to think, and time to get to know God.

"Besides," he added with a grin, "it wasn't all isolation. You should have seen the rendezvous, when we'd all gather to swap stories and sell the pelts we'd collected. My, those were shinin' times! Now, some of those old boys had stories your readers would love to hear. Bill Williams, Antoine Leroux, Pauline Weaver—I met 'em all, one time or another."

"So how did you wind up with a family, way out here?"

Jed chuckled, remembering. "Back home, where all those people were fussing at each other, there was a girl named Mary. No matter how long I stayed away, no matter how many mountains I crossed, I couldn't get her out of my mind. I'd see her face in the river, in the clouds, in my dreams.

"One day I chucked it all and went back to see if she remembered me. She just stood there, tapped her foot, and said, 'You took your own sweet time coming back, Jedediah. I'd about given up on waiting for you.' " He threw back his head and roared.

"That was some woman, I'm telling you! I stuck it out back there until Robert, Charlene's father, was about half grown. Then these old mountains started pulling at me again. Mary knew me so well, one day she said, 'We've stayed here long enough, Jedediah. You won't be happy unless you have both me and your mountains. Since we can't move the mountains here, it looks like we'd better start packing.'

"Two weeks later, we headed west. Set up our place over on the Verde River. After Robert was grown, he made a foray over to the California goldfields. He didn't make a strike, but he came back with a wife, and they settled right here. When I came to live with them, I helped them add on to this house.

"It's been a good life," he reflected. "A different kind of life, but a good one."

"I'd say it was a remarkable life," Matthew told him. He went on, hoping he was not being overly effusive with his praise. "What appeals to me most about your stories is that they're accurate, not romanticized. You haven't fallen into the trap so many have of exaggerating in order to capture the reader's interest, and thank goodness for that!

"Why they feel they have to stretch the truth at all is beyond me," he continued. "This country is so big, so wide open, just portraying it as it is makes it seem larger than life to readers back east. There's no need to embellish. The truth is astounding enough."

"So you like what you see, do you?" asked Jed, with a quiet smile.

Matthew took a moment to respond, framing his answer carefully. "It isn't often that reality lives up to your expectations. But in this case, it's everything I had imagined. . .and more," he added softly, thinking of the girl with the delphinium-blue eyes framed by a golden halo of hair.

Chapter Four

A determined shaft of sunlight broke through a tiny gap in the curtains and fixed itself on Charlene's right eyelid. She scrunched her eyes tighter and muttered in her sleep. Slowly, the knowledge that the sun was not only up but up high enough to be shining in her bedroom window penetrated her sleep-numbed mind, and she sat up with a start, clutching the bedclothes to her.

She shook her head, trying to clear away the dullness, and measured the sun's height with a practiced eye. She couldn't remember ever sleeping this late in her life! But then, she had seldom been up as late as she was the night before.

Slipping off while Jed and Matthew were engaged in conversation had given her valuable time alone, and the ideas flowed freely from her mind onto the paper. Charlene had become so absorbed in her writing that she didn't realize how much time had passed until the flame guttered and she saw that the lamp was almost out of oil.

Now, rubbing the last traces of sleep from her eyes, she swung her legs over the edge of the bed. It was a wonder Jed hadn't come banging on the door long before this to find out if she was ill. Maybe he and Matthew had overslept, too.

She hoped so. That would give her time to put things in order before they discovered her slothfulness. Charlene hastily pulled her brown calico dress over her head and emerged from its folds with her nose twitching. What was that tantalizing smell? Surely not coffee! Consumed with curiosity, she hurriedly dressed her hair and bolted out into the kitchen.

The smell was coffee, all right, the aroma itself strong enough to jolt her completely awake. The fire in the woodstove sent fingers of radiant warmth through the house. Jed sat at the table, contentedly nursing a mug of coffee.

"Must be nice to have someone take over your chores so you can spend half the day in bed," he grumbled, as though talking to himself. Seeing Charlene's stricken look, he burst forth with a loud guffaw. "Don't take on so, honey. I was only teasing."

His gaze rested on her fondly. "I saw the light under your door when I got up to throw another log on the fire last night. I figured you'd need some extra sleep."

"Is Matthew awake yet?"

Jed snorted. "He was up before I was. Had the fire going and coffee on by the time I got out here. Hear that?" He nodded toward the barn, and Charlene could hear the rhythmic blows of a hammer. "Said he noticed some loose boards that needed fixing when he was in there yesterday and thought he'd put it to rights to help pay for his keep."

He took a sip and mumbled, "If he keeps this up, *we'll* owe *him* before long.

"We had another good talk while he drank his coffee this mornin'," Jed went on, while Charlene began stirring up pancake batter. "It gave me a chance to get to know him a little better." He paused, then asked bluntly, "What do you think of him?"

The direct question caught Charlene off guard. "What do I think of him?" she repeated, trying to buy herself some time before answering. *I think of him entirely too much,* she admitted to herself. "He seems nice enough. Why? What do you think of him?" she asked brightly, trying to appear unconcerned.

"I think he's a decent man. I truly like him. You know I don't usually take to folks right off."

Charlene listened to make sure she could still hear the hammering from the barn before she asked the question that was on her heart. "What about letting him think you wrote the stories?"

Jed hung his head, looking uncharacteristically abashed. "I don't like it," he said flatly. "I thought it would be fine, since those stories were mine long before I ever shared them with you, but it doesn't feel right. I think we ought to set him straight." He glanced up at Charlene expectantly.

But Charlene knew she needed more time to consider his request. "He does seem nice," she said slowly. "But our livelihood is riding on the line. He can finish his trip, go back to Baltimore, and continue with his paper without giving us another thought." Her heart lurched at the idea of his leaving and forgetting about her. She pushed her emotions down.

"But we've got to get along somehow, and I don't know yet how he'll feel about having a woman writer." She fixed Jed with serious blue eyes, begging him to understand. "I want to tell him the truth too. It's just that I'm not sure I'm willing to trust him with our future. Not yet, anyway. We need to find the right time."

The unspoken question of when that right time would be hung between them for a long moment before Jed spoke. "You've got a point there, honey," he said quietly. "All right. We'll wait a while longer before we say anything."

The scrape of boots on the back porch alerted them to Matthew's arrival. When he swung the door open, Charlene was flicking water from her fingertips onto the griddle to see if it was hot enough. The dancing droplets announced that it was, and she poured out dollops of the batter. Behind her, she heard Matthew scoot a chair out from the table and sit down.

"Finished already, are you?" Jed chuckled. "I can't get over how handy you are. Not at all what I expected of a city boy."

"It must be this wonderful mountain air," Matthew said exultantly. "I feel like I could do anything." Charlene placed a platter stacked high with hotcakes in front of them, then slid into her chair.

"Try ignoring those delicious flapjacks," Jed suggested, and Matthew chuckled appreciatively.

"Where to this morning?" Charlene asked with forced cheerfulness. Now that she and Jed had agreed that Matthew must be told of their deception, she felt a barrier had been erected between them.

Matthew didn't seem to notice. "I think I would like to start with the place where Nick—that is, Jed," he amended with a grin, "talked his way out of trouble with that Apache hunting party. Is it too far away?"

❦

By the time they were halfway there, Charlene thought gloomily that she should have answered yes. Their route twisted, turned, and threaded along trails barely wide enough for the wagon to pass.

Normally, the leisurely pace along the turning route made this one of Charlene's favorite drives. Today, however, was hardly normal. Since her conversation with Jed, guilt over their misrepresentation of the truth swelled up, choking her with shame.

How could something that seemed so simple—was it only a couple of days before?—turn into such a complicated situation? *The truth shall set you free,* she chided herself. *The truth could also cost me dearly,* she argued back.

Fortunately, Matthew was too engrossed in their surroundings to pay attention to her brooding. They rode along in companionable silence, and Charlene was grateful that he seemed happy enough just drinking in the scenery.

❦

When they neared the top of a slope, Charlene stopped the wagon, allowing the horses a chance to catch their breath. "Just over the rise," she told Matthew, "is the place. Grandpa came along through those trees, following a game trail." She swept her hand to the southeast, indicating his route. Staring intently, Matthew could just make out the faint path.

"He thought he was all alone," she continued, "until he topped the rise. You'll see in a minute how it forms a hollow. And down in the center of that hollow were four braves, busy dressing out a deer. By the time Grandpa realized they were there, they'd already seen him.

"It was an awful fix to be in! Even with the bit of a head start he had, and with them having to run uphill to follow him, he knew he'd never be able to get away." She paused and Matthew tried to imagine what he would have done in the same situation.

"Is it true he got his inspiration from the Bible?" he asked.

Charlene laughed, a sound Matthew immediately decided he'd like to hear again. "He was quite a character, even back then. He'd read that morning about how David feigned madness before the Philistines. If it worked for David, he figured it might work for him, too. So, instead of running away, he rushed right toward them with a huge smile on his face, pulling his Bible out of his pack as he ran. He jumped onto a big rock, flipped open his Bible, and started preaching to those braves at the top of his lungs."

"And it really worked, the way it did in the story?"

"It worked, all right. They must have thought he was crazy as a loon, for they grabbed that deer and took off as fast as they could. Grandpa just kept on preaching, long after they were out of sight. He said he'd read that God's Word never comes back void, so he figured the Lord would be able to use it somehow in those Indians' lives."

Matthew threw back his head and laughed. "I can just picture him doing it."

"Are you ready?" she asked, her eyes still dancing with the excitement of the story.

Matthew nodded and stared in rapt attention as they crested the ridge, tracing the actions of the story in his mind. He stepped down from the wagon as soon as Charlene drew the team to a halt, and he walked slowly through the trees, his feet making little noise as they padded along the forest floor, pressing into the carpet of pine needles, grass, and the leaves from a hundred autumns.

In the center of the bowl-shaped depression was a clearing, perhaps two acres in size. Its grassy expanse was ringed by aspens, whose erect paper-white trunks with their distinctive black markings stood sentinel, swaying gently in the breeze.

A more pastoral setting was hard to imagine, but in his mind's eye Matthew could picture the Indians looking up, startled, from their work. He could see Jed stop abruptly as he realized the gravity of the situation and tried to think of a way out. That he had done so was a testament to the man's quick thinking and courage.

The aspens framing the clearing, backed up by the tall Ponderosas, the faint trail leading the unsuspecting

Jed into danger, even the rock where Jed had preached his "sermon"—everything was just as he had pictured it.

No, he corrected himself, *it was just as Charlie Matkin had portrayed it, painting a picture with words that was as vivid as a photograph.*

He shook his head slowly, marveling at the varied talents of the former mountain man. Who would have thought it possible an untamed spirit like that could prove to be such a gifted writer?

The descriptions in the Nick Rogers stories had fired his imagination. He had known after reading the first few that he wouldn't be able to rest until he had seen those places for himself. And to think he had the privilege of meeting and spending time with the man who had done all this!

Matthew closed his eyes and breathed deeply. The tangy pine scent and the more earthy smell of the aspens mingled into a sweet perfume far more enticing to his way of thinking than the Paris imports favored by the young ladies of his acquaintance in Baltimore. *There was nothing,* he thought, *absolutely nothing back home that can compare with this.*

Charlene had busied herself setting out a picnic lunch and was waiting patiently when Matthew wandered back, his heart and mind full of the wonder of this place. He lowered himself onto the blanket she had spread out and, after closing his eyes for a brief blessing, helped himself to fried chicken and biscuits, grateful that Charlene seemed to sense his disinclination to talk and enjoyed the quiet with him.

Early wildflowers dotted the clearing, bravely opening themselves up before their fellows to welcome this new season of growth and hope. Matthew noticed a plant growing within arm's reach and plucked a stem from it. "What is this?" he asked, showing Charlene the blossoms nodding from its tip.

"Lupine," she answered with a smile. "It's one of my favorites. It blooms early and keeps on blooming until fall. Look over there," she said, pointing. "See that mass of pale blue? That's blue flax. And up there on the slope—the bright orange spot—that's the first Indian paintbrush I've seen this year."

Matthew shook his head regretfully. "I'm ashamed to say I know almost nothing about wildflowers. You seem as knowledgeable about them as my mother and grandmother are about the flowers they grow in their gardens."

"Grandpa taught me most of what I know," Charlene said. "And in a way, I guess these flowers *are* my garden. I mean, I don't plant them or tend them, but to me, all of this is part of my home. Home doesn't end at the edge of the dooryard." Her hands fluttered as if she were embarrassed and her cheeks were stained with that pink flush that never failed to fascinate Matthew.

Does she know she looks like a flower herself? he wondered. What would she do if he told her so?

Instead of speaking, he turned to examine the lupine in his hand more closely, gently caressing the purplish-blue blossoms with a fingertip. *The petals are shaped something like miniature sweet peas,* he thought, so delicate, yet hardy enough to survive in this harsh climate and thrive year after year. *Much like Charlene,* he realized with a start.

He stole a look at her as she gathered the remains of their lunch. Those delicate features, that slender build—a casual observer would never guess what inner strength they concealed.

Having taken it upon himself to perform many of her chores, he was amazed at the amount of heavy work she did as a matter of routine. True, a lot of things had been left undone—apparently there were things too hard even for Charlene—but like the lupine, she thrived and grew sturdily in her element, adding beauty to the world just by being in it.

Looking up, Matthew watched the slender-trunked aspens sway in the wind. Seated as he was in the hollow, he only felt the slightest of breezes, but up above, the treetops waved back and forth as if nodding to one another. The soughing of the wind through the treetops waxed and waned, almost like the sound of breathing. Matthew looked again at Charlene, who had repacked their lunch things and was sitting, hands folded in her lap, as if awaiting his command.

❦

She rose when he did and they walked, as if by mutual agreement, up the slope to the far edge of the ridge that rimmed the hollow. From there, they looked down across a vast expanse of mottled greens. Matthew drew in his breath with wonder.

Charlene smiled, pleased by his response. "The dark

green areas you see," she said, gesturing with her arm, "are Ponderosas. Those clusters of yellowish-green are aspens. When the leaves turn in the fall, those spots will light up with the brightest yellows and oranges you can imagine, as if God put together an enormous patchwork quilt."

Matthew studied the rolling contours of the hills, and he was filled with yearning to see them dressed in their autumn finery, to see that and every other seasonal change, not only that year but the next, and the next. Before that was possible, though, there was something he had to tell Charlene, and he didn't know how to begin. He had kept up his charade for too long already. But how could he tell her the truth now that he'd misled her for this long? He turned and followed as she led the way back to the wagon.

～

As they descended, Charlene stepped on a small fallen branch hidden under a blanket of pine needles. It rolled under her foot, throwing her off balance. She flailed her arms in an effort to recover her footing, an effort she knew was futile as soon as both feet began sliding down the slope. Then she heard hurried steps behind her as she braced herself for the fall, but her descent was suddenly arrested.

Her chest heaving with quick, shallow gasps, she realized Matthew had caught her, turned her around, and now held her, both arms wrapped around her and one foot braced securely against the base of the trunk of an ancient pine. They stood like that, neither of them moving except to draw breath, for an endless moment, with one of Matthew's arms supporting her shoulders and back, the other wrapped protectively around her waist.

Charlene stared into his deep brown eyes and was sure Matthew's gaze would bore right through her. His lips were slightly parted, and she could feel his breath, as quick and ragged as her own, move the loose strands of hair at her temples. His arms tightened about her, and for one moment, Charlene was certain he was about to kiss her.

Instead, he drew her to her feet, setting her upright and steadying her until he was sure she had regained her balance. Then, without a word, Matthew took her by the arm and escorted her gently down the bank.

They crossed the clearing in silence through dappled sunlight that painted shadowy patterns on the ground, and Matthew helped her into the wagon as though she were a fragile piece of china that might shatter at the slightest touch.

Neither of them broke the silence on the ride home, each keeping as much distance between them as possible on the narrow wagon seat.

Chapter Five

The days fell into a pattern, with Matthew rising early to do odd jobs that had long been neglected, and the two of them going exploring most afternoons. Charlene often thought about the moment when Matthew held her in his arms and she had gazed into his face, only inches away from her own. Matthew never mentioned the incident again, and Charlene didn't plan to bring it up. There seemed to be a tacit agreement between them to bury the episode in the past.

Had he intended to kiss her? Had she wanted him to? She briefly wondered if he hadn't kissed her because he did indeed have a wife back in Baltimore. But he had never mentioned a wife, so she quickly dismissed the notion as her own paranoia. Charlene didn't know the answer to her questions, and wasn't sure she wanted to.

You're crazy even to consider such a thing! she told herself fiercely. *He could take not only your heart but your income if he chose to, and here you want to go swooning right into his arms!* But she couldn't truly picture Matthew doing harm to her or anybody else.

He'll be going back east anytime now. That much was

certain. *Besides that, you barely know the man. What kind of person are you, anyway?* She wasn't sure she wanted to know the answer to that question, either.

No one mentioned the topic of Matthew's departure. Matthew appeared content to fit into the routine they had established and showed no inclination to leave anytime soon. Jed was happier than Charlene had seen him in a long, long time. Having another man around the place was evidently good medicine for him. And Charlene found her life changing for the better in many ways.

Matthew's assumption of the heavier chores left her free to concentrate on the duties she enjoyed most. And the shortcuts she had developed enabled her to keep house in record time. As for her writing. . .Charlene found, to her amazement, that she had produced an astonishing amount during the uninterrupted times she had in the early mornings and in the evenings when Matthew and Jed talked by the fire.

Not only was she writing more, but the quality of her writing had improved markedly. Even she was aware of it. It was funny, she mused, that the very situation that had driven her to write in secrecy had also enhanced her work beyond her wildest dreams. She was almost grateful to Matthew Benson for disrupting the even tenor of her life.

With another story finished and ready to submit ahead of schedule, Charlene decided to take a well-deserved break one evening. Gathering her mending and her sewing basket after supper, she approached Jed, who was sitting in his favorite chair in the living room. "Mind if I join you?" she asked playfully.

"It's about time you poked your head out of your room," he responded, his eyes twinkling. "I've almost forgotten what female company is like. Sit down, honey. Matthew should be finished feeding the horses before long. We can all have a nice visit when he comes back."

"He's outside? Good." Charlene pulled a folded sheaf of paper from her pocket and handed it to Jed. "It's the latest story. Take a look at it and tell me what you think." She threaded a needle and began replacing a button on one of Jed's shirts.

Jed held the papers out nearly to arm's length and began to read, his lips moving silently as he scanned the pages. Charlene watched anxiously, unable to gauge his reaction. She suddenly felt unsure. Had she been wrong? Had she overestimated the quality of this piece? No matter how many stories she sold or how many complimentary remarks she received from Mr. Emerson, her grandfather's opinion was still the last word as far as she was concerned.

"What do you think?" she asked as soon as he lowered the papers, unable to contain her curiosity a moment longer.

His faded blue eyes held a faint spark of mischief. "I think it's a fine piece of writing." He folded the papers with care. "But that's just my opinion. Let's see what a real expert has to say about it." He tucked the papers between the arm and the cushion of his chair and settled himself more comfortably.

"Oh, no," Charlene said, perceiving his intent. "I've gone through too much already, hiding out and writing behind closed doors. So far, we've gotten away with it. I don't want to push our luck. Give me the story, Grandpa."

Jed patted the hand she held out to him. "Simmer down, honey. It'll be fine." Charlene was about to make a grab for the papers when the door swung inward and Matthew entered the room.

"Look who we've got for company tonight," Jed announced to Matthew as he smiled teasingly at Charlene, who glared back at him. Her irritation was somewhat allayed by the way Matthew's face lit up with pleasure at Jed's statement. After spending part of nearly every day together in the wagon, it was a welcome compliment to see his obvious delight at the prospect of spending even more time with her now.

Charlene bit off the tail end of her thread and picked up a new piece of mending. Matthew sank into an overstuffed chair as naturally as if he had lived there for years instead of only weeks.

"I've been a little curious about something," Jed said, breaking the comfortable silence. "How can you manage to take so much time away from the paper, especially when you just bought it? Aren't you worried about everything falling apart while you're gone?"

Charlene couldn't decide whether the ruddy hue on Matthew's face was due to a blush or the glow from the fireplace. He rose to add another piece of wood to the fire, prodding it with the poker until he had it arranged to his satisfaction.

"No, I'm not worried," he answered without turning his head. "I left it in very capable hands." He replaced the poker and resumed his seat.

"Speaking of the newspaper," Jed went on smoothly, "I've got something here that might interest you." He withdrew the story from his chair casually, as if he'd had it there all evening. "Nick Rogers's latest adventure. Would you care to hear it?"

Charlene gave an involuntary jump, barely avoiding jabbing herself with her needle. Her grandfather, she fumed, was treating this whole situation all too lightly. Didn't he understand what the consequences could mean for them?

Matthew perked up at Jed's offer, readily agreeing to listen. Jed cleared his throat and began to read aloud, pronouncing each word carefully. Charlene feigned deep concentration on the seam she was repairing, not daring to look at Matthew.

Thank goodness, Grandpa has at least read it once! It would have been awful if he'd stumbled over the phrasing. She listened as Jed continued, impressed with the way he made the story come alive.

Listen to the old faker! Why, I'd swear he really was the author, if I hadn't written it myself. No wonder he was able to bluff his way out of so many tight spots in his younger days.

The sound of Jed's voice ceased, and she realized he had finished reading. Her amused thoughts halted abruptly as she waited for Matthew's reaction. Here, as

Grandpa had said, was an expert. What would his honest response be?

She moved the needle in and out of the fabric determinedly, her eyes focused on the job at hand and the rest of her being on the words that would come from Matthew's lips.

"I'm not sure what to say, Jed." Her heart sank. "Just when I think you can't possibly top the previous effort, you get even better." Matthew leaned forward in his chair and clapped Jed on the shoulder. "That's the best Nick Rogers piece yet!"

A sigh of infinite relief whooshed from Charlene's lungs, and she looked up to see her own broad smile reflected on her grandfather's face. "Charlene can mail it off tomorrow," he said.

"May I see it first?" Matthew asked, holding out his hand. In response to Jed's puzzled frown he added, "I want to add a note of my own—telling the bookkeeper to increase the payment." Charlene looked down again at her mending to hide the happy tears that sprang to her eyes.

The evening went on peacefully, the men visiting companionably and Charlene adding her own comments from time to time. It struck her that the three of them together felt like a family.

Look at Grandpa, she thought with a guilty pang, seeing the way his face brightened at the opportunity to talk and share. *He hasn't had companionship like that since I started spending so much time writing.* It was just one more reason to be grateful to Matthew.

❧

"Are you sure you won't go to church with us, Grandpa? It's a beautiful morning, and you haven't been out for so long." Charlene tried to keep the pleading note out of her voice, knowing that Jed disliked being pressured.

"Not today, honey," Jed told her gently. "It's a mighty pretty morning, all right, but last night got cold enough that my old knee is acting up something fierce. You two go on ahead, though. I'll be fine."

Having Matthew accompany her to church was still something of a novelty to Charlene. True to his enthusiasm when he first met Brother Jenkins, he seemed to look forward to their simple services with relish.

Charlene enjoyed the congregational singing, but hearing Matthew join in beside her had enhanced it immeasurably. She had expected him to have a good singing voice, considering his rich baritone, and she wasn't disappointed. And far from looking down on Brother Jenkins's plainspoken preaching after being exposed to the learned ministers from the city, he listened intently during the sermons, as if unwilling to miss a single word.

Charlene appreciated his evident enjoyment and willingness to participate. She *didn't*, however, appreciate the curious looks being cast in their direction by other members of the congregation. To take her mind off them, she turned her attention back to the sermon.

"Spring is my favorite season," Brother Jenkins was saying, a broad smile covering the lower half of his square face. "It's the season of hope, of new life. It's the time our Lord chose to show us the most powerful example of new life—the Resurrection.

"You know," he continued, "every year, I watch as we make preparations for Christmas. Even out here in our remote area, we plan get-togethers and try to think of gifts we can share with our loved ones. It's a special season, and we spend a good bit of time getting ready for it."

Brother Jenkins leaned across the rough-hewn pulpit and peered intently at the worshipers. "We spend plenty of time remembering the joy of Jesus' birth. . . but what do we do in remembrance of His great sacrifice for us, the giving up of His own life so we might have life eternal?"

His gaze roamed over the attentive congregation, and Charlene felt he could see straight into her heart. "I would like to challenge each one of you. Each one of *us*," he corrected softly.

"As we approach Easter, let us plan to give a gift to our Savior. As we remember Jesus' sacrifice, may we prepare our hearts, striving to live our lives free from sin, in gratitude for what He has done. Make a special effort to live during these coming days as we should endeavor to live every day. . .pure and consecrated to Him."

Charlene, whose spirit had soared with thankfulness at the reminder of Jesus' great gift of love, felt the joy of the day dim at these words. She saw Matthew bow his head for Brother Jenkins's closing prayer, and she hurriedly ducked her own. The words she heard, however, were not Brother Jenkins's benediction, but her own tortured self-condemnation.

With her whole heart, she felt herself respond to the pastor's call to commitment. But how could she do it? A life free from sin, when she was deliberately living a lie? *Lord, I don't want to dishonor You. I know I have to tell Matthew the truth. Please show me the right time to do it, and give me the courage I'll need.*

She had better do it quickly, she realized. Not only was Easter almost upon them, but Matthew had been with them for several weeks already. He could go home anytime, and she wanted—*needed*—to have the matter cleared up before then.

The awareness that Matthew might indeed decide to return to Baltimore before long hit Charlene like a blow to the stomach. What was wrong with her? She ought to be relieved that her life would once more be back on an even keel.

Then why did that knowledge leave her feeling as cold and empty as an abandoned hearth?

The scrape of chairs and murmur of voices alerted her that the last "amen" had been said and the congregation was milling around, visiting with one another. She opened her eyes to find Matthew staring at her quizzically.

"Are you all right?" he asked, his eyes warm with concern.

Charlene nodded, not trusting herself to speak in her present state of confusion. She threaded her way through the crowd without talking to anyone and waited for Matthew in the wagon.

Several times during the day, Charlene opened her mouth to blurt out the truth about Charlie Matkin. Each time, words failed her and her mouth closed of its own accord. She knew Jed, after giving her permission to wait until she was ready, was expecting her to carry through on this. More, she knew the Lord expected her to be truthful.

She had every good reason in the world to own up to her deception. So why was she so reluctant to get on with it?

It wasn't just the money anymore, she confessed to herself in the privacy of her room that night. Knowing Matthew as she did now, she couldn't see him refusing to use her stories. Even if he did, God had taken care of her and Jed before, and He would continue to do so.

No, the reason for her reluctance was that she didn't want to see the look of disappointment she knew would appear in Matthew's eyes. He might agree to use every Charlie Matkin story she ever wrote, but she couldn't bear the thought that he might turn away from her in disgust when he learned of her duplicity.

And why should that matter? teased the annoying little voice in her brain. "Because we've become friends and I don't want to lose his respect," she muttered. *Are you sure that's all?* "Yes. No. I don't know," she moaned, throwing herself across her bed and burying her head under her pillow.

But she did know. Her feelings for Matthew had gone from cautious reserve to friendship, and from there had deepened into something she didn't care to explore.

"You're an idiot to feel like this," she rebuked herself. "He'll be heading back east anytime and you'll be staying here. There is no point in letting your heart get involved with a man you'll never see again."

It was too late, she admitted. Her heart was already involved, with or without her consent, and it was going to hurt terribly when Matthew left.

"It's ridiculous!" she scolded herself. "You only met him a few weeks ago. You can't possibly know him well enough to love him." She knew she was right, knew it made perfect sense.

But her heart argued with that logic.

Chapter Six

"Are you going to tell your old grandpa what's wrong?" Jed pushed his rocking chair gently with his good leg and stared at the snow-capped peaks in the distance.

Charlene ceased her restless pacing along the front porch and plopped into the chair next to him, pressing both hands against her temples. "I guess there's no point in telling you there's nothing wrong," she mumbled.

"Oh, I suppose you could," he answered, as imperturbable as the mountains he stared at. "Expecting me to believe it, though, that's another matter." He rocked on in silence, slanting a shrewd look at Charlene. "It wouldn't have anything to do with our guest, would it?"

Charlene threw a frantic look over her shoulder as if expecting to see Matthew standing right behind them.

"Take it easy." Jed patted her hand, chuckling. "He's still in town getting the lumber he wanted for fixing up the barn roof. Now, what's going on?"

"I'm. . .having trouble finding the right time to tell him about Charlie."

"Mm-hm. And that's all?"

"What more could there be?" Charlene asked, eyeing him suspiciously.

Jed pursed his lips, considering. "Hmm. How about the fact that you're head over heels in love with him?"

Charlene gaped at him in astonishment. She opened her mouth to deny it. Closed her mouth and opened it again for another try, but could form no words to contest what they both knew was true.

"Well?" she cried in frustration. "Aren't you going to tell me how crazy this is? I've only known the man a few weeks."

Jed spoke slowly, his sober tone contrasting with the merriment in his eyes. "I've been wondering how long it would take you to figure it out," he said. "I've known it from the moment he showed up at our door."

"You couldn't possibly have known anything of the sort," Charlene retorted. "Things like that only happen in fiction. Why, I wouldn't put something so ridiculous in one of my stories."

"Ridiculous? Hogwash! I saw the look on your face when you opened the door to him. The first time I met your grandmother, she had that same thunderstruck look. We both did. Sometimes love creeps up on you slowlike," he asserted. "Sometimes it just leaps out and grabs you."

He rocked steadily, eyeing the distant mountains. "In our family, it tends to leap out and grab."

"That's utter nonsense!" Charlene catapulted out of her chair and stalked off toward the chicken coop, muttering. The brisk spring air fanned her cheeks as she strode along, sweeping the cobwebs from her mind and allowing her thoughts to fall into order.

Scooping cracked corn into her apron, she scattered it with wide sweeps of her arm, watching the birds chase the grain as it fell, pecking eagerly and sometimes taking up gravel instead of corn in their haste.

"Look at you! You're no better than I am," she told them. "You want the right thing, but you're going about it the wrong way."

She sank down on an empty crate outside the door and buried her face in her hands. What was she going to do? Her grandfather had just confirmed what her heart had been trying to tell her—she loved Matthew Benson. Matthew Benson, who, in a short time, would be traveling back to Baltimore, a continent away.

As if the wrench of parting weren't bad enough, she had to tell him the plain, unvarnished truth about Charlie Matkin, and tell him soon. Almost a week had passed since Brother Jenkins made his challenge to the congregation.

Charlene pictured telling Matthew the truth. She could see herself twisting her fingers nervously, haltingly forcing out the words that would forever change the way Matthew felt about her.

In her mind's eye, she saw his horrified expression when he realized the charade she had carried out. The Charlene of her imagination clasped her hands together, pleading with him to understand, to forgive. But Matthew made a repudiating gesture and turned away from her with an expression of distaste.

Charlene gave a cry of despair, startling two hens pecking at the grains of corn that had fallen from her apron. To have discovered love at last, only to lose it as quickly as she found it! When Brother Jenkins had talked about sacrifice, he hadn't known the half of it.

❧

Charlene heard Matthew drive the wagon past the house and back toward the barn while she measured the ingredients for a dried-apple cake. She could hear him unloading the lumber for the barn roof while she beat the batter. Knowing Matthew, she could picture him sorting it into neat piles as she poured the batter into a pan and slid it into the oven.

She licked a dab of batter from her finger and busied herself cleaning an already clean kitchen, knowing it was only a matter of moments before Matthew would walk in the door, and knowing she was only cleaning to keep her mind occupied.

Jed sat at the table, cradling a steaming mug of coffee in both hands. After their confrontation on the front porch, he hadn't said a word. Neither had Charlene. She had reached a turning point, one from which there would be no going back.

She was just pulling the cake from the oven when the back door opened and Matthew entered the room, eyes shining from the exertion of unloading the lumber. What a picture he made! Charlene tried to fix his image in her memory for all the long, lonely years she was certain were ahead.

"What a glorious day!" he exulted. "Jed, with your permission, I'd like to borrow your granddaughter for a while. It's too beautiful a day to waste working on that roof. I'll get to it first thing tomorrow."

Charlene watched him, emotions warring within her, as he awaited Jed's answer. He looked so exuberant, it nearly broke her heart. What she would give just to revel in his company today! Instead, she had something to tell him that would wipe that joyful look from his face.

Jed took a slow sip of coffee. "I reckon that depends on what Charlene wants to do," he said, not looking at either of them.

Matthew turned to Charlene, his face alight with boyish eagerness. *I won't see him smiling at me again after what I have to say,* she thought with a pang. "All right, Matthew," she said dully. "I'll go."

~∂

Matthew let out a low whistle. "I don't know how you do it," he said in a wondering voice. "Every time we visit a new place, I'm sure you've brought me to the most beautiful spot on earth. Then you manage to find one even better the next time.

"But this—" He swiveled his head to take in the full panorama. "This has to be the absolute best."

Charlene managed a small smile, gratified by his reaction. Matthew had asked her to guide him to a place where they could enjoy spring in all its splendor. The spot Charlene had chosen was her favorite, one she had used as the setting for several Nick Rogers stories. It was a breathtakingly beautiful location at any time, but now, just awakened from its long winter sleep, it was especially magnificent.

Small clumps of aspens, pale trunks gleaming in the

sunlight, made a stark contrast to the darker pine trees. Underfoot, springy green grass just now sending out tender shoots cushioned their steps.

Charlene led Matthew to an open spot next to a stream fed by the melting snows, wondering if she had made a mistake bringing him here. Normally, seeing this place in the spring filled her with a sense of promise, of hope. Today, she felt only a sense of dread.

∼

Matthew settled himself comfortably next to the stream while Charlene took up a spot several feet away on a cushiony hummock of grass.

He leaned back on one elbow and feasted his eyes on the scene. Columbines of varied hues lent spots of color to the glade, and emerald green moss clung to the time-worn rocks that lined the icy stream. High up in this mountain pass, spring was slow in coming. And patches of snow still lingered here and there. Everywhere was nature's incomparable glory.

And then there was Charlene.

Matthew watched her trail her fingers in the water, then trace light patterns on the velvety moss. She seemed a natural part of this setting, at one with its beauty, and apparently oblivious to his presence.

His heart constricted. He had asked her to come out with him on impulse, spurred by the freshness of the day. He knew that now was the time to speak, before he lost his nerve. But how to start?

"You're as lovely as one of those columbines." The words were out before he could stop them, and he sat frozen, waiting for her reaction.

Charlene stared at him incredulously, lips parted, and shook her head slightly, unable to speak. Not knowing what else to do, she turned away and began plucking columbine blossoms from their stems, hoping he didn't notice the way her fingers trembled.

"I didn't know you had such a poetic streak in you," she said, trying to make her tone light to mask the emotion that washed over her at his words. Could it be that Matthew had feelings for her, too? She nearly groaned aloud at the poor timing. *Why here? Why now?* If only things were out in the open between them so they could explore their feelings freely!

She heard Matthew shift on the grass as he sat up. When he spoke again, his voice sounded closer. "I'd say you were the one with the poetic streak." His breath stirred the hair at the back of her neck, and she closed her eyes, trying to control the tingly sensations that flooded her being.

"This place is just the way I pictured it from reading about it." His husky voice swept over her like a caress. "You described it perfectly. . .Charlie."

Caught up in the struggle to govern her feelings, Charlene didn't catch his meaning at first. Then his words registered on her brain and she froze, trapped in a moment when time seemed to hang suspended.

She turned slowly, numbly, dreading what she might see, only to find Matthew's face glowing with an incredible compassion. And what looked like a glimmer of laughter in his eyes.

"How did you know? *When* did you know?" she faltered when she finally found her voice.

"I didn't figure it out right away," he confessed. "At first, I believed your grandfather had written the stories, just as you wanted me to." Charlene winced and he smiled, taking her hands in his and holding them lightly, stroking the backs of her hands with his thumbs.

"And in spending so much time listening to him reminisce, it was clear he knew the stories, all right. But he didn't use the same vocabulary. Jed can spin a good yarn," he said, "but he doesn't have the gift for painting a picture with words that Charlie Matkin has.

"So I began to wonder. Little things began to add up. I've seen Jed's handwriting and I've seen yours, and yours is definitely the handwriting on the manuscripts."

Charlene looked at him, surprised. "Oh yes," he said, laughing, "I'm very familiar with 'Charlie's' writing. I've made it a point to have the manuscripts come straight to me before anyone else reads them.

"I thought for a while," he went on, "that Jed might have you copy the stories for him, since your handwriting is obviously much easier to read. But again, the language wasn't Jed's. It was yours."

His voice was rough with suppressed emotion. His gaze locked onto Charlene's and held it fast. "You truly have the soul of a poet, and you use it to make poetry of this incredible land."

Charlene tried hard to make sense of what he was saying. "Do you mean—you aren't angry about the way we deceived you?" she asked timidly.

Matthew shook his head slowly and managed a slight smile. Eyes clouded with apprehension, he looked at her steadily. "I understand why you did it. Besides, it would be very wrong of me to be angry about that when I've practiced a deception of my own."

Charlene's eyebrows soared upward in disbelief and she pulled her hands away. "Deception? You?" Maybe he *was* married as she had feared earlier. Her confusion grew and she braced herself for the words he would say next.

Matthew moistened his lips and took a deep breath. "My name *is* Matthew Benson," he said, never taking his eyes off Charlene. "But it's Matthew Benson, *Junior.* My father is actually the one who purchased the paper. I merely run the day-to-day operations." He watched Charlene's brows knit together as she tried to sort out the implications of this news.

"I love the newspaper business," he continued, "but I loathe city life. I have for a long time." He leaned forward, willing her to understand.

"Your stories stirred something deep inside me, whetted my appetite to see the places where they happened. I could hardly allow myself to hope that the reality might be even a tenth of what you described. I never dared to believe it might be even more."

"But why not tell us who you were from the start? I don't understand." She flinched as she spoke the words aloud. Who was she to talk? She hadn't been truthful.

"If your beautiful West lived up to my expectations, I hoped to stay and start a newspaper right here. The territory is growing, and more people will come. The railroad will be here soon, and with it, the timber and cattle industries will flourish.

"The *Arizona Miner* down in Prescott is a good newspaper, but it's too far away. Someone needs to be right on the spot to help this area grow and mature. It was my hope to be that person." He gave Charlene a shamefaced look. "I wasn't sure what kind of reception I'd get as merely the son of the paper's owner, so I just mentioned my name, and let you two draw your own conclusions."

One corner of Charlene's mouth twitched upward. "There seems to be a lot of that going around."

Matthew gave her a wry grin in response. "Once I got to know you and Jed, once I'd been here long enough to know how much you both mean to me, I didn't know how to tell you the truth." He took her hands again and held them in a gentle grasp.

"Your stories made me fall in love with this land before I'd ever seen it." His grip on her hands tightened. "But it was being here that made me fall in love with *you*."

For the second time that afternoon, Charlene was struck dumb. She searched his face, looking for signs of reproach or condemnation, but all she found was love and assurance.

"Does that mean you forgive me?" she whispered.

The look of love in his eyes melted her heart. "If you'll forgive me, too."

Heart hammering wildly, she asked, barely daring to hope, "You're not going home, then?"

Matthew looked at her tenderly, framing her face with both hands. "I *am* home."

Epilogue

On Easter morning, Charlene dressed in her finest and arranged her hair with special care. She spread an armload of blankets in the wagon bed, forming a soft pallet, while Matthew helped Jed off the porch and into the wagon. Jed's company gave the day an especially festive air, and they sang hymns of praise as they drove through the predawn darkness.

Pulling the wagon close to the assembled group of worshipers so Jed could participate from the comfort of his pallet, Matthew jumped from the seat and lifted Charlene down to stand beside him. The congregation moved little and spoke less as they waited for Brother Jenkins to begin.

The pastor's voice broke through the gloom, retelling the story of the Crucifixion and burial on Good Friday, the grief and desolation of Saturday. Charlene, who had heard the story countless times, felt her eyes well up with tears as she followed the sorrowing women to the tomb and heard the angel say, "He is risen."

"He is risen!" Brother Jenkins repeated in a resounding, jubilant voice. "The grave no longer holds Him, and the power of sin has been broken. Hallelujah!"

"Hallelujah!" the people responded.

The first rays of light peeked tentatively over the mountaintops, then showered the gathered worshipers with the sun's radiance. Matthew slipped his arm around Charlene's waist and drew her close.

She turned a glowing face toward his and they exchanged joyful looks, full of gratitude for the *Son's* radiance. For His atonement and resurrection. For the wonder and promise of spring.

Carol Cox

Carol is a native of Arizona whose time is devoted to being a pastor's wife, home-school mom to her teen, active mom to her toddler, church pianist, and youth worker. She loves anything that she can do with her family: reading, traveling, historical studies, and outdoor excursions. She is also open to new pursuits on her own, including genealogy research, crafts, and the local historical society. She plans to write several historical inspirational romances in which her goals are to encourage Christian readers with entertaining and uplifting stories and to pique the interests of non-Christians who might read her novels.

The
Blessings
Basket

Judith McCoy Miller

Chapter One

April 17, 1906

S ing Ho plopped down onto the narrow, quilt-covered bed opposite her best friend, Hung Mooie. As the two oldest girls at the Mission Home, they were now entitled to the coveted small bedroom at the end of the hall—a bedroom they shared only with each other. It seemed fitting. Both of them had become members of the household at 920 Sacramento Street back in the spring of 1894, Sing Ho first and Hung Mooie two days later. Both had been rescued from slave owners who were members of the tongs, the Chinese gangs that victimized and preyed upon their own countrymen. Each of the girls had taken an instant liking to the other, and that had never changed.

"I am so tired! I thought we would *never* finish," Sing Ho stated, her almond-shaped eyes bright with excitement. She pulled her hair forward and began unbraiding the thick black mane.

"We have only a short time to rest before it's time to get cleaned up for the reception. Instead of talking, why don't we take a nap?" Hung Mooie suggested, her eyes already closing as she talked.

Jostling her friend until she finally relented and opened her eyes, Sing Ho gave her a look of disapproval. "Lo Mo is right! You're going to sleep your life away."

"Lo Mo is like all mothers. She never seems to need sleep," Hung Mooie replied. "And you are almost as bad. Why don't you let me sleep? After a week of cleaning and scrubbing every room in this house, I deserve a few minutes of rest."

"You make it sound like you're the only one who was working. Don't forget there are fifty of us living here."

"But not all *fifty* of us did the work," Hung Mooie quickly retorted.

Sing Ho chuckled and shook her head in disbelief. "You expect the three babies and little toddlers to help you scrub floors and dust shelves?"

"No, but the only reason Yuen Kim wants to stay with the babies is so that she doesn't have to do the hard work like the rest of us."

"You don't really believe that, do you? Taking care of the babies and watching all the little ones is *very* hard work. If you felt that way, why didn't you ask Lo Mo if you could trade off with Yuen Kim?" Sing Ho suggested.

"It's not that I *want* to watch the babies. I'm just saying it's easier work," Hung Mooie replied.

"Oh, so you just want to complain, do you?" Sing Ho jokingly countered. "Well, in only a few more days you won't have to worry about anyone else doing less work than you. Once you are married to Mr. Henry Lai, you'll be doing *all* the housework!"

"That's true. But it will only be for two people instead of fifty!"

"Remember, this housecleaning wasn't just for the Mission Board reception and meetings; it was for your wedding also. Perhaps we should have given you the privilege of cleaning by yourself," Sing Ho teased. "Come on! We need to get ready before the guests begin arriving," Sing Ho urged, pulling a white pleated shirtwaist and navy blue skirt from the cramped, pine-scented closet.

"Now look what you've done! You've cheated me out of my nap!" Hung Mooie replied.

"What is that Bible verse Lo Mo recites? Is it Proverbs 19:15? Something about an 'idle soul shall suffer hunger'? You wouldn't want to sit around and go hungry, would you?" Sing Ho asked and then giggled at her friend's contorted face.

"I prefer to quote the last line of Isaiah 32:18 that says 'my people shall dwell. . .in quiet resting places.' Not that anyone gets a quiet resting place with you around!"

Sing Ho laughed, a slight blush rising in her saffron-colored complexion. She was going to miss Hung Mooie. At ages twenty-one and twenty-two, the two of them had remained at the Mission Home longer than most. They knew that the younger girls already considered them old maids. At least they had until Hung Mooie announced her wedding plans last winter. Sing Ho was sure they still considered her a lost cause.

It was no matter to her what the other girls thought. She knew that one day God would send the right man into her life—a man with whom she could share her love and respect, someone who shared the same values and beliefs. After all, this wasn't China, where she would be subjected to an arranged marriage and have no say in the matter. Even though Miss Cunningham appeared to thoroughly enjoy matchmaking, she had never forced one of the girls into a loveless marriage. Besides, Miss Cunningham was always telling her she didn't know what she'd do without her, and, for now, she had no urgent desire to leave the only place she had ever considered a real home.

"How are things going between you and Du Wang?" Hung Mooie inquired as she donned a blue-striped shirtwaist with white linen cuffs.

Sing Ho shrugged her shoulders. "He's a nice man, but too old for me. I told Lo Mo he's too old, but she said to be patient—that he's a good Christian man," she answered, wishing that Lo Mo had not given the older man permission to call upon her.

"Did you invite Du Wang to the reception tonight?"

"No, it's only for the members of the board and a few others who have made substantial contributions to the Mission Home. Besides, with his farm so far away, you know he comes to San Francisco only once a month. I'm not sure how Lo Mo thinks we'll ever become acquainted. By the time he completes all his business, there's little time left to visit me."

"It's not fair. A man of forty years is too old for you. I know that Lo Mo wants us to marry good Christian men, but she needs to find someone better suited to you," Hung Mooie agreed. "I don't remember this skirt fitting so snugly. Do you think I've gained weight?" she asked, as she tugged at the waistband of the navy serge skirt.

"I warned you that resting all the time isn't good for you. Now maybe you'll believe me," Sing Ho bantered. "We'd better get downstairs. I'm sure Lo Mo would like us to be present before the guests begin arriving."

෴

The two eldest girls stood behind a lace-covered table laden with delicate cookies, pastries, and tea sandwiches, smiling and exchanging pleasantries with the guests as they passed through the serving line. "Who's that man over there who keeps looking at you?" Hung Mooie whispered in Sing Ho's ear, nodding toward the fireplace where a group of guests stood talking.

Sing Ho glanced across the room. "I'm not sure, but I think his name is Charlie Ming. I've seen him at church, and Lo Mo told me once that he owns several businesses in Chinatown."

"Now *he's* a nice-looking man! Is he on the Mission Board?"

"I think so, but—"

"It looks like he's coming over here. I think he wants to meet you," Hung Mooie interrupted as the two of them quickly looked back down at the serving table. "At least I thought he was coming to meet you."

Charlie Ming walked past the girls and stopped at the end of the table where Bertha Cunningham sat pouring tea from a sterling silver tea service. The two girls watched as he stood talking to Miss Cunningham, nodding and occasionally taking a drink of tea. A short time later, Lo Mo looked their way and then rose from her chair and led him to where they stood.

"Sing Ho, this is Mr. Charlie Ming, our newest member of the board. I'm sure you've seen him at church. And this," she continued while nodding toward the other girl, "is Hung Mooie, our bride-to-be."

"Hello," both of the girls replied in unison as Charlie smiled and nodded.

"Sing Ho, why don't you pour yourself a cup of tea and answer some of Charlie's questions about the Mission Home. Hung Mooie can take care of the tea table without your help. Can't you?" she asked the girl, leaving no doubt what answer was expected. Hung Mooie dutifully agreed and gave her friend a look of encouragement.

"Why don't we sit over here?" Charlie asked, giving her an engaging smile.

Sing Ho followed alongside and then seated herself beside him on the silk tapestry of the overstuffed sofa. She tried not to stare, but his jet-black eyes seemed to draw hers like magnets. It wasn't fair to draw comparisons, but she found herself unfavorably contrasting Du Wang, her suitor, with Charlie. Charlie's black hair was neatly braided into a long queue that hung down his back, and his broad shoulders and sturdy build made him appear larger than most Chinese men. Perhaps it was the way he held himself, but he certainly seemed much larger than Du Wang, who would typically appear at the front door of the Mission Home with strands of hair flying out from his queue, his loose trousers and jacket covered in dust, and his shoulders stooped over in an expression of total defeat.

"Do I have something on my face?" Charlie asked, breaking into her thoughts.

"What? No, certainly not," she replied, attempting to regain her composure. Carefully, she balanced the teacup in her hands and turned toward Mr. Ming, attempting to call into play all of the etiquette and elocution lessons she had mastered throughout the past twelve years.

Sing Ho had been one of the brightest students at the Mission School. Her ability to learn, coupled with her willing spirit, had allowed her to develop a close relationship with Miss Cunningham. After attending English classes for only a year, Sing Ho began acting as an interpreter on rescue missions. Miss Cunningham had told her that God would protect them, and Sing Ho never doubted that promise. He had not failed them.

"How are you enjoying our reception?" she inquired.

"It's very nice to have an opportunity to meet with the other board members before the annual meeting begins tomorrow," he replied. "It appears that all of you have been working very hard preparing for our visit," he continued, his eyes surveying the gleaming furniture and floors.

"Lo Mo wanted everything to be in good order for the meeting *and* for Hung Mooie's wedding," she replied, giving him a warm smile.

"I take it that all of you girls call Miss Cunningham, 'Lo Mo'?"

"Yes, eventually we all have—at least all of the girls since I've lived here. The babies just start out calling her Lo Mo because they mimic us. The girls who come when they are older are a little slower to use such an affectionate title. Of course, she was already known as 'Mother' when I came here.

"Miss Minnie, our housekeeper, told me one of the first girls Miss Cunningham rescued began the tradition as a way of showing respect and honor. Since Miss Cunningham is a substitute mother, she decided to call her the Chinese name for mother."

"And when did *you* come to the mission, if you don't mind my asking?"

"I don't mind at all. I've lived here almost twelve years. Lo Mo rescued me when I was only ten years old. This has become my home and my family, and I have been very happy here," she told him. "It looks as though I'd better get back to the serving table. It appears Hung Mooie is having problems keeping the trays filled."

"I'm sorry. I've been monopolizing your time when you have other duties to attend to. Perhaps we can visit another time?"

"Perhaps. I've enjoyed our conversation," she replied, giving him an engaging smile as he escorted her back to the table and then retreated. Sing Ho smiled when she glanced across the room and noted that his position permitted him a clear view of the serving table where she and Hung Mooie were performing their hostess duties.

By ten o'clock, the few remaining guests were gathering their wraps and visiting near the front door. The

184

older girls, having been relegated to the kitchen for dish-washing duty an hour earlier, were finally released by Miss Minnie.

"I thought we were never going to have a minute alone!" Hung Mooie complained as the two of them raced up the rear stairway. "Did you like him? How old is he? Does he live in Chinatown?"

"Yes, I liked him. But I didn't ask his age or where he lived, you silly girl. I would never ask such rude questions. He would think me impertinent. We talked about the Mission Home. After all, that's why he was at the reception—because of his interest in the home," she replied, revealing nothing further. "We'd better get to sleep. Don't forget, Lo Mo wants us up early in the morning to help prepare for the brunch she's serving the board members before the first meeting."

"I know, but I want to hear more about Charlie Ming," Hung Mooie countered.

"There's nothing more to tell. Besides, you're the one who always complains about not getting enough sleep," Sing Ho replied as she pulled a white cotton nightgown over her head and knelt beside her bed in prayer. A few minutes later, she pulled back the multicolored quilt and slid between the crisp sheets, inhaling a deep whiff of their fresh aroma.

"Good night, Hung Mooie. Pleasant dreams," Sing Ho whispered.

"Good night," her friend replied. Hung Mooie's deep breathing began within a few minutes, and Sing Ho smiled, knowing that her friend was already asleep.

❧

Charlie strode down the sidewalk of the Mission Home and stepped up into his waiting buggy. Come morning, his mother would want all the details of the reception, especially information dealing with any potential brides who might have been in attendance. He smiled to himself. Should he tease her just a little and say there was a minute possibility he had met a young lady that interested him, and then immediately leave for work? He laughed out loud, knowing she would order him back to the breakfast table and question him until she was satisfied he had divulged every tidbit. That was a sobering thought! What would he tell her? A beautiful young girl with sparkling eyes and a captivating smile had stolen his heart? She would think he had lost his senses.

Besides, there was the early morning meeting at the church, and his mother's delay tactics would certainly cause him to be late. He knew his mother well, and her questions would likely lead to an onslaught for which he held no responses. No, he wouldn't tell her—at least not until there was much more to reveal.

❧

A blazing orange sun was beginning to peek out of a pale tangerine early morning mist as an occasional newspaper cart clattered up the cobblestone street, and a milk wagon rattled along its delivery route. Bags of produce were piled high on the sidewalk, awaiting the vegetable and fruit vendors who would soon begin stocking their carts. An occasional trolley or cable car rumbled by, carrying a few early morning workers while a policeman, swinging a short wooden club, walked his beat. Suddenly a deep, thundering tremor began to sweep across the city of San Francisco—a tremor that swiftly wrenched away the anticipation of a glorious spring day.

"Sing Ho! Sing Ho! What is happening?" a tiny voice cried out.

"Stay there, Ah Chung. I'm coming," Sing Ho called, brushing back strands of hair that had escaped from the long braid hanging down her back. *At least I hope I am,* she thought to herself, trying to remain calm as the bedroom furniture began dancing about the room. Suddenly, shattering glass ricocheted off the walls, threatening bodily injury. "*All of you!* Cover your heads with your pillows!" she screamed, hoping the children could hear her command above the ever-increasing roar.

Bricks were being hurled across the street while telegraph poles rocked and wriggled, shooting off blue sparks into the gray dust-laden sky. The groaning house continued to twist and strain, fighting to hold firm against the quaking earth beneath it. Sing Ho clutched the door jamb, laboring to keep herself upright as she reached the bedroom of the younger children. Terror was written across the small faces of the children that greeted her, their almond-shaped eyes glistening with tears as they peeked from under their white cotton-covered pillows.

"I think it has stopped. Come quickly!" Sing Ho ordered, her petite frame only a bit larger than most of the children. "Bring your pillows, and put on your shoes," she added as they quickly began to desert their beds and run toward her.

"What happened?" Ah Chung whimpered.

"An earthquake, I think. We must gather with the others and move downstairs. Hurry along," she ordered and then watched as the roomful of young Chinese girls filed into the hallway and down the stairs. "Do you need help, Hung Mooie?" she asked her friend, who was leading another group of young girls toward the stairs.

"No, I have all of my group together, and nobody is injured. I think that all of the others have already gone downstairs."

Sing Ho nodded and followed her friend down the winding stairway and into the entrance hall and parlor, where the fifty occupants of 920 Sacramento Street were now gathered.

"Now then, is everyone accounted for?" Miss Cunningham inquired, her dark brown hair hanging loose and unkempt upon her shoulders.

"It looks like everyone is here, Lo Mo," one of the older girls replied, giving Miss Cunningham a half-hearted smile as the older woman began pulling her hair toward the back of her head and into a familiar bun.

"In that case, I want one of you older girls to stay with the little ones. Sing Ho and Hung Mooie, come with me," she commanded. The three walked onto the front porch of the red brick five-story house bearing the inscription "Board of Foreign Missions."

"Look!" Sing Ho stated, her voice a raspy whisper as she pointed toward the columns of smoke rising from the city below.

"The fires are moving this direction. We'll need to

feed the children and collect a few belongings. I think we'll be safer if we move to the Presbyterian church."

The two girls nodded. "Whatever you think is best, Lo Mo. Just tell us what we should do," Sing Ho replied.

"With both chimneys down, we can't cook breakfast. Why don't—"

"There's Miss Minnie," Hung Mooie interrupted, pointing toward a middle-aged woman briskly walking toward the house with a wicker basket over her arm.

"I managed to get some bread from Mr. Nettleson's bakery. Mrs. Poon Chew sent apples and is bringing a kettle of tea shortly. God has provided," Minnie called out with a grin spread across her face.

"So He has," Miss Cunningham called back. The three stood waiting as the stout matron hiked up the street and climbed the steep steps to the porch. "I don't recall sending you out for breakfast, Minnie."

"Nor do I," the housekeeper replied, brushing past the three of them and moving toward the front door. "Come along and help me wash these apples, Sing Ho. You watch for Mrs. Poon Chew to bring the tea, Hung Mooie," Minnie continued without further explanation.

"I see that this catastrophe hasn't impeded your ability to take charge," Miss Cunningham retorted, giving the housekeeper a grin.

"Just doing my job—feeding these children is my responsibility," Minnie answered, continuing on toward the kitchen.

"What we gonna do?" Bo Lin asked a few minutes later, holding tightly onto a chunk of bread and a bright red apple.

"Well, first of all, we're going to say grace and thank God for keeping all of us safe and providing a nourishing meal. Then we're going to dress and gather some of our belongings. After that, we're going to walk up to the First Presbyterian Church and stay there," Miss Cunningham calmly replied.

"Why?" Bo Lin inquired, her five-year-old eyes wide with fear.

"Because I think we'll be safe there. It's farther away from the fire," she explained in a quiet voice.

"I don't want to go," another small child whimpered.

"Neither do I. But we must do what's best, and I'll expect each of you to do as you're told. Sing Ho and Hung Mooie, I need to speak to you," she said, motioning the two older girls toward the parlor. "I want you to take the oldest girls upstairs and have them pack only their necessities. They must be able to carry their own belongings and those of one other child, so they can't take much. The two of you oversee them and gather your own things. I'll stay with the younger children. We must leave *soon*."

"If we try to rush the children, they'll become more frightened. It's only eight blocks to the church," Hung Mooie argued.

"It is eight *long* blocks, and all of them are uphill. We have fifty children to keep in tow during that uphill march. Even worse, the streets are already filling with curious sightseers and people who have been displaced from their homes. And you can be sure that some of the slave owners will be out there lying in wait to kidnap one of you girls. There have been enough small tremors that I don't want to take any chances staying here any longer than necessary. Hurry now!" Miss Cunningham commanded in her sternest tone.

Instructing the children as they ascended the stairway, the older girls watched as the little ones quickly bundled some bedding and a few garments, along with an occasional keepsake.

"What are you doing?" Sing Ho asked, keeping her voice low.

"I can't leave it. If I take nothing else, I'm taking my wedding gown," Hung Mooie answered, as she continued to frantically stuff the white gown into a small valise.

"Lo Mo will be unhappy with your decision," Sing Ho warned, her dark eyes flashing.

"She won't know unless you tell her."

"I won't tell her, but what do *you* plan to say when you need a change of clothing?" Sing Ho inquired. Without waiting for an answer, she motioned the children to hurry. "As soon as you have your belongings, go downstairs to the parlor and wait," she instructed.

An hour had passed by the time the group was assembled, tasks had been assigned, and they were able to get under way. The household formed a tight knot with Bertha, Minnie, and the older girls surrounding the younger children, all of them keeping a wary eye for any stranger that might draw near. Slowly, the procession picked its way up Sacramento Street toward Van Ness Avenue, past the ruined mansions on Nob Hill with their brick-and-stone grandeur now transformed into piles of rubble, and trudged on toward the church.

"You girls collect pew cushions and carry them to the basement. We'll use those for pallets to sleep on," Miss Cunningham instructed as they entered the church.

"Miss Cunningham! I'm relieved to see you and your girls," Pastor Browne called out from the front of the church. "Do you need some assistance getting settled?"

"We can always use extra hands," she replied, watching as the preacher began gathering several men to aid with their baggage.

"Sing Ho! Let me carry that," a man offered and then reached for the bundles that she was carrying toward the stairs.

Startled, she quickly turned toward the familiar voice. "Charlie! What are *you* doing here at the church?"

"Pastor Browne had arranged for the Mission Board members to meet for prayer before the annual meeting. I didn't sleep well last night and finally got up and began walking to the church shortly before five o'clock. You can probably guess the rest," he said.

"Were you already at the church when the earthquake hit?" she asked.

"I had just come inside when the first tremor began. Let me take your baggage," he urged.

"I can carry these. Why don't you help the smaller children?"

Charlie nodded and gave her a broad smile that reached his engaging dark eyes. His black queue was tightly braided and swung back and forth as he bounded down the stairs. Sing Ho watched as he quickly set down his burden and ran back upstairs for another load. Moments later, she spied him with an armload of pew cushions which he began to carefully arrange into make-shift beds on the floor. She didn't understand her feelings at that moment, but something stirred deep within her as she watched him speak quietly to one of the little girls, give her a reassuring hug, and then continue arranging the cushions as the child followed along behind him.

"There you are, Charlie," Bertha Cunningham called out as she approached her newest board member. "I can't begin to tell you how much we all appreciate your help."

Continuing down the aisle of cushions, Charlie placed a bundle of belongings atop each of the improvised cots. "I wish I could do more," he said, eyeing the group of toddlers, fearful and crying, wandering around the large room.

"I'm sure that opportunity will arise," she replied while surveying their unaccustomed surroundings.

❧

It was some time during the early hours of the morning when Charlie felt himself being roused from a deep slumber. Trying to blink away the sleep from his eyes, it took a few moments before he realized where he was. Bertha Cunningham was leaning over him and shaking his arm.

"Something terrible has occurred, and it must be resolved immediately. Will you help?" she asked, her tremulous voice barely audible.

Chapter Two

April 19, 1906

The wind changed as the couple turned onto Sacramento Street, the light breeze now showering them with ashes and stinging their eyes with smoke as they cautiously traced their way through the darkness and descended the steep hill.

"I wish we could have done this during daylight," Charlie stated just as Miss Cunningham lost her footing on a pile of loose rubble.

"So do I, but I didn't remember earlier in the day. I'm sure that God was warning me of the danger, and that's why I awakened. We have to remember that God doesn't always work on our schedules, Charlie," she stated, giving him a reassuring smile.

"Perhaps, but—"

"Hold up there!" a loud voice called out. "Don't take another step, or I'll shoot."

The pair stopped in their tracks as the soldier approached, his rifle pointed toward them as he looked them up and down with a menacing glare.

"Don't you know we're under martial law? Nobody's supposed to be out on these streets," he yelled. "Is this slant-eye trying to rob you?" He spat at Charlie's feet. "Dirty Ch—"

"Stop that!" Bertha commanded, straightening her shoulders and pulling herself into a rigid stance. "This *gentleman* is a member of the Board of Foreign Missions, and he is helping me."

"I don't care *who* he is. You two had better get off these streets, or you're gonna get yourselves shot. Do you understand me?"

"What's going on?" another voice called out of the darkness. "You have a problem, Private Morgan?"

"It's nothing, Captain, just some lady and a—"

"May I please speak with you, Captain?" Bertha called out in a firm voice, ignoring the threatening look of the young private.

"Yes, ma'am," he replied, taking long steady strides toward where they stood. "What can I do for you?"

"We need to get into the house at 920 Sacramento Street; it's the Mission Home," she explained.

"Can't do that, ma'am. We have orders to keep everyone out of the houses and buildings. It's too dangerous to go back in, what with the dynamiting and fires breaking out everywhere. Ain't nothing in your house worth dying over," he stated.

"Oh, yes there is," Bertha argued, "and I'm going to get in there, one way or the other."

"Just what could be so important that you're willing to risk your life, lady?"

"I've spent the last twenty-five years rescuing little Chinese girls from the hands of tong leaders who want to use them in their filthy brothels in Chinatown," she explained. "I've had to go to court and fight these evil men to establish my right to keep the girls. In our haste to leave yesterday, I forgot the papers."

"You want to go back for a bunch of papers?"

"They're not just *papers*. They're proof of my girls' identities and their guardianship documents. If fire consumes our home, I lose all the proof that grants me legal authority to keep the girls."

"Those tong leaders won't ever know your papers burned up," the Captain growled.

"You don't know these men. They're like animals sniffing after a bone. They won't hesitate to take me into court and challenge my rights. These girls are chattels to them, and they don't give up easily. I'm begging you to please show some charity toward these young children."

"So who is this?" the captain asked, poking his rifle toward Charlie.

"This is Charlie Ming, a respected member of our Mission Board and the owner of several prosperous business establishments in the community," she responded. "He, along with Pastor Browne and several others, helped us get settled in the Presbyterian church on Van Ness earlier today."

"Probably not safe to be traveling with a…Chinese man," he stated matter-of-factly.

"I think it's safer than traveling by myself on these deserted streets. Now, are you going to help us or not?" Bertha asked, bringing the conversation back to her intended objective.

"Come on. After all, who am I to interfere with your divine assignment?" he begrudgingly agreed, leading them down the hill until they reached the fortress of red brick with its domed top.

Bertha stood transfixed, staring at the home. It looked much as they'd left it, the subsequent tremors seeming to have had little effect upon the stalwart edifice.

"You just gonna stand there, or you going in?" the captain asked. "We can't be around here for long. You've got five minutes to get your papers and get back out here," he commanded while quickly scanning the area.

Bertha and Charlie scurried up the steps and into the house. The glare of the burning city lit up the rooms. "Why don't you grab some additional food while I get the papers," she hastily suggested as she ran up the steps to her office.

Locating the papers, she quickly stuffed them into a pillowcase, along with the ledgers, some jewelry, and a meager amount of money she'd not yet taken to the bank. Charlie met her at the foot of the stairway with two baskets of food, just as the anxious soldier called out for them to hurry.

"They're dynamiting in the next block. We've got to get out of here!" he shouted as Bertha reached the front porch.

"Thank you, Captain. I know you'll be rewarded for your kindness," Bertha said as he escorted them along the desolate pavement to the top of Sacramento Street.

"If anyone finds out about this, my reward will be a

197

court-martial," he grunted. "By the way, it's not going to be safe in that church for much longer. You'll need to get those girls moved somewhere else tomorrow," he warned as they passed a few scattered troops moving up the hill ahead of the dynamiting.

"Yes, sir. We will leave in the morning," she assured him.

"It's only a couple of hours until dawn. We'd better try to get some sleep. We'll make a decision about where to move in the morning," she said to Charlie as they walked into the church.

❧

Sing Ho spent most of the night going from pallet to pallet, attempting to comfort the younger girls, holding crying toddlers, and feeding the infants. Their strange surroundings and the deep resounding booms of exploding dynamite sent the young children trembling with fear to anyone who would hold them. She breathed a sigh of relief when morning eventually arrived.

"I'm looking for Miss Cunningham," a messenger called out as he entered the church shortly after they had finished a meager breakfast.

"She's over there," Sing Ho said, pointing toward the American woman surrounded by a group of small Chinese girls.

Shoving the paper toward Miss Cunningham, the young messenger rocked from foot to foot, reciting his assigned speech. "Mr. Knoxberry asked me to deliver this message to you. He said to tell you he and several other members of the board were burned out. They've temporarily relocated in Oakland, but he's found a place for you and these children to stay in San Anselmo. You want me to take any message back to him?"

When she declined, the boy took off as if he'd sprouted wings. "Sing Ho," Miss Cunningham called out as she folded the paper and shoved it into her pocket, "would you please go upstairs and ask Mr. Ming and Pastor Browne to come down here?"

Sing Ho nodded and quickly ran upstairs to the sanctuary. "Miss Cunningham would like to see you and Pastor Browne downstairs," she said, giving Charlie a bright smile. "You look tired. Were the benches too hard for sleeping?"

"No, the night was too short. Miss Cunningham requested that I accompany her on an errand early this morning," he confided, returning her smile. "Pastor Browne left a few minutes ago. I don't know when he'll be back, so we might as well go on downstairs."

"Where did you go with Miss Cunningham?" she asked, trying to hide her weariness.

"We made a trip back to the Mission Home."

"Why would she even consider going back?" Sing Ho asked, a look of disbelief crossing her face.

"She forgot the guardianship and identity papers for all of you. Her fear is that if one of the tong members ever takes her back to court, she won't be able to prove she has legal custody," Charlie explained.

Sing Ho shook her head in amazement. "She is such an unselfish person. To think that she would do such a thing isn't surprising. God seems to protect Lo Mo, even when she makes unwise decisions. What would we do without her? Thank you for going along to protect her," Sing Ho said, rewarding him with another radiant smile.

"*She* did the protecting," he said as he gave her a nervous laugh. "We were stopped by the militia."

"What happened?" Sing Ho asked, her eyes growing large as she reached out and took his hand. "Did they harass you?"

"Yes, but Miss Cunningham quickly took my defense," he replied while glancing at her hands that now embraced his.

She followed his eyes and quickly dropped her hold. *What am I doing?* she thought. *Lo Mo would be dismayed by such bold behavior.* "We should go downstairs," she said, struggling to regain her composure.

"Sing Ho, wait just a moment."

"Yes?"

"Would you...would it be—how do I say this—acceptable if I asked Miss Cunningham for permission to call upon you? When things have settled down a bit, that is," he quickly added.

"I don't know if she would permit it. She has already given someone else permission," Sing Ho replied, trying to hide her excitement at his interest.

"I see. I didn't realize that you are betrothed."

"Oh, no, I'm not betrothed. We are just getting to know each other. He calls upon me once a month," Sing Ho explained.

"Once a month?" he asked with a look of astonishment on his face. "At that rate, it will take the two of you years to decide if you are suited. Miss Cunningham does permit you girls to marry someone you care for, doesn't she? I mean, she doesn't arrange a marriage and—"

"No, she doesn't force us into arranged marriages, but she does encourage us to marry Christians," Sing Ho quickly informed him.

"And what do you think of this young man who is courting you?" he boldly inquired.

Sing Ho gave him a shy smile. "He's not so young, but I can say nothing ill of him. I think we should go downstairs now. Lo Mo will wonder what has happened to us," she replied, quickly changing the subject, knowing she dared not express her true feelings.

What would he think if I told him that Du Wang doesn't meet my marriage requirements? I wonder if he would be shocked to hear that I would dance with delight if given the opportunity to have him as a suitor instead of Du Wang. He would probably think that I was an ill-mannered, impertinent, uncharitable human being, Sing Ho thought, meeting Charlie's understanding eyes.

But she wouldn't say any of those things. She had been taught better. Such behavior was frowned upon, and, as the oldest girl at the Mission Home, Sing Ho was expected to set a good example. Instead, she pulled her gaze away from him, kept her lips tightly sealed, and walked resolutely toward the stairway.

Miss Cunningham, Minnie, and several of the older girls were gathered together in a small group when the pair entered the room. "Pastor Browne has left the church, and we don't know when he's expected to return,"

Sing Ho stated as the two of them walked toward the clustered women.

"Well, we won't wait. We've been advised that we must leave the church. I've received a message that there is an old barn in San Anselmo where we can make a temporary home. It's a four-mile hike, which will be difficult for the small children, especially since we have all these bundles to carry. We don't want to frighten the little ones, so let's attempt to make this seem as much like an adventure as possible," she suggested.

The group began their hasty preparations and it soon became apparent that much would be left behind. "There's so much we won't be able to take with us," Hung Mooie told her friend as they attempted to make assignments of what bundles each person should carry.

"I have an idea," Sing Ho told the others excitedly. "We can break the handles off the brooms and tie our bundles to them. If we balance the poles on our shoulders we can carry more."

"She's right," Minnie agreed. "Hurry! Find everything that has a wooden handle that we can use."

Working at a frantic pace, the anxious group soon organized their belongings and began their journey. The little girls' soaring spirits and excitement over their anticipated excursion to the boat docks were quickly subdued by thick smoke, flying cinders, and tired feet. Doggedly, they proceeded onward, a weary, unwashed, uncombed procession tramping through the stifling, crowded streets while the fires continued to rage. Farther on, they passed through the evacuated district that had already burned and lay still smoldering in the aftermath. It seemed an eternity before the group finally reached the foot of Van Ness Avenue.

"There's the pier," Charlie called back over his shoulder, waving them forward.

He smiled as the small children began clapping at the sight. As they drew closer, the winds from the ocean pushed the smoke back, and they watched an empty ferryboat churn through the bluish-green water and maneuver alongside the wooden pier.

"We need passage across the bay," Charlie told the captain.

"Get 'em loaded," he replied. "Haven't seen this boat so empty in two days," the captain remarked as the group began to board the steamer.

"God's watching out for us again," Bertha stated as she stood beside Charlie, who was helping to load the smaller children.

Forcing herself to smile as she approached where the others stood, Sing Ho silently began lifting bundles and passing them into the boat. "You are coming with us, aren't you?" she finally asked Charlie, secretly fearing his answer.

"No, but I've told Miss Cunningham I will come later in the week and bring some supplies. Take care of yourself," he said, giving her a warm smile while assisting her onto the boat.

She thought that he had given her hand a slight squeeze, but perhaps that was just her imagination.

Chapter Three

Positioning herself between two of the younger girls, Sing Ho slipped an arm around each and pulled them close, with her eyes remaining fixed on the pier where Charlie stood waving. She knew that she should stop thinking about him, but it seemed impossible. Unless Lo Mo was willing to terminate the courting arrangement with Du Wang, she felt certain that Charlie would keep his distance. *The only way to solve this is through Lo Mo. As soon as we get settled, I'll talk to her,* Sing Ho decided, glancing toward the household matriarch who appeared to be deep in conversation with several of the girls. Pulling her thoughts away from Charlie, Sing Ho gave them her attention.

"I still don't understand why God would do this to us. If He is a God of love, why didn't He prevent this earthquake?" Yuen Kim asked in a trembling voice, obviously close to tears.

"That's an excellent question, my dear, but I'm afraid I can't answer the whys and wherefores of God's plan for this universe," Miss Cunningham replied, giving her an encouraging smile. "However, it does seem that we begin to question God's love only when things are going wrong. I suppose it's human nature. But, if you would look at our situation from a different perspective, you would be assured that God loves you very much, Yuen Kim. In fact, He loves every one of us," she continued, stretching her arm outward to include all of them in her declaration. "Do you understand what I mean?"

The boat continued to slice through the calm waters toward the opposite shore. "Not exactly," a bedraggled Yuen Kim answered.

Miss Cunningham scanned the group of girls. "Anyone? Do any of you girls feel absolutely assured that God still loves us?"

"I do," Sing Ho quickly replied. "The Bible tells us that God's love is steadfast and never changing. But we're also told we will suffer and that our salvation is no assurance of an easy life."

"That's true. But can you give me an example of God's love in the midst of all this chaos?" Miss Cunningham urged.

"None of us were injured," Sing Ho replied. "So many people were injured or died during the earthquake, yet none of us suffered even a scratch."

"Exactly!" Miss Cunningham responded while beaming from ear to ear at her protégée's answer.

"And we had a place to stay," one of the other girls called out.

"And food to eat," another cried.

"I think that if we were to list all the blessings God has bestowed upon us since the earthquake, we would all be pleasantly surprised," Miss Cunningham told them.

"In fact, why don't we do that?"

"We don't have any writing supplies," Yuen Kim responded sullenly, obviously intent on remaining negative.

Sing Ho reached for the basket that was stowed beneath her feet and lifted it to her lap. "I don't have a paper or pencil, but I do have a small knife," she began.

"What good is *that?*" Yuen Kim asked, her voice now dripping with sarcasm.

"I can make a small notch in the edge of my basket for each blessing," Sing Ho explained as she directed her idea toward the others and avoided Yuen Kim's frown.

"Oh, yes," the smaller girls agreed, clapping their hands.

"I think that's a fine idea, Sing Ho. It will be our blessings basket," Miss Cunningham concurred. "Now, who wants to be first?" she asked, turning her attention to the group.

Sing Ho continued to carve tiny notches around the top of the basket until they arrived at their destination, and even as they disembarked the steamer at Sausalito, several of the girls continued to call out God's blessings. They all agreed, Lo Mo included, that the trip from the dock in Sausalito to the old barn in the countryside of San Anselmo was going to be grueling. But, in spite of their hardships, the girls continued to find blessings. Hung Mooie was first when she joyfully declared that she was claiming their picturesque surroundings as one of God's blessings, and she instructed Sing Ho to immediately carve another notch. Good humor remained intact for the remainder of the excursion, with only an occasional insolent remark from one or two of the girls.

As predicted by the ever-gloomy Yuen Kim, the barn was large, drafty, and uncomfortable. The group was plagued by inadequate bedding, food, and water, all of which Yuen Kim seemed only too pleased to point out. But when Lo Mo asked the other girls for their opinion, she received shouts of jubilation for a roof and dry hay; for the one tin dipper; for the dozen spoons and plates that they could share; for the crystal clear, bubbling stream that ran close by; and for the red beans that Miss Minnie had packed and set to boil over a fire shortly after their arrival.

Hung Mooie made her way to where Sing Ho was fashioning pallets in the hay for some of the younger children. "Would you pray that Henry will find us?" she asked, tears beginning to form in her eyes.

"Of course, I will. Everything is going to work out. I just know it," Sing Ho replied, tenderly wrapping her arms around Hung Mooie. "Come on now—help me with these beds, and then we'll go down to that stream and wash up. That will make both of us feel better."

A feeble smile tugged at Hung Mooie's lips as she leaned down and spread one of the blankets. "I didn't pack any clothes, remember?"

"I know, but I did," Sing Ho answered as she continued to work alongside Hung Mooie.

"Your clothes won't fit me!"

"I know that. When you insisted on filling your valise with your wedding gown, I went back and got two of your shirtwaists and skirts and packed them with my things."

"Really? You are such a fine friend that you make me ashamed of being so selfish," Hung Mooie replied, grabbing her friend's hands and dancing about.

What would it feel like to be so excited about your upcoming marriage that you would pack a wedding gown instead of necessities? What would it feel like to even know you were going to marry? Even more, what would it feel like to be in love and want to spend the rest of your life with another person? Sing Ho wondered as the two young women walked hand in hand toward the stream.

"You need to carve another notch in your basket," Hung Mooie said, interrupting her thoughts.

"Why is that?" Sing Ho asked as they reached the stream. Sitting down by the water's edge, she began to poke through her basket, pulling out several pieces of clothing and a hairbrush.

"For you—for our friendship. What would I have done all these years without you by my side, always a faithful friend?"

"You would have been fine! But I'm going to miss you when you marry Henry and leave for Ohio. I wish you weren't moving so far away."

"You mean *if* I get married. Henry's train was due to arrive on the eighteenth, the day of the earthquake. Even if he did make it to San Francisco, I doubt that he will ever find us," Hung Mooie lamented, running the brush through her long, black hair and then dividing it into three sections. Her supple fingers dove in and out, quickly plaiting the strands into a tight braid as she followed along behind Sing Ho.

Bedding and a few food supplies were being delivered from several of the local churches just as the girls reached the barn. "Another blessing," Hung Mooie giggled as they began to help unload the items.

They completed the task just as a light mist began to fall. Within several hours, it had turned into a raging storm, which soon gave evidence to a multitude of holes in the barn roof. Beds were moved to any dry spot they could locate while the wind whistled through the cracks in the deteriorating wood. And true to form, Yuen Kim gave them yet another facial expression that matched the gloomy weather conditions.

❧

Two days later, the rains abated and the sun began to peek through a crimson and gold horizon. Sing Ho smiled as she walked outdoors, her arms filled with laundry. The rains had transformed the hills and valleys into an exquisite panorama of reds, pinks, yellows, blues, and purples. The flowering blossoms of the hawthorn trees and a profusion of blooming wildflowers and budding acacia painted the surrounding expanse in a rainbow of color. It was going to be a good day; she could feel it. Maybe, just maybe, Henry would arrive and set Hung Mooie's worrying to rest. And perhaps even Charlie would visit them by tomorrow or the next day—at least she could hope.

Reveling in the beauty, she walked downstream a short distance and began scrubbing and soaking the multitude of small shirts and matching baggy trousers worn by most of the little girls. Carefully, she spread them across the nearby bushes and grass, the warmth of the sun assuring her that they would soon be dry. Sitting back on her heels, Sing Ho brushed a strand of hair behind her ear. It was hard to believe that only a few miles away such devastation existed.

Sing Ho had just finished washing the last shirt when she heard Hung Mooie calling for her. Waving toward her friend, she briskly started walking back to the barn. Was that a man standing beside Hung Mooie? She couldn't quite see. But then, a few moments later, the figure began to take shape. Was it Henry? Could it possibly be? She began to run. It was! Henry had found them. She ran forward and embraced Hung Mooie as she greeted Henry. "I told you he would find us," Sing Ho proclaimed. "This should be worth more than one notch in my basket!" Sing Ho declared as the two girls skipped about, unable to contain their excitement.

"You would think that Henry came to marry *you*," a voice spoke from behind where the happy trio stood.

Sing Ho whirled around. "Charlie! You came! And so soon." She could hardly catch her breath. Her heart fluttered at the sight of him, and her fingers trembled as he took her hand in welcome. "I'm so happy to see you," she blurted out, wishing that she could throw herself into his arms as she had done with Hung Mooie a few moments earlier.

"And I am *very* happy to see you, also," he replied, giving her hand a squeeze. "You're trembling. Are you ill?"

"Yes. No. I mean, no, I'm not ill. I'm just excited. When did you get here? How did you find us, Henry? I can't wait to hear *everything*," she exclaimed just as

Miss Cunningham walked out of the barn toward the two couples.

"Why don't you young people walk down by the stream and have a picnic lunch? Charlie went into Sausalito and brought us a supply of food. You girls pack some things and relax for a few hours," she suggested.

"Oh thank you, Lo Mo," Sing Ho replied, giving the matron a hug.

Lo Mo shook her head and laughed. "You're right, Charlie. You'd think *she* was the one getting married."

"Perhaps she will be," he replied, his remark causing Sing Ho to stop in her tracks. She turned toward him, a questioning look on her face, but he merely smiled and continued talking to Miss Cunningham.

Could it be that he cares for me? Or is he thinking that I'll soon marry Du Wang? she thought, running into the barn. Quickly, she grabbed some bread, cheese, and several ripe oranges and tucked them into her wicker basket.

"Where are you going?" Miss Minnie called out. "I'm making chicken and rice for lunch. Charlie brought us all this good food. You won't want to miss it."

"Charlie, Henry, Hung Mooie, and I are going on a picnic down by the stream. We'll have some rice for dinner."

"Ha! You think there will be any left by then? Go along, then—enjoy your picnic while we eat a good, hot meal," she replied, laughing and giving Sing Ho a pat on the shoulder.

Running from the barn with the basket swinging from her arm, Sing Ho joined the others. "I'm ready," she breathlessly announced as soon as Miss Cunningham had finished speaking.

"Then, off with you. Go and have fun, but be back by 3:00," she instructed. "You can bring the laundry back when you come."

"Yes, ma'am," Sing Ho answered as the group meandered down the slight incline toward the stream. "Let's go farther up this way," Sing Ho suggested, pointing upstream toward a small grove of hawthorn trees.

Together they ate and listened carefully as Henry told them of his trip across the country and the final miles into the outskirts of San Francisco. Fortunately, the passengers had been warned of the disaster, but there had been no way to prepare them for the shocking sights that they would see.

"The train stopped several miles outside the city and the railroad had a few horse-drawn drays to carry us into town. It was gruesome. Cable and trolley tracks sticking up, twisted in midair, injured and dead people lying in the streets, roads split open in great chasms—how do you prepare people for sights such as those?" Henry asked, shaking his head. "But why am I saying this to you? You lived through it," he continued, still shaking his head as if to chase the dreadful scene from his mind. "When I tried to make my way to the Mission Home, the militia stopped me. They said all the homes had been evacuated. When I asked how I would find you, they laughed. But then one man called me back and said most of the refugees had headed toward either San Mateo, across the bay to Sausalito, or toward Oakland. I decided a group of fifty girls would be noticed by at least a few people, so I began questioning anyone who would talk to me. When I arrived at the Embarcadero, there was a man standing on the pier looking out across the bay. It was Charlie."

Wide-eyed, the two girls looked at each other. "This is more than a blessing; this is a miracle," Hung Mooie stated, her voice a strangled whisper.

"It *is* a miracle," Henry replied, placing an arm around his fiancée's shoulder and drawing her close. "I still want our wedding to take place on schedule. I don't want to wait," he continued. "I've told Miss Cunningham, and she promised to check with Pastor Landon. She thought that perhaps we could be married in the chapel at the theological seminary."

Hung Mooie beamed at this suggestion. "I brought my wedding dress," she told him, obviously unable to contain her excitement. "It was the only thing I could fit in my valise, but I refused to leave it behind."

"It's true," Sing Ho acknowledged when both men stared at Hung Mooie in obvious amazement.

"In that case, we had better put it to good use," Henry replied. "I know it won't be the wedding that you planned, but it will still be beautiful."

Charlie and Sing Ho walked toward the fortress-like seminary, which stood several miles in the distance, neither of them saying a word. A screeching hawk flew overhead, and robins twittered about, obviously seeking worms for their newborn babies.

"Tell me about yourself, Charlie," Sing Ho asked.

"When did you immigrate to San Francisco, and where is your family?"

He gave her a subdued laugh. "I didn't *immigrate* to San Francisco—I was born here."

"*No!* Really? Your parents lived in California when you were born? That's hard to believe!"

"Why is that so hard to believe? My father was born in this country also. You see, my grandfather came to California during the days of the gold rush, back in 1850. Shortly after he arrived, he sent for my grandmother. My father was born in the gold mining country up around Placerville in 1852. My grandparents were very fortunate, in more ways than one," he explained.

"How is that?" she asked.

"Well, while panning for gold they met a young missionary couple who led them to the Lord. They soon became Christians and raised their children in a Christian home. In addition to that, my grandfather struck gold and became a very wealthy man."

"I see. So you've had a life of luxury and indulgence."

Charlie laughed a deep, resonating laugh that continued for several minutes. "No, far from it. Even though my grandfather became wealthy, his values and ethics remained the same. And those same values have been passed down to me. My family lives comfortably, but we are far from pampered. Much of my parents' time and money is spent in the Christian work of spreading the gospel," he told her.

"So is that how you came to serve on the board at the Mission Home?" Sing Ho asked.

"Yes. My parents have both been very supportive of the home, and when Miss Cunningham asked that one of them serve on the board, they deferred to me. You see, my father's health is not what it used to be, and my mother would never consider such a prominent position —she prefers to work behind the scenes. Miss Cunningham seemed pleased by the suggestion, so here I am, at your service," he joked, giving her a mock salute.

"What keeps you busy when you're not collecting food for our wayward group?" she asked as they turned and walked back toward the stream where Hung Mooie and Henry appeared to be deep in conversation.

"Many things, but I will be spending a large portion of my time rebuilding two of the family businesses. We own part interest in a shoe factory on the edge of Chinatown, and my father owns the telephone company in Chinatown. Both suffered tremendous damage," he explained. "Needless to say, there is more work to do than I care to think about right now. When we aren't fighting the devastation of earthquakes, I manage those interests, along with several others, for my family. I am an only son, which means my father relies upon me greatly," he explained.

Giving him a sweet smile, she contemplated her next question. She didn't want to appear bold, but she wanted to know if there was a woman in his life. From some of his comments, she felt that there was no one, but there was no way to find out for sure—no way but to ask. "And what of your evenings and weekends? Do you and your lady friend attend the theater and exciting social events?"

"I attend as few as possible. Those things really don't interest me. By the way, I almost forgot to tell you," he said, but then hesitated momentarily. "Henry isn't the only person who found me," Charlie finally remarked, breaking the silence.

"What do you mean?" Sing Ho asked, her curiosity piqued.

"Your gentleman friend, Du Wang, came looking for me. He asked if I knew where Miss Cunningham had moved you girls."

Sing Ho's breath caught in her throat. "Du Wang? How would he even know to look for you?"

"I'm not sure who, but somebody told him I was a member of the Mission Board. I'm not a difficult person to find—even after a major disaster. He found me at what remains of the telephone company, picking through the rubble."

She wasn't sure she wanted to know the answer, but she asked anyway. "What did you tell him?"

"I told him the truth—that I saw you off on a ferry headed for Sausalito and your final destination was an old barn in San Anselmo, near the theological seminary."

She nodded, keeping her head bowed, not wanting to meet his eyes. "And did he say he was coming here?"

"No, he merely scribbled down what I told him and scurried off without a word. He's a strange little man. He appears too old for you," Charlie added, "although I suppose that is not my business."

Chapter Four

Hearing Bo Lin's soft cries, Sing Ho rose from the rumpled, uncomfortable pallet and carefully threaded her way through the maze of sleeping children on the floor. She stooped down, lovingly gathered the small child into her arms, and began rocking her back and forth. As Bo Lin's whimpering ceased and her breathing deepened, Sing Ho's thoughts wandered back over that day's events.

It had been a good day. The plans for Hung Mooie's wedding were well under way before Henry's departure earlier that evening. The thought of their wedding filled Sing Ho with a strange mixture of excitement and anxiety. Then, too, Charlie had delivered the good news that there was a vacant home available for all of them in San Rafael. One of the board members had offered it as a temporary residence until final decisions could be made concerning rebuilding the Mission Home in San Francisco. But news of restoring the Mission Home had been promising, also. According to Charlie, funds were already pouring in toward repairing the brick edifice on Sacramento Street. In fact, his visit had been cause for several notches in her basket.

After the many struggles of the preceding days, seeing Charlie had provided a much-needed respite. She smiled, remembering how attentive and kind he'd been throughout the day. Yet he *had* masterfully avoided her question about escorting lady friends to social functions. Moreover, he'd told her about Du Wang's visit immediately after she had asked that particular question. Perhaps he was censoring her question, thinking it inappropriate—reminding her that she had no right to ask about his personal life when she had a suitor of her own. However, he had seemed pleased to go walking with her after the picnic and tell her about his family, apparently enjoying her company. It was confusing—that much she knew for certain.

The smart thing to do is put thoughts of Charlie aside, Sing Ho determined. *After all, Du Wang had obviously been concerned about our welfare. Why else would he have made a special trip to inquire about our whereabouts?* Those thoughts, however, did little to curtail her interest in Charlie Ming or the fact that he would be returning with Henry on Saturday. She wandered back to her makeshift bed and slipped into a restless sleep that was fraught with dreams of living on a small vegetable farm with Du Wang, only it was she that was stoop-shouldered with unkempt hair instead of Du Wang.

Miss Minnie's morning rituals were already in progress when Sing Ho awakened. "You're beginning to take up Hung Mooie's habits," Minnie teased as Sing Ho walked outdoors toward the crackling fire where the older woman sat tending breakfast.

"I didn't sleep well," Sing Ho replied, collapsing onto the ground beside Minnie.

"Somebody stolen your heart?" she asked, not looking away from her task. Bright orange flames licked upward around the bottom of the skillet as a large slice of ham resting inside sizzled and popped in protest.

Sing Ho eyed the woman. *How could she know? Is there some telltale sign?*

"I'll take your silence as a 'yes,'" Minnie chortled, obviously pleased with herself. "Can't say as I blame you. That young man certainly stole my heart, too."

"*What? You're* in love with Charlie?" Sing Ho asked in a shrill voice. How could somebody Miss Minnie's age possibly be in love with Charlie? It wasn't possible!

Miss Minnie laughed—loud and hard. She laughed until tears ran down her plump cheeks and spilled onto the bodice of her blue print shirtwaist. "I'm sorry, Sing Ho. I shouldn't be laughing at you," she sputtered, obviously trying to contain herself. "It's just that such a thought is so preposterous that I couldn't help myself," she continued, gasping to catch her breath as the giggles began to subside. "Can't you just imagine—oh, never mind," she stopped herself.

"No! You must explain what you meant about Charlie stealing your heart," Sing Ho insisted.

"Any man who would spend his time and money making sure this little band of vagabonds has food and shelter has my love and loyalty. He's a Good Samaritan, if ever I saw one," she explained. "You needn't worry about me trying to steal your beau!"

Silently, Sing Ho watched as Minnie tossed flour into the skillet and stirred until it turned a golden brown. Miss Minnie could make gravy better than anyone. Of course, it had taken several years before Sing Ho had grown accustomed to American food, but now she ate it as often as she ate the food cooked in the Chinese kitchen of their home. At least she had when they had a home.

"Did Lo Mo tell you anything about the house in San Rafael?" Sing Ho asked.

"A little. Why do you ask?"

"Does it have two kitchens like our house on Sacramento Street?"

Minnie tilted her head to one side and gave Sing Ho a kind smile. "She didn't say, but I would guess that it has only one. Most houses don't come equipped with more than one kitchen, but if we can adjust to living in a barn, we can adjust to cooking Chinese and American food in one kitchen. I'm just thankful that we'll soon have a roof over our heads that doesn't spring leaks. At least I hope it doesn't."

Sing Ho nodded and contemplated her next question. Miss Minnie didn't mince words when asked for advice. Not that she was unkind—but if she thought you were headed down the wrong path, a dose of her advice was akin to a spoonful of castor oil, and Sing Ho didn't feel up to that. She needed to word her question carefully, but it soon became obvious that she wasn't quite sure how to ask it.

Minnie finally broke the silence. "Something on

your mind, child?"

"Would you talk to Lo Mo about Charlie?" she blurted without further thought.

"Sure. But about what?" the older woman asked. She brushed a wisp of gray hair back from her face and gave Sing Ho an inquisitive look.

"I want her to give Charlie permission to call upon me—as a suitor. Instead of Du Wang," she quickly added.

Miss Minnie said nothing for several minutes. Instead, she sat staring at the bubbling gravy, stirring while quietly murmuring something under her breath. "So he really has stolen your heart. Is *that* what you're telling me?" she asked, breaking the early morning silence. Her tone of voice sent a reverberating signal, and Sing Ho immediately questioned the wisdom of seeking Miss Minnie's assistance. "What's going on between the two of you?"

"Nothing. Nothing is going on. He's a good man, and I find him much more to my liking than Du Wang. I can't help how I feel," she explained, sensing that she needed to defend herself.

"I see. Well, this matter might take care of itself without any interference," she commented as several of the little girls began to gather around, eager to begin their breakfast. "Du Wang probably won't pursue his courtship. He doesn't even know that we've come this direction," she continued.

"That's just it. He *does* know," Sing Ho replied. "He's already talked to Charlie and gotten directions to the barn. Why would he inquire if he didn't intend to continue our courtship?"

"You've got a point, but I think this is something best left in the hands of the Lord," Minnie advised as she pulled a Dutch oven filled with biscuits out of the fire.

"*What's* best left to the Lord?" Miss Cunningham asked as she approached the two of them.

"Charlie Ming," Sing Ho muttered, handing Bo Lin a biscuit.

"Isn't he a fine man? And not yet married, either! I may ask him if he'd like to call on Yuen Kim."

"You're going to give Charlie permission to call upon Yuen Kim? Why would you do such a thing?" Sing Ho squeaked. Fingers of overpowering panic began stretching and tightening their way around her heart. She struggled to regain her composure. "He's too old for Yuen Kim," she offered, stealing a fleeting glance at Miss Minnie.

"Yuen Kim is only a year younger than you," Miss Cunningham replied.

Sing Ho could think of nothing to say. Not one word of rebuttal would come to mind as she sat mutely staring across the fire into Miss Minnie's brilliant blue eyes.

"Your comment surprises me, Bertha," Minnie declared, giving Sing Ho a compassionate look as she spoke to Miss Cunningham.

"What? That Yuen Kim is only a year younger than Sing Ho or that I would talk to Charlie about courting her?"

"The part about Charlie. He didn't appear interested in Yuen Kim. In fact, if you'll forgive my saying so, he acted like a man besotted with our little Sing Ho."

"You may be right. I don't know what I was thinking to send them off with Hung Mooie and Henry. After all, Sing Ho is already spoken for."

Sing Ho's eyes darted back and forth between the two women until she could no longer restrain herself. "Spoken for? Du Wang has not spoken for *me!* I've seen him exactly eight times since you told him he could call on me a year ago. He has never spoken of marriage, but I now know I could never be married to him!" she exclaimed.

"Just what has occurred in the last few weeks to convince you of such a thing?" Miss Cunningham asked while taking Sing Ho aside and walking toward a small clump of bushes alongside the barn.

"Quite honestly, I never wanted him to be my suitor. I told you before that he's too old for me and I have no feeling for him. But you told me to be patient, so I have tried," she replied.

Miss Cunningham nodded her head, appearing to carefully listen to Sing Ho's remarks. "Yet I feel there's more to this than your earlier proclamation that Du Wang is too old. Is there something else you should be telling me?" she probed.

"It's Charlie. I would like Charlie to be *my* suitor," she honestly replied. "Is that so wrong? He's more my age, and we can talk together. Besides, I think he cares for me also," she quickly added.

"I see. Well, I know Charlie Ming is an honorable

man, and he would never interfere with another man's courtship. Besides, if he had plans for courtship, I'm sure he would discuss them with *me* before talking to one of my girls."

"He has said nothing about courtship and he knows that Du Wang is my suitor, but whether Charlie declares intentions to court me or not, I would like you to consider breaking my courtship with Du Wang. Would you at least consider it?" she pleaded.

"I think Miss Minnie was right. This needs some prayer," Miss Cunningham told the girl. Lo Mo placed an arm about Sing Ho's shoulder and led her back to where the rest of their family was hungrily eating breakfast.

⁂

If one couldn't be married in the Chinese room at 920 Sacramento Street, Sing Ho decided that the ivy-covered chapel outside San Anselmo was near perfect. It was a part of the theological seminary but stood far enough away from the other buildings to give the appearance of sitting alone among the flowering hawthorn and acacia. Sing Ho, Yuen Kim, and several of the other girls had spent the morning decorating the church sanctuary, which now stood in readiness for the afternoon nuptials.

"It looks beautiful, don't you think?" Yuen Kim asked as the group headed back toward the barn.

Sing Ho voiced her agreement and then busied herself talking to Bo Lin, her five-year-old shadow. She knew that it wasn't Yuen Kim's fault that Miss Cunningham considered her a possible bride for Charlie. But Lo

Mo's proclamation caused Sing Ho now to view the girl as an adversary, and even prayer had not assuaged those emotions.

"Oh, look—Henry and Charlie have arrived," Yuen Kim declared, a smile lighting up her face.

"Why are *you* getting so excited?" Sing Ho curtly inquired.

Yuen Kim glared at Sing Ho and grabbed her arm. "I want to know why you're treating me so rudely. What have I done to you?"

"Nothing! You've done nothing! Now let go of my arm. We need to get back to the barn," she ordered, attempting to pull her arm from Yuen Kim's tightening grip.

"If I have done nothing, then why won't you talk to me? You act as though I don't even exist anymore. You never used to treat me this way, and I don't see you acting impolitely with anyone else," she persisted. "Is it because I told Miss Cunningham I had no interest in being courted by Charlie Ming? I know he's become your friend and you think he's a wonderful man—not that I don't think he's nice, too," she quickly added, "but I don't want to get involved with *any* man. I told Lo Mo I've decided I want to go to college."

"You do? Oh, Yuen Kim, I think that's a wonderful idea—your going to school, I mean," Sing Ho replied, embracing her in a giant bear hug and giggling.

"You've been acting strangely for the past several days. It must be Hung Mooie's wedding. I know you're going to miss her!"

"I *am* going to miss Hung Mooie," Sing Ho agreed.

Yuen Kim's pronouncement that she held no interest in Charlie was more than Sing Ho could have hoped for. She wanted to take off in a headlong run toward where Charlie stood, but she knew that she dared not make a spectacle of herself. At least part of her prayer had been answered.

It was a beautiful spring day, Hung Mooie would be married in a few hours, and, best of all, she could enjoy the festivities in Charlie's company.

Sing Ho headed directly for where Charlie stood talking with Miss Cunningham, but her thoughts were interrupted by Miss Minnie's declaration that Hung Mooie wanted her assistance in the barn. "She needs you to help her get dressed, so hurry along," she continued, turning Sing Ho toward the barn door and away from where Charlie stood staring at her. Their eyes locked momentarily before Miss Minnie took her by the arm and escorted her inside.

Hung Mooie sat waiting in one corner of the barn, her wedding dress hanging neatly from a nail in one of the wooden braces. "Hurry! You know I want you to fix my hair. What took you so long?" she asked in a voice filled with agitation.

"You need to calm yourself. We have plenty of time. Besides, you wanted the church to look nice, didn't you? Well, that's what I was doing—decorating the church. I see that you found someone to press your wedding gown. It looks lovely," Sing Ho rambled on as she began brushing Hung Mooie's long black hair. Carefully she divided the hair in half and plaited it into two plump braids, which were then coiled on either side of Hung Mooie's head and embellished with wildflowers and ribbon. "There!" Sing Ho proclaimed when she had finally finished the task. "You look especially lovely, and, once we get you into that dress, there won't be words to describe your beauty."

"As long as Henry finds me a worthy bride, I will be happy," Hung Mooie replied. "You'd better hurry and get dressed."

"I wish I had packed the dress I was to wear for your wedding," Sing Ho complained, remembering the royal blue silk print. "But since I didn't, I suppose you must be satisfied with an attendant dressed in a simple skirt and blouse."

"Just so long as you are there with me, I don't care what you're wearing. Did Miss Minnie tell you that Mr. Haslett from the church in San Anselmo sent over a horse and buggy for my ride to the chapel?"

"No. That's wonderful! Isn't his wife the lady who pressed your gown?"

"Yes. They've been very nice. Mrs. Haslett found out about the wedding, and within two days she had organized the ladies who made the food for the reception! Everyone is being so helpful and kind, that it's hard to believe we're a displaced group of nomads."

"I gathered some lovely flowers for your bouquet—they match what I've put in your hair. We can leave the stems long, and Lo Mo gave me some ribbons I can use to tie around them into a bow. They're over in my basket if you want to see them," Sing Ho remarked while braiding her own thick hair and coiling it into a bun at the back of her head. "Once we remove the flowers, it sounds as though I need to carve a few more notches in the basket."

The flowers looked beautiful lying in the basket—a profusion of colors and sizes mixed with a variety of ferns and green, leafy stems. Hung Mooie stared at them momentarily and quickly walked back to where Sing Ho had just finished styling her hair.

"Instead of making a bouquet, why don't I carry the flowers in the blessings basket, as a remembrance of all the good things God has provided since the earthquake? When I walk down the aisle carrying the basket, it will cause all of us to reflect upon God's mercy," Hung Mooie suggested, holding the basketful of flowers in front of her. "How does it look?"

"It looks splendid! I'll just tie the ribbons to the handle, and I think it will be much more lovely than anything we could possibly create."

They heard Mr. Haslett arrive with the horse and buggy just as Sing Ho finished tying the ribbons. Miss Minnie scurried into the barn, announcing the men had already gone to the chapel and rushing the two girls toward the waiting carriage. They rode in silence, Sing Ho contemplating her life without Hung Mooie's ever-present friendship while Hung Mooie's trembling fingers clung to the flower basket. From the number of buggies tied outside the chapel, it appeared that most of the residents of San Anselmo had decided to attend the wedding.

"I'm starting to get nervous," Hung Mooie confided as they stepped out of the buggy.

"Then you're doing fine. I would have been nervous way before now. Just think how much better you're doing than I would," Sing Ho soothingly replied. They both giggled—a shrill, nervous, cackling noise that sounded strange in Sing Ho's ears. Miss Cunningham met them in the church vestibule, gave final instructions, and then ordered Sing Ho to begin her walk down the aisle. With halting steps, she walked down the long, narrow passageway between the pews.

Henry stood waiting for his bride at the front of the church with Charlie standing beside him, obviously acting as best man. His eyes met hers, and Sing Ho wondered why Hung Mooie hadn't mentioned that Charlie would be Henry's best man. Of course, who else would be? She really hadn't given the matter any thought, but somehow she hadn't expected to see him standing there waiting beside Henry. Something deep inside made her wish that Charlie was waiting for her to meet him at the end of the aisle and become his bride. But this wasn't her day—it was Hung Mooie's, and wishing wouldn't change anything.

Turning, Sing Ho stood with Pastor Landon, Henry, and Charlie and then watched as Miss Cunningham escorted Hung Mooie down the aisle. Poised and stately in a green and gray cheviot dress, Lo Mo tucked Hung Mooie's arm through her own, and together they slowly walked toward the front of the church. No one could deny the fact that Hung Mooie, in her off-white silk gown and gossamer veil trimmed in blond lace, was the focal point of the afternoon.

Several times throughout the ceremony, Sing Ho glanced toward Charlie. Each time she found him staring at her. It pleased her, yet she hoped that Lo Mo and Miss Minnie weren't watching them. Miss Minnie already seemed intent on keeping the pair separated, and she wanted to spend at least a little time with him during the reception. Chords of joyous organ music brought Sing Ho back to the present. She watched as Henry kissed his bride and the newlyweds began walking back down the aisle. Charlie walked toward her and offered his arm. Her heart fluttered, and a slight shiver ran down her back as she took his arm.

Chapter Five

Three of the girls from the Mission Home stood at white linen-covered tables and proudly served fruit punch and thin slices of buttery pound cake topped with a translucent raspberry glaze. At another table, sterling silver trays were laden with delicate tea sandwiches, fresh fruit, and cheese. The guests mingled and visited, most of them devout members of the San Anselmo church, who had become enchanted by the wedding plans from the moment their assistance was requested. Who could refuse a young couple determined to overcome one of nature's most devastating obstacles in order to proceed with their nuptials?

Miss Minnie fluttered from table to table while dispensing orders and filling trays, her cheeks flushed with excitement. Outside the church, the little girls played in the small fruit orchard. Their shouts of pleasure blended with the polite conversation of the adults who had gathered inside the church parlor to watch the bride and groom open their wedding gifts.

Charlie stood beside Sing Ho as Hung Mooie began to unwrap one of the beribboned packages. "It was so kind of these people to purchase wedding gifts for Henry and Hung Mooie. They don't even know them, yet they've done so much," Sing Ho stated.

"That's one of the many benefits that come with having a Christian family. The family extends and embraces all members of the faith, helping each other wherever and however they can. At least that has been my experience, and I believe it's what Christ planned for His church," Charlie replied, offering her a cup of punch. "Any word from Du Wang since I last saw you?" he asked, surprising her by the abrupt change of topics.

"No, although I'm not surprised. I still can't imagine why he went to the trouble of finding you and requesting information about my whereabouts. He never seemed like a man who would do such a thing."

"Perhaps he cares very deeply, but has difficulty showing his emotions—a lot of men are like that," he commented. "It looks as though the bride and groom are about ready to leave. You'd better get over there, or you'll miss your chance to bid Hung Mooie farewell."

Hung Mooie's arms reached out to hug her approaching friend. "I was beginning to wonder if you would tear yourself away from Charlie to tell me goodbye," she teased as they tenderly embraced.

"You know better than that!" Sing Ho replied, pulling her tighter. "I will miss you so very much, but I know that you and Henry are going to have a wonderful life with lots of lovely children. You must make him promise to bring you back to visit us, and I'll expect letters—lots of them! You can tell me all about Cleveland and those other big eastern cities."

"You know that I'll write to you. I'm going to be lost without all the noise and activity—at least for a short time!" she replied, with a mixture of laughter and tears.

"You'd better go. Henry is waiting, and we're just going to cry if we keep talking. I love you, Hung Mooie, and I know I'll never have a better friend. You'd *better* be happy," Sing Ho said, shaking her finger.

Hung Mooie flashed her friend a bright smile and then took Henry's arm and walked out the double wooden doors of the ivy-covered chapel, into her new life as Mrs. Henry Lai.

❧

"Sing Ho! Come here, please," Miss Cunningham called out, motioning the girl toward where she stood.

"Yes? Do you need help?" Sing Ho inquired obligingly.

"Would you please go outdoors and check on the little girls? I'm sure that they're fine, but I don't want them wandering too far away from the church."

"Certainly. I'll be glad to," Sing Ho replied, unaware that Charlie followed close on her heels.

"Where are you rushing off to?" he asked, running the last few paces to catch up with her.

"Lo Mo wanted me to check on the children. I suppose it comes from all those years of worrying that one of them will be kidnapped. Quite frankly, it's easier to do her bidding than argue. Besides, I never win an argument with Lo Mo," Sing Ho told him and laughed.

The girls were in a large circle, playing drop the handkerchief, and Sing Ho quickly counted heads. And then she counted again, her eyes carefully scanning the little faces.

"Where are Bo Lin and Yoke Lon?" she asked while attempting to keep her voice calm. Her fists were clenched, and she could feel her fingernails digging into the flesh of her palms.

"They went to play over by those trees," one of the girls said, pointing toward a small grove not far off. Hiking up her skirt, Sing Ho took off, her feet flying through the grass and her voice piercing the air as she called the two girls' names. Panting and out of breath, she was unwilling to believe her eyes. She continued to run between the trees, certain that Bo Lin's head would pop out from behind a bush at any moment. "They're hiding from me. It's just a game," she frantically cried to Charlie, who was searching nearby.

"Keep looking! I'm going back to the church and get some of the other men to help us search," he instructed before rushing back in the direction of the church.

"Bo Lin, *please*. Come out here right now. This isn't funny anymore! Bo Lin, *please, please!*" Sing Ho wailed.

The men flooded out of the chapel doors and came running toward Sing Ho. By the time they reached her, she had fallen to the ground weeping, no longer able to convince herself that the girls were merely hiding. Miss Minnie and Miss Cunningham followed closely behind, fear etched on their faces as they obviously attempted to retain their composure. Meanwhile the children's game had ceased, and, their curiosity piqued, they now began to wander toward the adults who were spreading across the grassy acreage.

"You must gain control of yourself, Sing Ho. We also need to think about the other children. I don't want to frighten them. After all, this may be a false alarm. Now tell me—who is missing?" Miss Minnie pleaded.

"Bo Lin and Yoke Lon," she managed to croak through the lump that had formed in her constricting throat. "My little Bo Lin," she wept, falling into Miss Minnie's arms.

"They may have gone to play over at the stream," one of the men yelled. "Three of you men come with me, and we'll check along the water's edge."

"That's it!" Sing Ho announced, brightening. "They have gone to play in the water. You know how Bo Lin loves the water, Miss Minnie."

"Yes, dearie, I know she does. And perhaps they're having themselves a gay old time splashing in the stream. Now, you need to settle yourself. We need to question the other children and find out if they know anything. Can you help?"

"Yes," she staunchly replied, sniffing one last time before wiping her eyes.

And so they began questioning the children, one by one. *How long had Bo Lin and Yoke Lon been gone? Why did they leave the group? Had they seen the pair after they went toward the trees? Had anyone strange been lurking about? Had anyone heard either of the girls scream or cry?*

The replies were surprisingly similar. The two girls hadn't wanted to play games and decided that they wanted to sit under the trees where it was cool. They had been in view for a while, but then had disappeared. Nobody had heard them make any noise, nor had they seen any strangers in the vicinity.

"It sounds as though they may have wandered off—at least that's what I want to believe. Since none of the girls saw anyone or heard any noises, it's just possible," Miss Cunningham confided in Sing Ho and Miss Minnie. "I don't want to believe that members of the tongs have tracked us down. You would certainly think they would have more pressing matters to take care of following an earthquake—wouldn't you?"

Minnie nodded her head in agreement. All three of them knew that there were a multitude of ways the tong members could busy themselves. But none of those would prove as profitable as securing several girls who could soon work in their brothels.

"I didn't risk my life to save those little girls to see their Christian lives cut short by those evil men," Miss Cunningham angrily proclaimed. "And I don't believe it is God's plan for those children to grow up and be forced to lead lives of depravity and disgrace. If they've been kidnapped, I'll find them and get them back if it's the last thing I do!"

Sing Ho had no doubt that Lo Mo would be true to her word. While accompanying Lo Mo on many of her rescue attempts, Sing Ho had learned long ago why Miss Cunningham was called *Fan Quai,* the "white devil," by the tong members. They found the American woman's uncanny ability to locate their slave girls and spirit them away to the Mission Home abhorrent—and her lack of fear was without dispute. It was because of that success they called her the white devil, certain that if she were merely human, they could stop her.

Sing Ho and the other girls had taken courage as Miss Cunningham had consistently refused to succumb to the terroristic threats and plotting by the tong. Whenever the men came to their residence at 920 Sacramento Street, screaming curses and attempting to instill fear, Lo Mo met the challenge with the Word of God; when they sought to intimidate with the evil messages they attached to rocks and hurled into the windows, Lo Mo placed iron grilles across the glass; when they lurked about attempting to kidnap one of the children, Lo Mo obtained police protection; and each time they took her to court attempting to prove that she had stolen a child, Lo Mo succeeded in producing the necessary adoption papers. In her heart, Sing Ho knew that Miss Cunningham would do everything possible to protect Bo Lin and Yoke Lon—but would it be enough?

Watching as Charlie crossed the grassy field and walked toward them, Sing Ho was sure of his message. With faltering steps, slumped shoulders, and a solemn face, he took Miss Cunningham's hands in his own. "We've found nothing, except this," he told them, holding up a pink satin ribbon that Sing Ho had woven into Bo Lin's hair earlier in the day.

Horror seized Sing Ho as she pulled the ribbon from between Charlie's extended fingers. She screamed inwardly, a prolonged, excruciating wail that never reached her lips. As hard as she tried, she could say nothing. Her voice wouldn't come. She merely nodded when Charlie asked if the ribbon belonged to Bo Lin. She stood mute, listening to Miss Cunningham ask where the ribbon had been found, and Charlie's answer that it was discovered near the road that ran by the barn.

"We think that the girls were kidnapped and that the men headed back toward the dock," Charlie explained. "It's certain they'll want to get the pair back to San Francisco as quickly as possible. Some of our men have already gone in that direction. Mr. Weaver took his horseless carriage. I'll join them shortly, but I wanted to report our findings to you," he told them.

"The girls would scream and holler if they tried to take them on the ferry. Surely the other passengers would be alerted," Miss Minnie suggested.

"You're right, it would be impossible to keep the girls quiet. They wouldn't risk traveling with other people. My guess is that they traveled in a small boat that they rented or perhaps borrowed," Charlie agreed. "Our only hope is that they don't reach the bay before we catch up with them. If I don't return before nightfall, don't worry. I promise you that I will return and report to you—no matter what the news," he assured them.

Without warning, Sing Ho's voice returned, loud and clear. "I want to go with him," she told Miss Cunningham. "I must," she said, so sadly and so simply that Miss Cunningham merely nodded her agreement.

"You're not going to let Sing Ho go off unescorted with the *men,* are you?" Minnie asked, her voice filled with shock.

"Minnie, there's a time to worry about propriety and a time to do what your heart knows is honorable. It is crucial to Sing Ho's welfare that she help find the girls," she replied as the young couple walked away. "I think that I'll head back to the chapel and pray. Care to join me?"

୶

Charlie and Sing Ho climbed into Pastor Landon's buggy and the threesome soon caught up to Mr. Weaver and the other men near Sausalito. The pastor said a quick prayer with the young couple and the searchers for the safe recovery of the girls before he returned to the church.

"We've talked with several people who have seen Chinese men with a cart of hay headed toward the bay," Mr. Weaver explained, "but none of them have seen any Chinese *children*."

"We've no time to waste," Charlie said.

"Let's go," Mr. Weaver nodded and helped Sing Ho into his horseless carriage.

Within minutes, the search group spotted some Chinese men with a hay cart stopped by the side of the road just ahead.

"There! There's the hay cart!" exclaimed Sing Ho.

"We'll drive on past them and wait just ahead where we can watch them," Mr. Weaver stated. He slowed down and added, "You two had better get invisible while we pass them or they are likely to get nervous. We don't want them doing anything stupid if they have the children."

Sing Ho and Charlie ducked down as they passed the hay cart. "Can't we just stop and search the wagon?"

Sing Ho asked.

"We can't take the chance that they would hurt Bo Lin and Yoke Lon," Charlie answered. "First, we must see what they are doing, then we will know what to do."

The closeness of Charlie's warm breath and encouraging smile made Sing Ho want to hold onto him to drive off the chill of fear.

The searchers stopped in a small group along the road, feigning trouble with one of the buggies while they observed the hay cart. Apparently confident that the group ahead was not watching them, the Chinese men moved some hay aside and appeared agitated as they talked.

"Bo Lin and Yoke Lon are in there, Charlie. I just know it," said Sing Ho.

"If you are right, we will need assistance from the police," Charlie answered. "Mr. Baker has the fastest horse, perhaps he could go into Sausalito and alert the police?"

"I'm on my way," Mr. Baker said as he spun on his heel and headed for his buggy.

"And I'll see if these men would like to sell me some hay while Mr. Baker is gone," Mr. Weaver said. "You all stay here unless I tip my hat back. That's the signal the girls are in the cart." He turned and casually strolled down the road.

As Mr. Weaver approached the hay cart, the Chinese men hastily pushed the hay back into place. Mr. Weaver walked past them to the back of the cart and they followed him. He reached in, grabbed a handful of hay, and inspected it. The men gestured for him to stop, but he reached in again, dredging deeper. Sing Ho gasped as Mr. Weaver leaned back and pushed his hat far back on his head. Charlie and the other men rushed toward the cart with Sing Ho on their heels.

Mr. Weaver reached deep into the hay and the kidnappers tried to feign shock when he pulled Bo Lin and then Yoke Lon from under the hay and the rescuers collected around them. Sing Ho heard them claim the girls must be runaways trying to escape a cruel master.

"Then perhaps you can explain the ropes around their ankles and wrists and the gags over their mouths," Charlie countered.

The kidnappers tried to run away but were detained by the rescuers and led away from the hay cart. Sing Ho was both relieved and outraged as she helped the girls loose from their bindings. Frightened but unharmed, both girls were talking and crying, apologizing and thanking Sing Ho for finding them.

The police finally arrived and Sing Ho and the girls watched until the kidnappers were taken away to Sausalito. Charlie returned to the hay cart where the three girls sat hugging, awash in tears of relief.

❦

Shortly before sunset, Miss Cunningham saw plumes of dust billowing in the distance. Squinting into the late afternoon sun, she finally made out Mr. Weaver's horseless carriage lumbering down the dirt road toward her. An arm was waving out the window, and she could hear excited shouts from the passengers as the car drew closer.

"Please, Lord," she whispered, "let my girls be in that car." Eventually, the automobile was within sight, and she thought she could see Bo Lin. Or was that her imagination? No, it *was* Bo Lin. In fact, she was perched on Charlie's lap, clapping her hands and laughing. But where was Yoke Lon? Surely they hadn't come back with only one child. Surely they had remained and searched further. Rushing toward the car, she grabbed Bo Lin from Charlie before the car came to a complete stop. Tears streamed down her cheeks.

"Thank You, Lord. Thank You," she repeated over and over, clinging to the child while her eyes continued to scan the vehicle that was now stopped a short distance from where she stood. She held her breath as the passengers piled out, one by one.

Sing Ho appeared haggard and near exhaustion as she moved toward Miss Cunningham, a half-smile upon her face. "As you can see, we've returned safe and sound," she quietly reported.

"At least part of you," Lo Mo replied, her voice cracking with emotion. "And what of Yoke Lon? Do you hold any hope that we'll be able to recover her?"

"Oh, Lo Mo, I am so sorry. Yoke Lon fell asleep in the car. I was weary and she was sleeping so soundly that I let her remain there. You thought—"

"Yes. I thought you had recovered only one of the girls. Praise, God! Our family is reunited!" she shouted.

Before long, all of the girls were outdoors, talking and laughing, shouting questions and showing fervent interest in every detail of the kidnapping.

"Girls, girls! Quit your shouting! I know you all want to know what happened, and so do I. Why don't we all gather together in the barn? That way they can tell the story, and, after they've finished, we can ask any questions we may have."

Quickly, the girls began to scamper back toward the barn. Miss Minnie lifted Yoke Lon from the car and carried her inside as the other adults followed and seated themselves in a circle. Once the group was settled, Miss Cunningham looked toward Sing Ho.

"I'd rather that Charlie tell you what happened," she said in answer to the older woman's look.

"Charlie? Would you care to enlighten us?" Miss Cunningham asked after giving Sing Ho a nod of understanding.

"It's much as we had thought. The girls were playing in the stand of trees away from the church. After a short time, they decided to get some water from the stream. They had gone only a short distance when they spotted the men. Thinking that the men were members of the local community, the girls weren't frightened. Even when the men approached them, they remained calm. It wasn't until they were seized and were being pushed under a pile of hay in the back of a small, horse-drawn cart that they realized they'd made a gigantic error in judgment."

"Apparently, I've failed to make the girls understand the seriousness of their plight," Miss Cunningham lamented as Charlie shifted and crossed his legs.

"This isn't your fault," he consoled her. "The girls need to have *some* freedom in their lives."

"I suppose. I'm sorry for interrupting. Please continue," she urged him.

Charlie spared no details explaining how the girls were discovered in the hay cart.

"The hay kept tickling my nose, and we could hardly breathe," Bo Lin chimed in.

"Who were these men? Were any of them from the brothels in Chinatown?" Miss Cunningham inquired.

"They were opportunists attempting to earn a bounty from the slave owners. It seems that even something as disastrous as an earthquake will not stop these men from their evil ways. In fact, they've already set up their ugly businesses in Oakland and other communities where large groups of Chinese men have begun to relocate. And, as you know, whenever they think they can find girls who will someday be useful to them, they are on the prowl," Charlie replied.

"It seems strange they would come to San Anselmo. So few Chinese migrated in this direction that I'm surprised they chose to search this area. Doesn't it seem odd to you?" Miss Minnie inquired.

Sing Ho and Charlie exchanged a look. "Is there something that you're not telling us?" Miss Cunningham asked.

"I'll tell them," Sing Ho quietly replied as Charlie gave her an encouraging smile. "When the police arrived, one of the kidnappers claimed to have been forced to participate in the kidnapping, in repayment of a debt, and soon divulged everything. It seems that Du Wang conducted business with several of these men, selling them produce whenever he came to San Francisco. And during one of those visits, Du Wang told them he was courting a girl who lived at the Mission Home."

"That was certainly foolish. What could he have been thinking? I can't imagine why he would even conduct business with such people, let alone tell them his personal business," Miss Cunningham interjected.

Sing Ho gave her a weak smile. "It seems that Du Wang met one of the men when he came to San Francisco after the earthquake. The man offered him a large sum of money if he would tell where the girls from the Mission Home had gone after the earthquake. That's why Du Wang went looking for Charlie and wanted to know our whereabouts," she stated.

"Are you telling me. . .do you mean to say. . .surely Du Wang would not consider doing such a thing," Miss Cunningham stammered.

"Not only did he consider doing it—but he did it!" Charlie stated, his voice filled with outrage. "How he could have done such a thing is beyond me, but apparently his love of money was greater than—"

"Than his love for *me*," Sing Ho stated softly.

"Sing Ho, this is certainly no reflection upon *you*," Miss Cunningham quickly interjected. "If anything, it's a reflection upon my judgment of character. I'm the one who gave Du Wang permission to court you. The last thing I want is for you to feel any responsibility for what has occurred," she continued, giving Sing Ho a warm smile.

"Does this mean that Sing Ho's courtship with Du

Wang is over?" Chow Kum, one of the older girls, asked as she walked from the side of the room and sat down beside Yuen Kim. All eyes turned toward Chow Kum.

"Well, of course," Miss Cunningham replied. "Why would you even need to ask such a question?"

Ignoring Miss Cunningham's question, Chow Kum looked at Sing Ho. "Now you can carve another notch in your basket, can't you?" the girl asked, a furtive gleam crossing her face.

"What *are* you talking about?" Miss Cunningham inquired.

"Because now she's free of Du Wang. *That's* a blessing, isn't it, Sing Ho?" Chow Kum persisted stubbornly.

"If your remarks are made in an effort to inform Lo Mo that I never cared for Du Wang and that I wanted the courtship to end, she already knows that. I told her of my feelings long before this incident," Sing Ho asserted, her eyes darting back and forth between Yuen Kim and Chow Kum.

"And have you already told her of your feelings for Charlie and that *he's* the one you want to court you?" Chow Kum inquired, her eyes dancing in delight at the surprised gasps from several of the older girls.

Sing Ho jumped up and ran outdoors, unable to withstand the embarrassment of sitting there any longer. Why had Chow Kum said those things in front of everyone? Especially Charlie. How would she ever face him again? And how did Chow Kum know of her feelings toward Charlie? That is, unless Yuen Kim had surmised the truth and discussed it with Chow Kum.

Sing Ho didn't hear the approaching footsteps and was startled when Charlie lightly touched her arm. "Please don't let Chow Kum's foolish actions embarrass you. She has humiliated herself by this reckless behavior. In fact, Miss Cunningham is speaking with her now." Taking hold of her shoulders, Charlie turned her to face him and gently lifted her chin until their eyes met. "However, I hope that what Chow Kum said just now is true, because I would be honored to know that you care for me. And I want you to know that the *only* reason I hadn't requested permission to court you was because of your prior relationship with Du Wang. Surely you've come to realize that I care for you—haven't you?"

"I have hoped for that," she replied, a blush rising in her cheeks.

"Then if I request Miss Cunningham's permission to court you, I need not fear rejection?" he asked while giving her a warm smile.

"No, you need not fear rejection. In fact, Chow Kum is right. I would probably sit up all night carving notches in the blessings basket!"

"One day, you're going to have to explain just what that blessings basket is all about. But for right now, I think I'd prefer to settle for this," he told her, gently gathering her into his arms and placing a tender kiss upon her lips.

Her arms seemed to automatically slip around his neck as she returned his kiss and her heart beat with excitement.

Chapter Six
April, 1907

The golden poppies, pink rockroses, and woolly blue curls were all in bloom, and the beautiful, ivy-covered chapel at San Anselmo looked much as it had a year ago. "Here we are," Miss Cunningham announced to the group of fifty girls. "You older girls, get busy and begin picking flowers—you little ones, stay close at hand," she ordered. "And be careful," she called after them. "Don't get out of my sight!"

She smiled as they scattered into the field, quickly gathering an array of blossoming wildflowers to be used as decorations in the small chapel. She had tried for several months to convince Sing Ho that the larger church in San Rafael would be more suitable for her wedding, but to no avail. The girl was convinced that the vows should be exchanged at San Anselmo. And, of course, whatever Sing Ho desired was fine with Charlie. Throughout the past year, their dedication and love had developed, becoming a constant source of delight to everyone who knew them, and he seemed unable to refuse any of her wishes regarding the wedding plans.

The Ming family was well-known in the San

Francisco area, and their guest list had been extensive. That fact, combined with the number of members of the Mission Board, their families, and Sing Ho's fifty-member family, had initially convinced Miss Cunningham that the chapel was out of the question. The Ming family had agreed. That is, until Sing Ho spent an afternoon at their home explaining all the events that had occurred the previous year and the significance of the barn and chapel located in San Anselmo. The Mings had never heard the entire story of the attempted kidnapping and how it had eventually brought Charlie and Sing Ho together. And in the end, they had agreed with Sing Ho that the wedding should be held at the chapel, even if the guests were a bit uncomfortable.

Minnie assured her that this arrangement would work if Miss Cunningham would leave things in her hands. And so she had—everything except decorating the church and arranging the flowers. Sing Ho had specifically requested that Lo Mo have the children decorate the sanctuary and fill her basket with wildflowers. She had sent along ribbons to tie a small bouquet for Hung Mooie, who had arrived from Cleveland only yesterday to act as matron of honor.

The sound of approaching horses' hooves and rumbling buggy wheels pulled Miss Cunningham back to the present and she watched in delight as Sing Ho stepped out of the carriage in her ivory satin gown, followed by Hung Mooie and little Bo Lin in pale pink silk.

"Come see what you think of the decorations," she

said, greeting the girls as they walked toward her. Three large silver candelabra stood at the front of the church, entwined with lavender and pink rockroses. Two large baskets of wildflowers bursting in a profusion of colors rested on marble pedestals between the candelabra. Large white ribbons were tied to the end of each pew, with different colored wildflowers nestled in the center of each bow.

Taking in the full effect of the decorations, Sing Ho placed an arm around Miss Cunningham. "It looks beautiful!" As soon as she'd made the pronouncement, she began to giggle.

"What? Have I missed something?" Lo Mo asked, quickly surveying the room.

"No," Sing Ho replied, attempting to squelch her laughter. "I was thinking back to a conversation I had with Charlie's mother about Chinese weddings," she sputtered, still unable to contain herself.

Miss Cunningham was clearly concerned that something was wrong with the decorations, and Sing Ho couldn't seem to stop giggling.

"I think she has wedding jitters," Hung Mooie interjected. "The church looks lovely," she added. "It reminds me so much of my wedding to Henry. Don't you think, Sing Ho?"

Sing Ho nodded her head and wiped away the tears that had pooled in her eyes. "I'm sorry, Lo Mo. The church looks absolutely stunning."

"Well, now that you seem to have composed yourself a bit, what was it that Charlie's mother told you about Chinese weddings that you found so humorous?"

"She asked me if I had ever witnessed a Chinese wedding ceremony or knew any of the Chinese wedding rituals. I told her I hadn't attended a wedding, but I knew that the bride wore a red gown and that gifts of money were wrapped in red paper because red is the Chinese color of joy."

Miss Cunningham nodded. "I still fail to see anything funny about that."

"That's not the funny part," Sing Ho replied. "Charlie's mother explained to me that when the bride is dressed in her red gown, a female member of the groom's household staff comes to the bride's house to escort her to the groom's home."

"And?" Miss Cunningham impatiently urged when it appeared Sing Ho was going to once again burst into laughter.

"This woman that the groom sends as an escort is required to carry the bride *piggyback* out of the house to the awaiting sedan chair. Then when they arrive at the home of the groom, the woman must once again carry the bride into the groom's house, because the bride's feet are not allowed to touch the ground until she reaches the home of the groom. Can't you just see me in a billowing red gown with Hung Mooie carrying me on her back into the church?" All three of them broke into gales of laughter, Sing Ho holding her sides as tears streamed down her face.

"What else did she tell you?" Hung Mooie sputtered, attempting to catch her breath.

"Nothing else that was quite so funny as that. The rest was about the hair-combing ritual to find good fortune and the fact that the emphasis of the ceremony is on worshiping ancestors and the heavens and earth instead of God. She told me that all of it now seemed strange to her, too."

"I think we had better quit our chattering before our guests arrive. Here are your bouquets," Lo Mo said, motioning for one of the girls to bring the flowers. The blessings basket was filled with every variety of wildflower that could be found, and lavish white ribbons matching those at the ends of the pews had been tied to each side of the handle. A large coordinating bouquet and ribbon had been made for Hung Mooie, and Bo Lin received a small basket filled with rose petals, which she would scatter down the aisle. "We've even matched the ribbons and flowers on the serving tables for the reception," Miss Cunningham confided, pleased with Sing Ho's delighted reaction.

"It's *beautiful,* Lo Mo! How can I ever thank you?" Sing Ho asked, pulling her surrogate mother into a loving embrace.

"Just be happy and always remain close to the Lord. That's thanks enough. And by the way, you were right," she replied, returning the hug. "This chapel *is* the proper choice for your wedding. I don't know why I ever thought that you should consider any other."

Sing Ho stood in the vestibule of the church, peeking around the corner to gain a view of Bo Lin as she preceded her down the aisle. She looked so grown-up in the pink silk dress, with her head held high as she took slow, halting steps, and inched her way toward the front of the church. Carefully, she dispersed the rose petals, a few at a time, until she reached her designated spot beside Hung Mooie.

"It's time," Lo Mo stated. "Are you ready?" she asked, tucking Sing Ho's arm into the crook of her own.

"I think so," she replied, the basket of flowers visibly shaking in her hand as they walked into the back of the church. She took a deep breath and exhaled slowly. There were so many people, and all of them were staring at *her*. Immediately, she began scanning the front of the church, searching for Charlie. Suddenly their eyes met, and he was looking at her with such love and adoration that her heart skipped a beat. She returned his gaze, keeping her eyes fixed upon him as Lo Mo slowly escorted her to where her groom stood waiting.

"Who gives this woman in marriage?" Pastor Landon asked, looking toward Lo Mo, who was positioned to the left of Sing Ho.

"As a blessing from God, *I* give this woman," Lo Mo replied, her voice unfaltering as she kissed Sing Ho's cheek and then released her to Charlie.

The remaining vows were exchanged in loving tenderness, followed by a gentle kiss, which drew applause from the crowd. Turning the young couple toward the assembled group, the minister proclaimed, "Honored guests, I present to you Mr. and Mrs. Charlie Ming."

❧

"Who would have ever believed that out of the devastation of an earthquake one year ago, our lives would have been so filled with blessings?" Sing Ho asked the small group that remained at the end of the afternoon.

"Certainly not Yuen Kim," Miss Minnie replied, causing them all to burst into laughter.

Yuen Kim nodded her head in agreement. "You're right! I've learned much about God's faithfulness this past year. I just hope that He doesn't need to take such drastic measures to get my attention in the future," she joked.

"I don't think that the earthquake was arranged solely for your benefit, Yuen Kim. I think there are a lot of us that needed that same lesson!" Miss Minnie replied as they moved about the room, packing up dishes and cleaning the tables and floor.

"It's time for us to leave," Charlie stated, giving his bride a smile. "We'll miss the last ferry across the bay if we wait any longer."

"Just a moment," she said, walking to a nearby table and picking up the basketful of flowers. "Come here, Bo Lin," she called to the child, who was carefully watching her every move. "I have a very special task for you," she explained. "Now that I'll be leaving to make my home with Charlie, I'd like for you to be in charge of the blessings basket. Do you think you can do that?" she asked in a solemn voice.

"I might cut myself. Maybe you should stay and live with us," she said, giving Charlie a doleful expression.

"I can't do that, Bo Lin, but Charlie has told me that you can come and visit us as soon as we return from our trip to China. It would make me very happy if I knew that you were taking care of the basket. And perhaps Miss Minnie will help you make the notches. How would that be?" she cajoled.

"If you're sure you can't stay with us, then I promise we'll take care of it," Bo Lin replied while glancing toward Miss Minnie, who was nodding her approval.

"Thank you, Bo Lin. I know that you are the very best choice to take care of the basket," Sing Ho replied, gathering the child into a tight embrace.

"I'm ready," she said, moving toward Charlie. His arm encircled her waist as they walked to the buggy waiting outside the church.

"I've made a decision," he told her as the horse trotted down the dirt road away from the church.

"And what is that?" she asked, giving him a bright smile.

"To purchase a big basket for our home. I think a blessings basket is *exactly* what we'll need!"

A Note to Readers

Although a Mission Home for Chinese girls actually existed at 920 Sacramento Street in San Francisco, California, and served the purpose of providing a Christian home for many homeless Chinese girls, this novella is a work of fiction and the names, places, people, and events have been created to serve the purpose of this story.

Judith McCoy Miller
Judith makes her home in Kansas with her family.
Intrigued by the law, Judy is a certified legal assistant
currently employed as a public service administrator in
the legal section of the Department of Administration
for the State of Kansas. After ignoring an "urge" to
write for approximately two years, Judy quit thinking
about what she had to say and began writing it, and
then was and has been extremely blessed! Her first two
books earned her the honor of being selected **Heartsong Presents'** favorite new author in 1997.

A Valentine for Prudence

Darlene Mindrup

Chapter One

Good morrow! 'tis St. Valentine's Day
All in the morning betime,
And I a maid at your window,
To be your Valentine.

(SHAKESPEARE)

Prudence Hilliard stared out the window at the bleak winter Boston landscape. Snow was falling steadily, giving the streets a pureness that reached a chord deep inside the not-so-young girl watching it as it flaked steadily downward. Blowing upon the pane, she smiled at the round frost on the glass before quickly drawing a heart with an arrow slashing through it.

"Did you know that in Italy, an unmarried woman stands at the window on Valentine's morn and watches the roads until a man appears? Supposedly, the first man she sees will be the one she marries, or at least someone who looks like him, within the year," Prudence told Constance, her sister, who was glowering at her from across the room.

"Oh, really, Prudence. Stop mooning around the window and help me get ready. Devlin will be here soon."

Constance struggled a moment with her whalebone hoops before glaring in exasperation at Prudence, still standing at the window, obviously not having heard a word she had said.

"Did you know that in England, they believe the birds will choose their mates this day?" Prudence asked.

"You've been at Papa's library again! Now give me a hand with this thing! You're a hopeless romantic."

"And you're not?" Prudence asked, still watching the road below.

"A romantic, certainly. But not, I trust, hopeless."

Suddenly, two figures came into view from around the corner, their derbies the only things visible above their morning coats. From this distance, they both struck Prudence as fine figures, though one stood out more than the other, due mainly, she supposed, to the fact that he was against fashion and was clean shaven. While Prudence studied him, he suddenly looked up at the window as though he knew he was being watched, and Prudence caught her breath in a slight gasp.

"What is it?" Constance wanted to know, momentarily forgetting her fight with the stays on her petticoat.

"N—nothing," Prudence told her, quickly coming to give her sister an assist. "Devlin is here."

"What!" Squealing, Constance turned this way and that, suddenly in a furor over what to do next.

Taking her sister by the shoulders, Prudence pulled her to a stop. "Be still, do."

"But I'm not ready," her sister wailed and Prudence

was hard put getting the lively young woman to stay in one position.

Pushing Constance's hands aside, Prudence began to tighten the ribbons on her sister's slip after having adjusted it over the hoop below. Although Prudence preferred the newer, more tailored look with the front flat and the back more full, Constance still preferred the rounder look of previous years.

She helped her sister lift her morning dress over her head, all the while murmuring soothingly as she fastened the tiny pearl buttons in the back.

"Aren't you the one who says that one must keep a man waiting so as not to show too much eagerness?" Prudence asked.

Constance fixed her sister with an eloquent look. "And what, pray tell, do you know about men?" she asked, not meaning to be unkind.

Refusing to answer, Prudence stood back and eyed her sister critically. Constance surely knew how to choose her clothes. The blue satin of her dress set off to perfection the golden blond of her curls hanging down her back, and her ice blue eyes glowed back, awaiting the appreciation she knew was sure to come. She was not disappointed.

"You are truly a vision," Prudence told her, handing her sister her fingerless white lace gloves.

Smiling, Constance slid them over her hands. "Let us hope Devlin thinks so."

Prudence would have remained behind, but Constance took her firmly by the arm and propelled her not so gently down to the parlor. Sighing in resignation to another morning of playing gooseberry, Prudence tried to arrange her features into some sort of acceptable greeting.

As they made their entrance—it was the only way to describe how Constance entered a room—Prudence became aware of another man waiting with Devlin. When she had seen them from the window, she had not realized that the other man was coming in with Devlin. She had assumed they were only acquaintances who had met on the street and happened to be going in the same direction.

Devlin's dark, good looks brought a little thump to Prudence's heart, which she quickly quelled. She had no hope of attracting such a handsome man, even if she had desired to do so. Besides, Devlin belonged to Constance.

Simultaneously, both men rose to their feet, and Prudence took the time to covertly study the other man. He was young, probably younger than Devlin's twenty-five years, but he had a bearing of confidence that gave an impression of early manhood. Unlike Devlin, this man had succumbed to the fashion of the times and was sporting both a beard and a mustache. His hair was the color of wheat, whereas Devlin's was as dark as the coal that filled their coal scuttle. Both men were incredibly handsome.

Constance sailed forth, fluttering her fan demurely. "Why, Devlin, you've brought company."

Devlin bowed low, taking one of her hands into his, raising it to his lips, and bestowing a kiss upon it. "I hope you don't mind. This is my cousin, Terence Scott, just arrived from England. I thought it only polite to introduce him around Boston, and I could think of no finer beginning than to have him make the acquaintance of three of the loveliest ladies this side of the Atlantic Ocean."

Constance dropped her lashes before extending her hand to Terence. "Devlin, how gallant. The pleasure is surely mine, Mr. Scott."

"Oh, Terence, please." Devlin turned to Prudence who hastily placed her hands behind her back. Lips twitching with amusement, he introduced his cousin.

Terence stared from Constance to Prudence in what could only be considered unflattering amazement. Prudence was used to the reaction, for her own dark brown locks, pug nose, and too-wide mouth had nothing in the way of beauty. Whereas her two sisters favored their mother, Prudence was the image of her father, in more ways than one.

Nodding her head, she gave him a brief curtsy. "Mr. Scott."

No one heard the footsteps descending the stairs, so it came as a surprise when a cool voice spoke to them from the doorway. "Company so early in the morning?" Jessica, their sister, asked.

Constance colored hotly at the rudeness of the remark, while Prudence sighed with impatience. Jessica was in one of her moods. She must have attended another suffragette rally last evening, for every time she did, she found fault with all men and with any woman willing to yield to their charms. Fortunately, her moods did not last long, but they were trying nonetheless.

Trying to head off the confrontation she knew was surely to come, Prudence slipped to Jessica's side, giving her a slight pinch. "Father is in his study," she warned softly, and watched the storm clouds gather in her sister's eyes. Still, even Jessica would not dare to make a scene with Father around. He had told them more than once that they were still not too old to turn over his knee, and even though Constance was seventeen, Jessica eighteen, and Prudence twenty-two, none of them doubted that he would do it.

Jessica's lovely blue eyes, a replica of her younger sister's, glared first at Devlin, then at Terence. The younger man's eyebrows lifted in surprise, obviously wondering at Jessica's antagonism toward him when they had only just met.

Prudence pulled Jessica forward, introducing her.

"I say, Devlin, you were certainly right about these young ladies. I have never seen lovelier," Terence offered.

Prudence flinched, knowing that was the wrong thing to say when Jessica was in one of her feminist moods. Jessica's eyes took on fire, but when she opened her mouth to retort, Prudence hastily interrupted her. "May I offer you gentlemen some refreshments?"

Devlin's eyes were alight with laughter and Prudence realized he was secretly amused by the exchange. After all, Devlin had been seeing Constance for some time now, and knew fairly well the temperaments of all in the household. It irritated her that they seemed to amuse him.

"No, thank you," Devlin answered for both of them. "We stopped by only to see if perchance we could prevail upon your mother to allow my cousin to attend her Valentine's party this eve. I know it's very poor manners to ask, but—"

Constance came at once to his assistance. "Of course not." Touching a bellpull by the fireplace, she turned to the servant who answered her summons. "Please ask Mrs. Hilliard if she could possibly come to the parlor."

Bowing, he left. As soon as he disappeared, Jessica turned to her sister angrily. "What Valentine's party? I have heard nothing of it!"

"Neither have I," Prudence agreed.

Constance, fanning herself with her little ivory fan, flushed a becoming red, but she refused to answer, studiously avoiding her sisters' eyes. It was then that Prudence realized that Constance and their mother had deliberately evaded any mention of a party.

Brows knitting in confusion, Devlin turned to Constance. "I'm sorry. Have I made a mistake?"

Before Constance could answer, Mrs. Hilliard swept gracefully into the room. At forty-three years of age, she was still a beautiful woman. Her blond hair was parted in the middle and pulled back into a lace snood whose color matched the burgundy of her morning gown. As with Constance, Mrs. Hilliard preferred the rounder look of skirts.

"Devlin," she smiled, lifting her hand for his kiss.

Bowing low, he clicked his heels together. "Mrs. Hilliard. May I present my cousin, Mr. Terence Scott?"

Terence took her hand and performed the same act, though Prudence thought privately that Devlin's greeting had more panache.

Jessica took her mother to task immediately. "What is this about a Valentine's party, and why weren't Prudence and I informed?"

Mrs. Hilliard gave her young daughter such a look of disdain it would have quelled a lesser individual.

"Knowing how much you and your sister dislike parties, why should I bother you with the details of helping to arrange one?"

"Mother!"

Devlin cleared his throat and everyone turned his way. "My apologies, Mrs. Hilliard, but I came only to beg your favor in letting my cousin attend your affair. Of course, you have already received my acceptance, but I feel honor bound to attend to my cousin who has just arrived from England."

"Oh, see here," Terence interrupted, "I can take care of myself for one evening, Dev."

"Not at all," Mrs. Hilliard told him. "We shall be pleased to have such a handsome gentleman attend our little function."

"In that case," Devlin told her, glancing uneasily from one sister to another, "we shall see you at seven." There were undercurrents here he did not quite understand, but he recognized the need to get his cousin away from the gathering storm.

All four women watched silently as the men made their departure. The door had no more than closed behind them when Jessica launched her verbal attack.

"You planned this deliberately, didn't you, Mother? You knew I wouldn't want to go! I hate going to parties and having to watch all the men fawn and preen to get a woman's attention!" She glared at her parent. "But you expect me to attend, don't you?"

"Of course," her mother told her, walking over and seating herself on the chaise near the fire.

Stamping her foot slightly, Jessica gritted through clenched teeth. "I won't go!"

Unperturbed, her mother silently awaited her acquiescence.

"I won't, Mother! Do you hear me?"

The voice that answered her was not feminine. "I hear you just fine," Mr. Hilliard said.

Prudence saw her mother settle back in relief. Reinforcements had arrived.

Mr. Hilliard glared at his daughter. "You will apologize to your mother."

Although he had not raised his voice, the color left Jessica's face. If there was one thing their father had never tolerated, it was disrespect to their mother.

Jessica stared mutinously back at him before finally dropping her eyes. "I'm sorry for yelling, Mother."

Prudence noticed that Jessica had not apologized for what she had said, merely for raising her voice. Would Father accept such an apology? She saw her father's shoulders relax slightly.

Her mother hastily intervened. "Thank you for apologizing, Jessica."

Mr. Hilliard's eyes went from Jessica to Prudence. "Your mother and I have discussed this matter, and we are agreed. All of our daughters *will* attend. Your mother has spent much time and money on this affair, and though I see no reason to interfere in your lives, I have allowed her this concession." His glance rested on Jessica. "I think you would agree that your mother and I have not been overly strict and we have allowed you more than your share of escapades. We have not interfered unduly with your wants and desires, although at times my own inclination has been strongly to do so." His look became fierce. "You will allow your mother this moment of your life."

Prudence dropped her gaze to the floor. Her father was right. Jessica and she had flaunted many of the conventions of their time and had been allowed more freedom than many of their contemporaries. Father had always felt that they should be allowed to live their own lives, within reason. He had never cared whether the gossiping tongues clicked over him or not. It was important to him that his daughters be allowed to grow and reach out. Feeling more than a little guilty, Prudence glanced at her sister. Jessica must have been feeling much of the same thing, for her manner was subdued.

"Yes, Father," Jessica told him meekly.

After glancing from one to another, his eyes rested on his wife. There was just the slightest softening there. "I will leave you to explain this soiree, my dear," he told his wife.

Smiling back at him, she waited for him to leave the room before she glanced hesitantly at Jessica. "I have ordered a dress for each of you. They will be delivered within the hour. At the party, every guest will have a decorated box for valentines. I am telling you this so that you may prepare them and have them ready. A copy of my guest list is in my morning room and you can decide from it to whom you wish to give."

Jessica's eyes grew flinty. "I don't need to see the list. There is no one I wish to give valentines to."

"Not even your sisters?"

Jessica had the grace to blush.

"Many of your own friends will be there, too," her mother continued. "If you choose not to give any to a man, that choice is, of course, your own."

Mrs. Hilliard's eyes rested briefly on Prudence. "You are not getting any younger, you know. It is time you settled down and began to raise a family."

Chance is a fine thing, Prudence thought. Having lived in the shadows of her beautiful sisters for many years, Prudence had no illusions about herself. She was doomed to remain an old maid. At twenty-two, she was already considered a bit long in the tooth. Of course, she did not feel old, but that was not saying anything where men were concerned.

"Darlings," their mother told them softly, "I only want you to know the joys of being the woman God intended you to be. He has said that it was not good for man to be alone. That goes for women, too. I only want

271

you to know the joys of love, for without it you will never feel truly fulfilled."

Jessica snorted but refrained from comment. The timbre of their mother's voice told them that she believed with all of her heart the things she was saying. Even Jessica could not deny it, and would not dare to hurt her mother's feelings by ridiculing her.

Prudence went quietly to her room while the servants began preparing the house for the coming festivities. She was amazed that her mother had accomplished so much without either her or Jessica's knowledge.

Constance followed her into her bedroom, her manner more quiet than usual. "Are you angry, Pru?" she asked, using the nickname her mother detested.

Prudence shook her head. "No, not angry. But I'm not exactly delighted, either."

"Why do you hate parties so much?"

Prudence sighed. How could she explain to her sister that parties were lonely times for her? A wallflower who kept the older matrons occupied while their children danced and flirted. Normally, Prudence did not mind, but just lately she had become more dissatisfied and frequently begged off attending the various affairs. She knew her mother worried about her, but her father had not. He had told her forthrightly that she had inherited his looks and that on a woman they were less than flattering, but he had also told her that one day a man would see past the outer adornments and would look at her spirit.

"I don't hate parties, Constance. I would just rather

not attend them," Prudence said.

A maid, carrying a large dress box, entered the room. "This just arrived, miss. Your mother said to bring it up."

Squealing with delight, Constance leaped off the bed and ran to Prudence's side. "Your dress, Pru. Open it!"

Feeling a sudden apprehension, Prudence slowly opened the box, her sister dancing anxiously at her side. Pushing aside the tissue, Prudence gasped at the beauty of the gown within. Lifting it carefully from the box, she shook it out slightly, holding it against her chest and peering down at the beautiful red silk that extended to just past her knees. The underskirt was still in the box and Constance pulled it out, *aahing* over the lovely pink organza.

"Oh, Pru," Constance breathed, "that color goes beautifully with your hair."

Eyes widening, Constance flew out of the room, her voice floating behind her. "If your dress is here, then mine must be, also."

Prudence watched her sister leave, her mind not fully on what she had just said. Her thoughts were on the night to come. Constance would be with Devlin, she knew. Suddenly a picture came to her of Devlin this morning, looking at her from the street below. She had been watching out the window as the Italians did, but instead of some stranger she had expected to see, the first face she had seen had been Devlin's.

Chapter Two

Prudence eyed the valentine critically. Was it too fancy? Her mother had always said that she had all the artistic talent in the family, but she attributed that to motherly prejudice. Still, the red heart she had painted on the pink paper was perfectly symmetrical, and the small yellow roses she had painted over the heart looked almost real. She had curled a ribbon into a bow and had attached it with glue to the right corner. Prudence's tongue tip protruded slightly from between her teeth as she frowned over the results of her artistic endeavor.

Constance peeked over Prudence's shoulder. "Oh, Pru. That's lovely. You should consider going into the card-making business like Esther Howland. I bet you could make as much money as she does."

Prudence grinned at her sister. "Thank you, kind mistress. But I'm afraid I haven't the time."

Constance looked at her sister slyly. "What *do* you do with your time?"

"Never you mind," Prudence told her, placing the valentine aside and pulling another sheet of paper toward her.

"Are you going to make valentines for everyone?" Constance demanded. "That will take hours! Why don't you just buy them like everyone else?"

"Not *everyone* buys valentines," Prudence argued. "Many people still make them. Who wants to pay ten dollars for a valentine?"

"Well, if you can afford to, why not? Besides, not all store-bought valentines are that expensive. I bought all of mine."

Prudence studied the paper before her, her mind only half on what her sister had just said. "I think it means more when someone takes the time to make something by hand."

"Oh, honestly, Pru. You're so old-fashioned."

Constance lifted the *Valentine Writer's Handbook* from Prudence's desk and began to flip through it, reading some of the quaint sayings. Shaking her head, she laid it back on the table and went toward the door. Before leaving, she told her sister, "By the way, Devlin has asked Terence to escort you to the dance."

Constance quickly vacated before her sister could react, which was a fine thing, for Prudence came quickly to her feet, ready to deny any such possibility.

"Oh, bother," Prudence groused, flinging herself back into her seat. "And in a red dress, too!"

❧

Terence studied his cousin Devlin, sitting across from him in his aunt's parlor. He was a handsome man, no doubt about that, and rich as well. So how had his American cousin managed to stay free from the marriage net that his mother and aunt seemed determined to draw him into?

"I say, Devlin, that Constance Hilliard is one fine-looking woman. You're a very lucky man."

Devlin grinned a lopsided grin. "How so?"

"Well. . .I mean. . .isn't she yours?"

"If you mean do I have matrimonial intentions toward the aforementioned lady, then no, she does not belong to me."

Terence frowned. "I don't understand."

"I dare say you don't," Devlin agreed. He had no intention of discussing his relationships with anyone, much less a cousin he hardly knew.

Trying another tack, Terence mentioned Constance's sister, Jessica. "She's as lovely, if not lovelier, than Constance."

Devlin watched his cousin, his eyes devoid of any emotion. "Agreed. But watch out for Jessica."

Intrigued, Terence leaned closer. "Why?"

"She's a suffragette."

Eyebrows flying upward, Terence sat back against the settee. "Ye gads, what a waste!"

Devlin grinned mischievously. "Aren't you glad I asked for Prudence to be your escort instead of Jessica?"

If anything, the eyebrows went higher. "The homely one?"

Devlin's eyes darkened, the smile freezing on his face. "Watch what you say about Prudence. She's the only intelligent one of the bunch."

"I take it she's a personal friend of yours?" Terence asked, more than a little nonplussed by his cousin's attitude.

"You take it correctly."

Thinking he understood, Terence made haste to apologize. "Sorry, Dev. I suppose one day she will be your sister-in-law and you feel the need to defend her. I didn't mean to be offensive."

Devlin did not answer. He studied the cup of tea in his hands, wondering what Terence would say if he knew the truth of the matter. In the beginning, he had gone to the Hilliards' to see Constance, true. But before long, her simplemindedness caused his interest in her to pall. Constance's main goal in life was to look beautiful and have fun.

But then, hadn't his been the same? When had it changed? Maybe when he had started having long conversations with Prudence. Now, there was a woman who knew what she wanted out of life. Never had he met a woman he could converse with, or even argue with for that matter, as he could her. Often her logic had swayed his own opinion. Prudence had set goals for herself and was striving to attain them. Education was important to her.

It bothered him more than a little, knowing that everyone seemed to consider her so homely. She wasn't that exactly, she was just overshadowed by two beautiful butterflies.

Terence's voice penetrated his musings. "Did you hear me?"

"What?"

"I asked what time we leave for the party tonight?"

"The party is at seven. Unlike most people, I believe in being unfashionably early. We shall leave here at half past six."

Rising to his feet, Devlin rang the pull cord beside the fireplace. A servant entered, bowing before Devlin. "Sir?"

"Raglan, we would like to dine early today. How about five?"

"As you wish, sir."

Devlin watched his butler exit the room before turning to his cousin. "Now, Terence. Let us discuss ways and means about this party."

❧

Prudence was the first to descend the staircase. Constance would still be another hour at least, and Jessica, who disdained what she called such folderol, would take almost as long. Regardless of what Jessica said, when it came to appearances, she was as much a woman as Constance.

Prudence entered the parlor, her pink organza swishing around her feet. The red overdress was pulled up at the center bottom by a lovely white silk rose. Tugging at the bodice, Prudence frowned down at the neckline.

"Leave it, Prudence," her mother called softly from the other side of the room. "You look lovely."

At Prudence's entrance, her father had risen and now stood studying her, his eyes shining. His voice was slightly husky when he spoke. "You are a sight, lass," he told her, and for the first time in her life, Prudence actually felt like she was lovely. She seated herself across from her mother, in the other wing chair next to the fire.

Her mother was as beautiful as her two sisters.

Often, people mistook her for a sister instead of their mother. Her blond hair was stylishly arranged in ringlets hanging down her back, although for the most part, they were false hairpieces. Constance would wear the same, but Jessica and Prudence disliked such artificiality. Prudence's own hair was artfully arranged in shorter ringlets, a spray of red roses tucked neatly into the top.

Before long, the first of the guests started to arrive. Devlin and Terence had made their appearance long before any others, but Mr. Hilliard was quite content to entertain them.

When they had first entered the parlor, both men had stopped short at the sight of Prudence, the light from the fire casting brilliant fingers of red and yellow across her gown and giving a red tint to her normally mouse-brown hair. Terence blinked once before glancing quickly at Devlin, whose face was an inscrutable mask.

Mrs. Hilliard rose gracefully to her feet. "Devlin, Terence. Come in."

They talked for a few minutes before Prudence's mother excused herself to see how the preparations for the party were proceeding. Mr. Hilliard began questioning Terence about England and asked after Devlin's mother.

Devlin walked over to where Prudence was seated, gazing into the fire. He turned his head toward her, his eyes raking her from head to foot.

"So, Cinderella has awakened from a long sleep. You look lovely," Devlin said.

Prudence blushed, her cheeks matching the color of

her overdress. "Haven't you mixed your fairy tales?" she asked him.

"I think not," he answered her softly, bringing more color to her face.

Her own thoughts were on how well Devlin looked in his own evening clothes. He had removed his top hat, overcoat, and gloves upon entering the house and Prudence thought he looked magnificent with his long tails.

His waistcoat was of black velvet and had wide silk lapels, and his white shirt with its high collar accented his dark skin. He had chosen a cravat instead of a tie and the black of it matched his other evening wear. Even his hair was black, so black it shone with blue highlights. When his dark eyes turned their inspection to her face, she colored hotly, having been caught staring.

"Constance will be down soon," she told him, dropping her eyes to her lap.

His lips tilted at the corners, but he said nothing. Prudence had never known him to be so lacking in words. She stumbled about for an area of conversation she thought would not seem trite. "So, Devlin, what do you think of Mr. Seward's Folly?"

"To make Russian America part of the United States? I think it's a great idea."

Prudence's father interrupted. "I agree. Think of all the fur and fishing to be had, and for two cents an acre. It seems a great bargain to me."

"Not everyone would agree with us," Devlin told him, and Mr. Hilliard laughed.

"True. Perhaps it's the thought of spending seven million, two hundred thousand American tax dollars that upsets them so."

Terence whistled. "That's quite a bit of money."

They became embroiled in the conversation, not noticing when Constance made her grand entrance. She coughed quietly to gain their attention, and four pair of eyes swiveled her way.

Prudence heard Terence's quick intake of breath, but her eyes were on Devlin. His appreciation of her sister's beauty was registered in his eyes, and suddenly Prudence felt very dowdy in comparison.

Constance drifted into the room, flicking her fan open as she reached Terence. Certain of his admiration, she made her way to Devlin's side. She batted her eyelashes coyly, taking the arm he held out to her.

"Miss Constance," he told her smoothly, "you are as lovely as ever."

And she was, Prudence realized. The rose pink of her gown added color to the youthful bloom in her cheeks, her china-blue eyes sparkling with feelings.

Jessica entered the room after her sister, her red silk gown rustling as she moved to her father's side. Terence and Devlin exchanged glances and Terence moved to Prudence's side.

"Miss Prudence," he addressed her, "I understand I am to have the pleasure of your company tonight. If you agree, of course."

Prudence had not missed the fact that Jessica had been overlooked in the introductions and Jessica's eloquent blue eyes told her that she was aware of the slight, also. Seeking to pacify, Prudence motioned toward Jessica. "Mr. Scott, I don't believe you have met my sister, Jessica."

"I believe we were introduced this morning," he told her coolly, turning back to Prudence, who dropped her mouth open in surprise. She had yet to meet the man who was not bowled over by her sister's beauty, but it would seem she had met him now. Jessica was less than pleased, her fuming eyes looking like chips of blue ice.

Mrs. Hilliard came sweeping into the room. "Our other guests are arriving, John. Girls, places, please."

Terence and Devlin moved with the others into the entryway. As the family took their places in the receiving line, the young men made their way from the parlor into the ballroom that had been prepared for this night.

Shimmering candelabra hung suspended from the ceiling, the flaming candles sending sparkling prisms of color around the room. Red, pink, and white roses flowed everywhere, adding a delicate scent to the rapidly filling area. Although the men were dressed in black evening attire, all the women wore shades of pink and red.

Mrs. Hilliard's idea, no doubt, Devlin thought. *She must surely know that her daughters look exceptionally fine in those colors, even Prudence.*

Devlin's eyes searched for and found Prudence as she mingled among the guests. She truly looked lovely this evening, yet she made no attempt to draw attention to herself. For some reason, he wanted to make this evening memorable for her.

To that end, he made his way to where a group of young men were huddled together whispering, their eyes following Constance and Jessica who were no doubt the belles of the ball. He joined the group, shaking hands all around since he knew all the young men present.

"Beauties, aren't they?" he suggested, his eyes on the two sisters.

The men hastened to agree. Devlin's eyes searched again for Prudence and found her sitting on a settee talking to his own mother. She glanced from time to time at the dancers on the floor, but she politely listened to her guest's conversation.

"You know," Devlin told the group, "one way to win the favor of the two charming Hilliard sisters might be to show favor to their sister, Prudence."

Four pairs of eyes swung to where Prudence sat, still listening to Devlin's mother, then back to her two ravishing sisters.

"I have heard it said," Devlin continued, "that Constance and Jessica will not countenance a young man's favor if they think their sister has been slighted."

"Oh." Four pairs of eyes followed Constance and Jessica longingly before straying back to Prudence.

Clearing his throat, one of the men, Thomas, moved away from the others. "If you'll excuse me," he told the others, and Devlin watched as he made his way to Prudence's side. Before many seconds passed, the others quickly followed suit.

Devlin grinned at Prudence's surprised expression as she stared bewildered at her determined suitors. Each man signed her dance card, Thomas pulling her to her feet while she excused herself to her guest.

As they danced around the room, Devlin continued to watch them, an unreadable expression in his eyes.

"Devlin?"

He looked down to find Constance by his side. Straightening, he smiled and held out his hand. "My dance, I believe."

They twirled among the other couples, Devlin searching the crowd. His attention was caught by something Constance had just said. "What did you say?"

"I said, I told Prudence that if she didn't always hide behind those dowdy day dresses of hers that she would be charming. It would seem the young men here think so, also."

"Does it bother you?"

She looked surprised. "Heavens, no. I'm thrilled. Prudence needs to be married and have a family. She's the type to have a whole brood of children."

"And you're not?"

She gave him an appalled look. "One or two, maybe, but not more than that." She shivered delicately.

Devlin studied the beauty he held in his arms and wondered what had ever attracted him to her in the first place. She was selfish and spoiled and, on top of that, vain. To be tied to one such as her for a lifetime appalled him almost as much as the thought of children had appalled her.

"Do you know who that man is?" Constance questioned, her eyes following a blond giant walking around the room, introducing himself to people.

"Yes," he told her, smiling down at her. "Would you like to be introduced?"

Color flooded her face, but Devlin paid it no heed as he danced them to where the stranger stood, talking to his cousin Terence.

He made the introductions brief. "Gaylord, this is Miss Constance Hilliard. Constance, Mr. Gaylord Fyfe."

Devlin left them together and then took Terence by the arm and propelled him across the room. "Isn't it about time you danced with Jessica?"

Surprised, Terence frowned at his cousin. "I thought you said it would be better to ignore her. Besides, I don't want to get involved with a suffragette."

"One dance won't kill you," Devlin argued, watching for an opening before pushing his cousin to Jessica's side.

Devlin then made his way to where Prudence was still talking to one of the young men she had danced with earlier. He seemed engrossed in what she had to say, so much so that neither of them heard Devlin's approach. He tapped the young man on the shoulder.

"My dance, I believe, Miss Prudence."

He gathered her into his arms, waltzing her around the room and smiling down at her briefly. "Enjoying yourself?"

Her narrowed gaze watched him thoughtfully. "Immensely. How ever did you manage it?"

"Manage what?" he asked, nearly choking at her obvious insight.

"I saw you talking to those gentlemen. It didn't take much to put two and two together."

He grinned down at her unabashedly. "Surely you

don't think *I* had anything to do with your obvious popularity."

Shaking her head in exasperation, she turned to watch the other couples sailing around the room. When she frowned, Devlin followed her look toward Jessica and Terence who were having a heated discussion that was rapidly drawing attention to them.

Devlin danced them in that direction. As they drew closer, they could hear the heated exchange.

"What kind of man are you?" Jessica sneered, her look flicking over Terence disdainfully.

"The question is, what kind of woman are you? I've heard of these so-called suffragettes. Rather loose women, so I am told."

"Of all the nerve!"

Devlin stepped between them. He gave Prudence a quick look and she interpreted it correctly. She pulled Jessica away, while Devlin took his cousin in the opposite direction. Tears shimmered just beneath the surface of Jessica's eyes and Prudence knew that Terence's words had stung.

"He didn't mean it," she told her sister soothingly.

"I don't care if he did. I hate men! All men!" She ran out of the room and Prudence rolled her eyes at her sister's histrionics.

Hoping no one else had noticed her departure, Prudence found her mother and gave her an edited version of what had happened. Her mother quickly left the room. Prudence only hoped that her mother could do something with Jessica. She was still so young, and had a lot of growing up to do.

Sighing, Prudence made her way to where the decorated valentine boxes waited for their cards. She lifted the top of the box that had her name on it, and then dropped it again. Already there were a few cards inside and Prudence knew they would be from her family. No one else had ever given her a valentine, except once at a Valentine party her mother had given when they were just children.

She could still remember that card. A penny dreadful, they were called. How did the verse go? Oh, yes:

Some are lovely as a rose,
Others smell divine,
But you could never find a clod
To be your Valentine.

How hurt she had been, especially when the young boy who had given it to her had started laughing and the others had joined in. What had hurt so much was that he had pretended to be her friend, and then she had found out that it was just so he could get close to Constance. At ten years of age, her little heart had been broken.

She lifted a beautiful card from inside the box, awed by the handcrafted design. Slowly, she stroked her fingers across the card, touching the mother of pearl petals on the roses and the silk fern used as leaves.

Hesitantly, she opened the card. She knew she was not supposed to until her mother gave the word, but something about this card had her turning the page without another thought. Probably it was from Constance. Hadn't she said she had bought all of her cards?

The verse inside was written in beautiful scroll lettering.

> 'Tis you I look for when I search for the stars,
> For surely the diamonds of your eyes are set in the
>   heaven's glory.
> But, alas, my love, your jewels are for another,
> You can never be mine, thus a sad ending to a
>   beautiful story.

It was signed, "A secret admirer."

Devlin was there to catch Prudence when she crumpled slowly to the floor.

Chapter Three

Prudence squirmed as she settled into her pew. She knew it was her imagination, but it seemed everyone was looking at her. After last night's party, she thought she would never be able to hold her head up in public again. Gritting her teeth, she decided to try and forget last night's fiasco. Easier said than done.

The first face she had seen when she had opened her eyes after her faint had been Devlin's, his worried eyes staring down into her own confused ones. She had not asked where she was or what had happened, like some melodramatic female in a novel. Instead, she had glared up at Devlin and told him in no uncertain terms, "Don't you dare laugh."

His lips had twitched in response, his eyes taking on a merry sparkle, but all he had said was, "I assure you, miss, that I had no such intentions."

Her mother had come into the room, wringing her hands in agitation, her father following with a glass of water. After that, Devlin had disappeared and Prudence had been sent to bed.

Of course, the card had caused no end of speculation. Even her father watched her with a somewhat suspicious eye. Who had sent it, and why? Or was it perhaps meant for one of her sisters?

Without meaning to, she began to search the faces around her, wondering who might have sent it. When a young man looked up and caught her eye, then turned hastily away, Prudence sent up a silent prayer. *Oh, please, Lord, not James Cavell.*

Not that there was anything particularly wrong with James. He was nice, kind, and quite handsome in fact, but his only interest lay in shipping and ships. Prudence did not think he had another thought in his head.

Her family's pew was empty this morning, except for Prudence herself. The others had chosen to remain abed, but Prudence never missed an opportunity to attend church services. She loved the singing and the preaching, and oh, just everything.

The stained-glass shepherd smiled down on her and Prudence thought again how her Puritan ancestors would have disapproved of such a symbolic display. As for herself, she loved the color and light. Her artistic soul embraced such beauty.

Her thoughts were interrupted by a commotion at her side. Turning, she fully expected to see her father, for he rarely missed a service, either. Instead, she met the laughing brown eyes of Devlin Drake.

Surprised, Prudence could only stare. As far as she knew, Devlin never set foot inside a church. She knew it had something to do with the Civil War now past, but so far she had been unable to get him to talk about it. Her questions were answered a moment later when

Terence appeared next to Devlin.

"Terence would like to know if we might join you in your family's pew today," Devlin told her.

Prudence smiled at the young man being discussed. "Of course." She moved to the side to allow both men access to the pew, but excusing himself, Devlin stepped over her feet and Prudence found herself sandwiched between the two gentlemen.

Prudence could already hear the whispers start, and her face colored hotly. Pulling the hymnal to her lap, she opened it and began studying it as though it held the means of salvation in its depths.

She almost dropped the hymnal when the young blond giant she had seen Constance with at the party stepped up to the pulpit. Her eyes widened in surprise when he introduced himself and informed them that he would be replacing Brother Michaels, who had chosen at this point in his life to retire due to failing health.

Prudence felt a sinking sensation in the pit of her stomach. She loved Brother Michaels. His sensitive sermons nudged her gently to become the woman of God she was intended to be. She fervently prayed that this giant of a man with the booming voice was not a fire-and-brimstone preacher.

If there was anything Prudence hated, it was yelling, of any kind. She had always been the peacemaker between her two sisters, and often between them and their father. Perhaps that was one thing she had inherited from her mother, because her mother was exactly the same way.

Gaylord Fyfe was nothing like Prudence expected. Though he had a resonant voice, his sermons were much like Brother Michaels'. However, there was one difference: His voice held the kind of power and authority that made you feel convicted by what he had to say.

He spoke to them of Jesus' love and the need for every Christian to grow to be the kind of Christian whom God could use in His service. He spoke of the need to do something with their lives instead of wasting the time God gave people here on this earth.

By the time he finished his sermon, Prudence had fallen under the young minister's spell. He made her hunger to know more about God and His kingdom.

She turned to say as much to Devlin, but found him unusually somber. His dark eyes plumbed the depths of her own curious hazel ones, and then he turned quickly away.

For the remainder of the service, Prudence thought about what Gaylord Fyfe had said. Resolved to do more with her life, she sang the hymns with greater gusto.

As they left the church, Devlin on one side of Prudence and Terence on the other, Prudence again became aware of the speculative looks cast her way.

Well, let them look, she thought, lifting her chin just a fraction.

They continued to the doorway where Brother Fyfe waited to shake their hands. Awaiting her turn in line, Prudence took the time to study the young man. So caught up in his words and his voice had she been, she had failed to notice his looks.

He was huge, that much was certain, but he was definitely not handsome, at least not in the conventional sense of the term. His eyelashes were so pale as to be practically nonexistent. They framed sky-blue eyes that sparkled with life. No, he was not handsome, but he was definitely attractive. What was the word she was looking for? Oh, yes, he had *charisma*.

Devlin took her by the arm when she would have stayed to talk, pulling her out the doorway. Exasperated, she turned on him. "I wanted to talk to him a minute!"

The twinkle was back in his eyes. "You and a hundred other people."

Glancing back, Prudence realized he was right. The man was positively being mobbed.

Terence took Prudence's other arm and smiled at her charmingly. "May we have the pleasure of escorting you home?"

Since tongues were already wagging, Prudence decided she had nothing to lose. They fell into step beside her, since it was her custom to walk unless her father was with her or the weather was unbearable.

Somehow, without Prudence being sure of how it had happened, the two managed to finagle an invitation to lunch. She sighed. Jessica was not going to be pleased.

When they entered the house, Mrs. Hilliard was surprised, but her good manners quickly overcame that and she graciously invited them to lunch.

Had their father not been home, Prudence felt sure that Jessica would have refused lunch, but with their patriarch present, she did not dare. Instead, to show her displeasure, she ignored the young Mr. Scott.

He did not seem to mind. Indeed, he spent the afternoon paying very close attention to Prudence, who was becoming increasingly uncomfortable under that young man's regard.

After the two had left, Prudence sighed with relief. Jessica was studying her thoughtfully. "I think we may have solved the riddle of Prudence's secret admirer," she told the room at large.

Their mother looked up from the canvas on which she was stitching an elaborate sampler. Her face creased in a worried frown. "Do you think it wise to encourage such a young man?" she enquired of Prudence.

Surprised, Prudence glared first at Jessica, then at her mother. "I never! I haven't encouraged anyone."

Her father came to her rescue. "I agree. I saw no such sign from our Prudence. If the young man is taken with her, then that must surely rest at the young man's door. For my part, I like the lad. I think he would make a good match."

Four pairs of female eyes stared at him in shocked surprise. Grinning at them all, he left the room.

Jessica turned to her sister. "How could you, Pru? He's. . .he's. . ."

Prudence tilted her nose in the air. "Well, I agree with Papa. I like him. Just because he dislikes suffragettes doesn't mean he's all bad."

Jessica left the room in a huff, her hoop skirts bouncing angrily around her.

Prudence sighed. Even in a rage, Jessica was

beautiful. More so, for her eyes sparkled and her cheeks grew flushed. No wonder Terence Scott was so taken with her.

Prudence had not been fooled by all his attention for his eyes had wandered often to Jessica, who had been sitting in the corner of the room, ignoring everyone. She decided she would do what she could to encourage this romance, but with Jessica it would not be easy.

Putting her thoughts into action, Prudence followed Jessica to her bedroom where she found her younger sister staring out her bedroom window at the garden below. Unlike Prudence's room, which faced the street, Jessica had a lovely view of their back garden.

Prudence seated herself on her sister's four-poster bed, smoothing the satin coverlet with her hands. "Jessica, do you really want to be a suffragette?"

Her only answer was a sniff. Prudence got up and went to her sister's side, handing her a lace-edged handkerchief. She studied the tears on Jessica's face.

"What would God have you do, Jess?"

Jessica flung away from her sister. "I'm not like you, Pru. I don't live my life worrying about what God would like or not. For years, religion has been used to keep women in their places."

"That's your Elizabeth Cady Stanton speaking, not Jessica Hilliard."

Jessica turned to her sister. "You don't understand. I want a *life*. I don't want to be just some man's chattel!"

Prudence smiled at her sister's vehemence. "Like Mother, you mean?"

Snorting, Jessica frowned at Prudence. "Mother is no chattel. She dances rings around father. Why, he would give her the moon if he—" She stopped abruptly, realizing what she was admitting. Glaring defiantly at her sister, she dared her to say anything.

Prudence smiled her gentle smile. "That's called *love*, Jess. It's the greatest gift God has bestowed upon us. Don't throw it away without giving it a chance."

Prudence left her sister so she could think about what she had just said. Jessica watched her go, her shoulders slumping wearily.

Chapter Four

Prudence slipped out the side door of the house and hurried out of the yard and down the street. It was early yet and she had hopes that no one would see her.

As she flew along, she struggled with the equipment she was carrying. It was not far to the Boston Common, but she was late already. She hurried faster. Her stomach growled in protest at having been denied the opportunity to partake of breakfast, but they were depending on her. It had been hard enough to slip out without anyone seeing her. Mother would have a fit if she saw her now; Father would, too.

She had left the house with relief, not only at having escaped for a while, but also for having evaded Terence Scott. He had been to her house every day for the past two months and it was beginning to wear on her nerves.

And Devlin had teased her unmercifully about her strange valentine. He watched her closely, as though trying to ascertain if she perhaps knew the sender. Well, she did not and she would just as soon forget it. Probably it was someone's practical joke.

She frowned in thought. And then there was Constance's sudden interest in church. She had gone the past two Sundays, her attention fixed raptly on Gaylord Fyfe. Was she perhaps interested in the man himself, or was she really interested finally in hearing God's Word? She would hate to see Brother Fyfe caught in her sister's web.

She loved her sister dearly, but Gaylord was such a man of God he was needed to preach God's Word. Already their church was beginning to grow. Even the men listened attentively to his words.

Constance could change all that. She had seen it before, a man's fire quenched when he fell in love and chose to please the woman he loved.

Prudence arrived at the Common and hurried to where she knew the others would be waiting. Eleven young boys ran to greet her, relieving her of the awkward equipment.

"Hi, Pru!" Ben, the oldest, greeted her as he always did. He felt he had a distinct advantage over the others since he had known her the longest.

"Hi, Ben. Is everybody here?"

"Everyone except George," he told her. "He's in bed with the flu. Sister said he had to stay there for a while."

Prudence was instantly sympathetic. "I'll go by and see him later." Her eyes went around the ragtag group. "Is everyone ready to play?"

"Ready!" they all shouted in unison.

"Okay. Ben, you captain one team. Michael, you captain the other."

Handing Ben the bat, Prudence stood back and watched as they moved their hands upward on the bat until Michael's crowned the top.

"Right. Michael, you choose first."

After the players were distributed, with only a minor argument over who would take William, the youngest, they made their way to their favorite spot to play.

Michael had chosen Prudence first, and she smiled at Ben, who glowered at the young man. For a long time, he had considered Prudence his own personal property. Funny how such possessiveness showed up even in one so young.

Prudence may not have had any men her own age seeking her hand in marriage, but her eleven devoted followers here promised they would love her forever. She grinned to herself. *Oh, to be young again.*

Prudence was designated catcher to replace George, and she took her place behind the first batter. "Okay, Pete. You can do it," she whispered, then raised her voice. "Come on, Mike. Strike him out!"

Pete turned to her, giving her a big wink. Prudence alternately encouraged and catcalled. The boys took it all in good part, knowing that Prudence loved them all, regardless of which team they were on.

When it was Prudence's turn at bat, Ben turned to his teammates. "Back up!" he shouted, and the outfielders scrambled to obey.

Prudence hefted the bat, giving a few practice swings. Pete grinned behind her. "Knock it out of the park," he whispered before shouting to Ben, "Come on,

Ben. Strike her out!"

The ball flew through the air and connected with Prudence's bat. Then it sailed high in the air toward the third baseman.

"Run, Pru!" her team shouted, and Prudence needed no other encouragement. She rounded the bases one by one and was headed for home plate when little Willie snaked the ball toward the catcher. As Prudence dove for the plate, the ball flew through the air; Prudence heard the ball connect with Pete's hand just as her own hand touched the plate.

"Safe!" Pete called, grinning down at her.

The team never argued about such things as ties and other questionable plays. Prudence had taught them well that the fun was in the playing, not the winning.

Prudence got to her feet amid cheers from the other players. Brushing the grass and dirt from her outfit, she smiled at them all. The smile left her face as quickly as it had come, for there, not ten yards away, stood Constance. And beside her stood a grinning Devlin and a horrified Terence.

Prudence stood quietly, waiting while the boys moved close beside her. They sensed something amiss and surrounded her in an unconscious effort to protect her.

"Prudence Hilliard!" Constance seemed at a momentary loss for words.

Devlin stepped forward, his glance raking over the boys surrounding Prudence. Eleven boys stared defiantly back at him.

"Won't you introduce us, Prudence?"

Prudence could have hugged him. She began the introductions and Devlin took the time to shake each boy's hand. His glance came back to rest on Prudence, who cringed in embarrassment.

Constance finally found her voice. "Wherever did you get those bloomers? You know Father refuses to allow them. Besides, they went out of fashion years ago."

Prudence brushed the dust off the offending articles. The Turkish trousers had a slight tear near the right gathered ankle, but other than that, they seemed to be intact.

"They were Jessica's. I dug them out of the trash where Father threw them." Looking for her cloak, Prudence remembered that she had left the house in such a hurry, she had forgotten it. Shivering from cold and nervousness, Prudence tried in vain to keep warm.

Devlin took off his own cloak and wrapped it around Prudence's shivering shoulders. His eyes sparkled merrily and Prudence could have cheerfully throttled him.

She turned to the boys. "Okay, guys. That's it for today."

"Aw!" They grumbled good-naturedly as they picked up the gear and handed most of it to Prudence.

Devlin in return took it from her and handed her his handkerchief. "You have dirt on your face."

Prudence watched in embarrassment as the boys gathered up their belongings and, looking back over their shoulders, headed for home. It was obvious they were reluctant to leave her; she felt warmed by their chivalry.

Prudence handed Devlin his handkerchief and turned to her sister, who was tapping her satin slipper in obvious disapproval. She flicked a glance at Terence, but his face was devoid of emotion, to say the least.

Devlin turned to the two of them. "Why don't I walk Prudence to my house? It's just across the Common and you can bring her something more. . .um. . . appropriate to wear. Constance, Terence will see you home safely. Take my carriage."

Prudence sighed as she watched them walk away. "I suppose she'll tell Mama and Papa."

"Most likely," Devlin agreed.

She turned to him then. "I wish you would wipe that silly grin off your face."

He tried, but without much success. "Tell me about them." He nodded to the boys disappearing in the distance, still turning back every once in a while to see that she was okay.

"They're from St. Anne's Orphanage." Her eyes softened. "They're really great kids."

Devlin's lips twitched again. "Children, I assume you mean. Tell me. Where did you learn such language? From the boys?"

Prudence's brow wrinkled. "Many people say kids instead of children."

"Undoubtedly," he returned. "I was referring to your rather extensive baseball vernacular. Like, 'kill the ball'?"

Prudence flushed. How long had they been standing there? She glanced at Devlin, strolling along at her side, and realized it must have been quite some time.

He took her arm to help her up the front stairs to his home. Although Devlin's father had chosen to live on Beacon Hill, Prudence's father had chosen the Back Bay area that the city's landfill project had created from a marshy section of the Charles River. Both, however, lived in townhouses, and Prudence could only hope that Devlin did not have nosey neighbors.

Devlin took her to the drawing room and indicated that she have a seat. Realizing for the first time just how cold she was, Prudence huddled near the fire.

Ringing for the butler, Devlin waited until he had ordered tea before seating himself beside Prudence on the settee. His eyes delved into Prudence's and she felt her mouth go suddenly dry.

"Tell me about them," he commanded softly.

Swallowing hard, Prudence told Devlin how she had become involved with the boys from the orphanage and about her work there. How she tried to help the nuns by finding activities for the children to keep them out of trouble.

"Boys are naturally competitive," she told him. "Given an outlet for their desire to conquer, their energy can be channeled into a more fun way of competing."

Devlin's face remained grave, but his eyes twinkled. "And how did you happen to learn so much about baseball?"

Dropping her eyes to her lap, Prudence began picking at her Turkish trousers. "Constance was seeing a gentleman who was a player in the sport. He. . .he agreed to help me learn the game."

"I'll just bet he did," Devlin grinned.

Prudence gave him a look that would have curled the hairs of a lesser man. Devlin took her hand and began stroking it with his fingers, and suddenly Prudence forgot everything she was going to say.

"You're a curious mixture," he told her softly. "Half man, half woman."

Affronted, she rounded on him angrily. "I am not!"

His lips twitched. "I meant it as a compliment."

She studied him from his black curly hair to his shiny black boots. Her look returned to his face. "I fail to see the compliment."

"I meant, you think like a man, but you look like a woman."

His husky voice did funny things to her pulse. Jerking her hand from his, she rose to her feet and went to stare out the window at the street in front.

"No wonder Jessica has embraced the suffragette movement so thoroughly," Prudence derided. "Only men are considered intelligent."

Devlin came quickly to her side. "I didn't mean that at all," he disagreed.

She cut her gaze toward him. "Then just what did you mean?"

Devlin was unable to answer her. Hadn't that been exactly his thoughts? He knew many intelligent women, but their intelligence showed itself only in the way they manipulated and managed people. Prudence was different. Her innocence gave her a special quality that attracted him. His eyes fastened on her lips, soft and inviting. Remembering Constance's cool little kisses on his cheeks, he wondered what kind of kiss Prudence would bestow.

"Have you ever been kissed, Prudence?"

Cheeks flaming with color, Prudence glared angrily up at him. "What a question to ask! What manners!"

"Have you?" he continued, undaunted by her growing anger.

She stared up at him furiously, her huge hazel eyes giving an elfin quality to her face. She was debating with herself whether to tell a small fib. Ashamed of her thoughts, she shook her head and turned away.

He caught her arm and turned her back to face him. His eyes were dancing with mischief. "We can't have that now, can we? All young women should be able to say they've been kissed at least once."

Sliding his large palms against her cheeks, he moved his lips down to cover hers. Her small sigh of capitulation sent the blood rushing through his body and what had started out as a jest became a very serious business.

His kiss was soft, gentle, but when he felt her lips tremble beneath his in response, his own lips became harder, more demanding.

Alarmed, Prudence began to struggle against him. What was she doing? This man was practically engaged to her sister, yet she knew with perfect honesty she had courted the kiss.

He released her slowly, his arms dropping to his sides. "I think, Miss Prudence," he told her huskily, "there is more to you than meets the eye."

What she would have answered she did not know, for at that moment the drawing room door opened and Constance walked in followed by Terence.

Chapter Five

For days, Prudence had studiously avoided Devlin, who came frequently to the house with Terence. She was becoming increasingly annoyed with Mr. Scott, for he never failed to start an argument with Jessica and they always ended up in a yelling match—but never when Mother or Father was home.

Prudence's head was already pounding and she had as yet to go downstairs for breakfast. When she did, she found her mother still in her dressing gown.

"Are you not feeling well, Mama?" Prudence asked.

Mrs. Hilliard gave a feeble smile. "I have a pounding headache. You'll just have to go to church without me."

Prudence sighed. Not again. Soon her mother wouldn't attend services at all.

Constance came into the room looking lovely, even though the somber gray dress she was wearing was hardly her style. Surprised, Prudence studied her sister's face and wondered about Constance's sudden change in her clothing. The demure neckline was nothing like the lower necklines she normally preferred. Even her earrings were sedate. Instead of the dangles she normally wore, she had on small pearl studs.

Prudence raised her eyebrows at Jessica, who only shrugged her shoulders. "Are you going to church today, Jessica?" Prudence asked.

Jessica pulled apart the roll on her plate, picking pieces with her fingers and slipping them into her mouth. "I thought I might," she answered.

Prudence stared at them all in wonder. Her father came in through the doorway, stopping by his wife's chair to give her a kiss on the cheek. "Hello, my dear. Not feeling well?" He continued to his seat, watching his wife carefully as he sat down.

"No, John. I have a dreadful headache. I should like to go back to bed, I believe."

Prudence became instantly alarmed, for it was not like her mother having once gotten out of bed to return to it. "Would you like me to stay home with you, Mama?"

Her father answered instead. "Not necessary, Prudence. I will stay with your mother. You girls go and enjoy."

"Are you sure?" Prudence was unconvinced.

"Do you think me incapable of caring for my own wife?" her father asked in exasperation.

"No, Papa."

"Well, then, let's hear no more about it."

The three sisters left, although Prudence was reluctant. Constance insisted they take the carriage and Prudence climbed in beside her sister, hoping against hope that Jessica and Terence would not have one of their fighting matches in the church.

Devlin had continued to attend, but Prudence suspected it had more to do with Terence than any desire to be closer to God. Feeling ashamed of herself for such a judgment, she promised herself to take the first opportunity to find out what Devlin had against God.

That opportunity came sooner than she expected. After services were over, Constance stopped by Gaylord's side. "We would like to invite you to a picnic," she told him. "Prudence, Jessica, and I were going to have one on the Common. Perhaps you would join us? And you and Terence, too, Devlin."

Jessica and Prudence exchanged glances. Now what was Constance up to? Neither of them knew anything about the said picnic.

"I'd be delighted, Miss Constance," Gaylord conceded, smiling at them all.

Oh well, Prudence thought, *at least nothing much could happen with the preacher in tow.*

When Constance pulled a picnic hamper from the back of their buggy, Jessica and Prudence exchanged surprised looks. Obviously, this was no spur-of-the-moment decision.

Surprisingly, Terence affixed himself to Jessica's side, and Jessica seemed not to mind. For the first time Prudence could remember, they actually acted congenial toward each other.

After Gaylord spread out the blanket and Constance set out the food, Devlin sat down next to Prudence. He nodded his head at his cousin. "It seems we're making progress."

Prudence nodded, watching her sister. "So it would seem."

Devlin's eyes studied her face. "And how about you, Prudence. Have you forgiven me for the other day?"

Color flooded her face, but she looked him in the eye. "Are you asking forgiveness?"

Devlin studied the soft mouth before him. Was he asking forgiveness? Given the opportunity, he knew he would do the same thing again. "Perhaps not," he told her, grinning when her eyes sparked with temper.

"Devlin Drake, you are impossible!"

Unrepentant, Devlin continued to grin at her, amused by the easy way he could fire her temper. He loved the way her eyes glowed when she was angry, and the blush that came to her cheeks was most becoming.

He decided not to push his luck and hastily changed the subject. "I've been meaning to ask you. What happened with your. . .um. . .baseball attire?"

The color that had receded from her cheeks flew back into them again. She glanced over to where Constance and Gaylord were deep in conversation. "Father had them destroyed."

"That's too bad," he empathized, and he truly sounded sympathetic. "I understand bloomers have started making a comeback and are being used in all kinds of sports."

Prudence looked back at him. "Father has forbidden me to play baseball, or to wear bloomers."

He leaned back on his hands, studying her from where he sat. The shade from a majestic oak tree added moving shadows to her face as she continued to avoid his eyes.

"Perhaps I could help," he offered.

Startled, she stared at him in surprise. "You? However could you help?"

He continued to study her thoughtfully. "I know I am no substitute for you, but perhaps the boys would allow me to take your place as a coach. You are the coach, are you not?"

A dimple formed in her cheek as she smiled at him. "Such as I am."

"You don't give yourself enough credit, I think. From what I saw, you have done exceptionally well."

Unused as she was to compliments, Prudence struggled not to blush. Devlin had been the cause of enough color in her face. She turned to study him where he was reclining. Whatever could Constance be thinking to turn from such a man? Or had she?

Prudence noticed that Constance seemed oblivious to everything around her, but was she? Was it possible that Constance was trying to make Devlin jealous? He had certainly refused to become just another one of Constance's conquests. He was different from anyone Prudence had ever met.

"I think maybe they would like that, Devlin. And perhaps you would be good for them. They have no man to look up to."

"Do you play with them every Saturday?" he wanted to know.

She nodded her head. "I'm the only one who has a bat and ball."

Devlin's lips twitched. "And where did the boys

happen to get the uniform shirts?"

Prudence bit her lip and turned to watch some children playing in the distance.

Devlin awaited her answer, fairly certain she would not give him one. "Never mind, Prudence. I think I already know."

She turned back and their eyes locked. Devlin saw confusion in the deep hazel depths of her eyes and wondered if it had anything to do with him.

The six of them ate their food leisurely, enjoying the tepid warmth of the April sun. Afterward, Constance began clearing the picnic things, while Terence and Jessica went for a walk.

Devlin helped Prudence to her feet then shook out the blanket and draped it over his one arm, offering Prudence the other one. She hesitated a moment before she placed her hand on the proffered appendage. Constance did not seem to mind, for she had taken Gaylord's arm and they had started across the Common.

Prudence rode home in silence, her thoughts on the man by her side. She was bewildered by the strange feelings she had whenever Devlin was near. When he was not near her, she could think more objectively, but at times like these she wanted. . .what?

She shook her head to clear it of confusing thoughts. She would have to talk to Constance about her attitude toward Devlin and tell her that if she were not very careful, she would lose him. Having settled the matter in her mind, Prudence leaned back, a frown forming on her face.

❧

Devlin was just crossing the street on his way to the Hilliards' when he noticed Prudence slip furtively out the side gate near the front yard and cross the street quickly. In a moment, she would be gone from sight.

Curious, he decided to follow her, and before long, the reason for her stealthy actions became apparent. Devlin found himself in one of Boston's seedier sections of town, and he felt himself grow angry at Prudence's complete disregard for her own safety.

When she reached a large brownstone house and disappeared inside, Devlin waited a moment before following her up the steps. A sign beside the door read: SARAH FULLER'S SCHOOL FOR THE DEAF.

He stood wondering what Prudence's connection was with this establishment. Was it possible she was secretly meeting a man on the sly without her parents' consent or knowledge? Could it be he was a teacher at this school? His face settling into tight lines, Devlin used the bell to ring for admittance.

A young maid dressed in black opened the door and lifted an inquiring face to his. "May I help you?"

Suddenly, Devlin felt very foolish, for what could he say to justify his presence here? "Yes. I. . .um. . . wondered if I might speak with the proprietor of this establishment."

"Of course." She studied Devlin's obviously expensive clothes before motioning for him to follow her to a room just off the side hall. She knocked softly, waiting for an answer before she opened the door slightly and peeked her head inside. When she pulled back, she opened the door wider. "Principal Baker will see you now."

Fully expecting to see some handsome young man with Prudence, Devlin was surprised to find himself face-to-face with a short, rotund little man with a balding pate. And Prudence was nowhere to be seen. Frowning in annoyance, Devlin hastily rearranged his features into a smiling mask when the gentleman introduced himself.

Mr. Baker waved him to a chair. "Please have a seat, Mr. Drake, and tell me how I might assist you?"

Devlin's eyes quickly studied the scrupulously clean room and he noticed that the furniture was simple and the room itself rather spartan. In fact, the only furniture was the desk behind which Mr. Baker sat, the wing chair into which Devlin lowered himself, and a large table, scattered with books and papers, sitting in front of the window.

Mr. Baker remained silent, his little gray eyes rather piercing in their intensity. Only his eyebrows rose as he waited for Devlin to explain himself.

"I wondered," Devlin told him, clearing his throat, "if you might tell me something about your school?"

Eyes twinkling, Mr. Baker relaxed back against his own chair. "Our school is a *total communication* school. We teach not only sign language but lipreading and Visible Speech."

Devlin sat back in surprise. He had not even known that such schools existed. And what exactly was Visible Speech?

Mr. Baker continued enthusiastically to expound the merits of his fine establishment. Devlin only interrupted him once. "But the sign on the door reads 'Sarah Fuller's School for the Deaf.'"

Nodding his agreement, Mr. Baker went on to explain how Sarah Fuller had a larger school in another part of Boston, but that this school was for those who could ill afford to send their children to such a fine establishment.

Devlin still could not fathom the reason for Prudence's coming to this school and he was becoming more curious by the minute. "Would it be possible for me to have a tour of your school, Mr. Baker?"

Realizing by the cut of his clothes that the gentleman standing before him was extremely wealthy, Mr. Baker readily agreed. It was not uncommon for the wealthy to find outlets on which to expend their wealth. It gave them the feeling of contributing without having to leave the comfort of their homes. A panacea for their guilt, no doubt. If this young man could be persuaded to give a donation, then perhaps he would be able to go ahead with some of the plans he had been formulating for a while now.

"At this time, we cannot afford a live-in establishment. Our children come, as in regular school, for several hours a day to learn their lessons. They are usually attended by one of their parents because it is necessary for the parents to learn to communicate with their children in the same way that they are being taught."

The old brownstone had been converted into a

school, each door containing a large pane of glass that allowed visual access to the classroom. In the first room, Devlin watched as the teacher moved her lips carefully, while signing the word. Fascinated, he stayed and watched. The children ranged in ages, the youngest being no more than six. Each child was concentrating on the teacher's mouth instead of her hands.

"Mrs. Thomson is teaching the children to read lips." Mr. Baker explained. "She first signs the word with her hands, and then shows them how to mouth the word with their lips. These children already know sign language."

There were only ten children in the classroom. "How many children do you have in your school?" Devlin wanted to know.

Mr. Baker continued on down the hallway, talking over his shoulder. "About thirty, right now. We could teach more perhaps, but we haven't the finances to be able to do it. As I said, these children are from poor families."

When they reached another room, Mr. Baker paused and, while Devlin watched, he explained that the teacher in this class was teaching the children sign language. Although she was an older matron, her fingers moved with the grace and rhythm of a ballerina.

First, she would show them a picture and then she would sign the word. The children signed each sign after her and the teacher would continue with that word until she felt certain the children thoroughly understood. Several older people sat on the periphery of the room, and Mr. Baker explained that those were the parents of some of the children. When the teacher signed a sign, not only the children followed, but the parents, as well.

At the last classroom, Devlin was brought up short, for there, sitting on the floor and surrounded by children, sat Prudence.

Chapter Six

Devlin watched as one young pupil got up from the floor and went to Prudence and placed one hand on Prudence's mouth and the other hand on her throat. The little girl bent close to watch the movement of Prudence's lips. Devlin could hear no sound from this distance, but he watched as the child struggled to imitate the sound.

He watched as Prudence's eyes lit up while she reached out and hugged the little girl enthusiastically. The other children applauded, although Devlin knew they could not have heard the sound, either.

Mr. Baker was beaming at Prudence, a soft glow warming his eyes. "Miss Hilliard was sent to us by God Himself, I'm sure, for she has been such a blessing. The children adore her."

From the look on the speaker's face, Devlin was sure the principal did, also. Devlin frowned. "Prudence is a teacher here?"

Surprised, Mr. Baker turned to him. "You know Miss Hilliard?"

Devlin hesitated. "Er. . .yes. I am a friend of the family."

"Then you already know of the work here."

One black eyebrow winged its way upward. "I'm afraid not. Miss Hilliard hasn't discussed it with me."

Puzzled, Mr. Baker frowned back at him. "How odd."

"May I speak with Miss Hilliard for a moment?" Devlin asked.

The principal was reluctant. "I hate to interrupt a class."

"I assure you, I won't take but a moment of her time."

Relenting, Mr. Baker opened the door and went inside. Devlin could see him talking to Prudence and then she crossed the room and came out. When she noticed who her caller was, her face drained of color.

"Devlin, what are you doing here?" she asked.

"I saw you leave your house and I followed you here," he answered.

His whole bearing told Prudence he was displeased with her. Shrugging her shoulders, she tried to sound defiant. "What do you want?"

Devlin looked past her to where the principal stood, watching them while also trying to teach the children. Devlin's eyes came slowly back to hers. "I would like an explanation." Seeing the flames burst in her eyes, Devlin knew he had just made a big mistake. Still, it was too late to back down now. "I will wait for you outside with a carriage. What time will you be finished?"

"I don't wish to ride home with you, Devlin Drake. And what time I leave is none of your concern."

"Perhaps I should discuss this with your father." He heard the wind rush out of her.

Prudence glared at him for several seconds before gritting her teeth and answering, "Four o'clock."

He nodded his head. "I 'll be here. And, Prudence. . . ?"

She turned from the door and glowered back at him.

"Don't leave without me. I would hate to have to come searching for you."

She understood his threat. Turning, she left him frowning after her.

୶

When Prudence descended the stairs at 4:00, Devlin was awaiting her in the hallway. Mr. Baker was standing by his side, warily eyeing the larger man.

"Prudence, Mr. Drake has informed me that he will be escorting you home."

Prudence locked eyes with Devlin, before nodding to the principal. "That's right, Mr. Baker."

Still unsure, the principal nonetheless handed Devlin Prudence's cloak. Devlin took it and placed it around Prudence's shoulders. He held her shoulders a moment too long and Prudence squirmed out of his hold.

As Devlin helped Prudence into the carriage, he tucked a blanket around her legs. Although the weather was not nearly so cold as before, it was still only the end of April and relatively cool.

Prudence had remained silent while Devlin attended her. Now she turned to Mr. Baker and smiled, though the expression never reached her eyes. "Mr. Baker, I will return tomorrow to help with class."

Mr. Baker studied Devlin uncertainly. "Are you sure?"

"Of course, I'm sure," Prudence told him with no small amount of irritation. Devlin and she would have a talk and she would let him know in no uncertain terms what she thought of his high-handedness. After that, he could very well stay out of her life.

They started off at a brisk trot, which Devlin quickly slowed to a walk. Before Prudence could say anything, Devlin told her in a rather amused voice, "How your parents came to name you Prudence, I have no idea, for you certainly haven't any."

Immediately riled, Prudence turned on him. "I've done nothing wrong!"

His own anger came quickly to the surface. "Then why are you skulking around the back streets of Boston like some low-class thief?"

"I wasn't skulking!"

"Do your parents know where you were?" When she quickly turned away, he had his answer. "Why not?"

She lifted her nose in the air, and for a moment Devlin was distracted, for she had the cutest little pug nose. But that cute little nose could have very well gotten itself into big trouble. Anger returning, he pulled the carriage to the side of the road.

Prudence noticed they were close to the Common. She turned blazing, guilty eyes to his face. "This is not my home."

"You and I need to have a talk," Devlin told her, and she knew by the set of his chin that that was exactly what they were going to do.

Going on the defensive, Prudence told him, "You

are not my brother yet. I don't need you to look after my life, nor anyone else for that matter."

"You need someone to keep you out of trouble, that's for certain."

She pressed her lips tightly together. "I am not in trouble," she told him, her voice softening as she continued, "at least I won't be if you don't tell."

Devlin studied her head, bent down beside him. Prudence was twisting her fingers together in her lap, awaiting his decision. She looked so innocent. His anger cooled.

"You are one incredible woman," he told her softly.

The color rushed to her face and slowly she turned to face him.

Devlin sighed. "Promise me you won't go to the school alone again."

The flames were back in her eyes. "I'll do no such thing!"

"Prudence—" He gripped her elbow with his hand and she slapped it away.

"I won't! They need me." She turned beseeching eyes on his. "Please, Devlin. They need me, and I want to help the children."

Devlin studied those beautiful hazel eyes with their speckles of brown showing through the green, and swallowed hard. Constance had never been able to melt his heart the way this young woman could. Without saying anything, he lifted the reins and slapped them across the horse's back.

"Where are we going?" Prudence knew they were

headed away from the Back Bay area.

"We're going someplace where we can have a little talk."

Devlin said no more and they sat in silence as they drove on. Prudence watched the houses flash past and knew they were heading out of the city. Finally, Devlin pulled to the side of an isolated road and he stopped.

Prudence eyed him uneasily and Devlin saw the hesitation in her eyes. A devilish sparkle entered his own.

"Worried?" he asked. "What can I do to you that some tramp from the streets couldn't do?"

"Devlin—" she began but was interrupted when Devlin reached across the seat and drew her into his arms. He crushed his lips against hers and Prudence began to struggle.

Lifting his head, he glared down into her frightened eyes. "Is that what you were worried about? Your puny strength is no match for mine, so how much more so a cunning fugitive from the streets. What would you do if you were attacked?"

Fear was rapidly turning to anger. "I could scream!"

"Try it."

She opened her mouth to do just that and Devlin covered her mouth with his lips again, snuffing out the scream before it began. Prudence struggled ineffectively against his superior strength, finally relaxing against him when she realized she could never break his hold.

When Devlin lifted his head, there were tears running down Prudence's cheeks. Feeling like an animal, he released her. Brushing a trembling hand back through his hair, Devlin let out a long breath. "I'm sorry."

Prudence said nothing, wiping at the tears with her hand. Devlin produced a snow-white handkerchief and handed it to her. She took it, but refused to meet his eyes.

"Prudence," he implored softly, "I'm sorry. It's just that when I think of what could have happened to you, I see red."

"That's no excuse," she told him.

"You're right." He waited until he was sure he had himself under control before he looked at her again. "Just promise me you won't go to the school again unless someone accompanies you."

"That's ridiculous. Nothing has happened to me yet."

Devlin went very still, but Prudence was too distraught to notice. "How long have you been going there?" he asked her very softly.

She studied the maple trees to the right of the path. "It's been. . .let's see. . .two years now, I think."

"Two years!"

Prudence immediately realized her mistake.

Devlin grabbed her by the arms, glaring fiercely down into her face. "You will give me your word or, so help me, I'll go straight to your father."

Clashing gazes. Clashing wills. Yet Prudence felt she had the most to lose. She dropped her eyes to her lap. "I really feel like God wants me to do this, Devlin."

Devlin felt his anger drain away. "I am not suggesting that you don't go at all, merely that you don't go alone. Can't you see the sense in that?"

She looked back at him. "I go only in the daytime."

He pressed his lips together. "Just two blocks from your school a man was murdered. In broad daylight. . . for his money." He let the words sink in and watched the color slowly drain from her face.

"If I ask anyone at home, Father is sure to find out. I can't take that chance."

"What makes you think your father would object?"

She twisted her lips. "Didn't you?"

He was already shaking his head. "No. I think what you are doing is wonderful. I wouldn't think your father would object, either. Why don't you talk to him?"

"And if he objects?"

"He won't."

She shook her head again. "I can't take that chance."

His lips tightened. "Then I want your promise not to go alone."

She remained stubbornly silent.

"Fine," he told her. "Then I'll take you."

Surprised, she began to chuckle nervously. "You?"

"Me."

Prudence knew he was determined to have his way. Maybe if she could make him understand. "I go to the school only twice a week to help in any way I can. Today was an exception because Miss Turner, the regular teacher, was ill. It seems she will have to stay abed for several days. I believe she has a bad cold."

Devlin watched Prudence and wondered, not for the first time, how she could possibly be related to her two butterfly sisters. "How came you to know about the school in the first place?"

Prudence grinned, feeling her uncertainty vanish under Devlin's obvious interest. "I met Sarah Fuller at a tea. She told me about her schools and it seemed such a fine thing to do that I wanted to help. She offered to let me learn along with the children. Now, I know almost as much as the other teachers, at least enough to help out when one or the other can't be there."

"What do you do otherwise?"

"Oh, I help Mr. Baker prepare charts and draw pictures. I have been able to put to use the talents of drawing and painting that God gave me."

Devlin stared at her in surprise. "Did you paint those pictures the teacher was using to sign?"

Embarrassed, Prudence nodded. She had not meant to reveal so much. Had it seemed to Devlin like she was bragging? Venturing a glance at his face, she decided that it had not.

Devlin was shaking his head. "You are right, Miss Prudence Hilliard. You must be allowed to continue the work God so obviously meant for you to do."

Amazed that Devlin would make such a suggestion, Prudence again determined to find out what had turned Devlin from the God he once knew. Before she could do so, however, he made an amazing declaration. "Tell me which days you need to go, and I will escort you."

Mouth dropping open, Prudence argued. "You can't."

"Why not?"

"Well, you. . .what about your work?"

"My business can survive without me for an hour or

two. Besides, I can drop you off on my way, and pick you up on my return."

Devlin saw the stubborn glint enter Prudence's eyes and one followed in his own. "It's either that or I tell your father."

Sighing, Prudence capitulated, "So be it."

Chapter Seven

Devlin kept his word and never said anything to Prudence's father about the school for the deaf. He did, however, talk to her father about the boys from St. Anne's and was able to receive permission to take Prudence along with him when he went to spend time with the boys.

After hearing of the good that Prudence was trying to do, Mr. Hilliard even went so far as to make a large donation to the boys' home, with the stipulation that some of the money be used for sports equipment. Prudence was thrilled, and although she was disappointed not to be able to play baseball, she was glad that she could watch and share time with the boys she had come to love.

Devlin was an excellent coach and it surprised Prudence that he knew so much about baseball. One day when they were walking across the Common to Devlin's house on Beacon Hill, Prudence asked him about it.

He grinned. "I didn't know too much about baseball before the Civil War," he told her. "There was a man in our unit who had played for the Knickerbocker Club. Have you heard of them?"

Prudence nodded. "Hasn't everybody?"

He tapped her lightly on the nose. "Not everyone is as interested in baseball as you are," he told her, chuckling. "Anyway, he taught us how to play and, to keep loneliness and boredom at bay, we would play whenever we had the time."

"Tell me about the war, Devlin."

His eyes grew cold. "What's to tell?"

Refusing to back down from this golden opportunity, Prudence pushed him for answers. "You fought for the South, didn't you?"

"I fought *in* the South," he told her coolly, "not *for* the South."

"That's what I meant," she agreed. "But something happened to you there, didn't it? Something made you turn your back on God."

"I don't want to talk about it," he told her firmly.

Stopping, Prudence placed a hand on his arm and drew him to a stop with her. "Please, Devlin, I want to know."

His angry brown eyes glared down into her own curious hazel ones. For a moment he was about to refuse, but then he thought better of it. Maybe it would help to share his pain with someone, because up to this point he never had.

His eyes took on a distant look. "I was with Sherman when he marched across Georgia."

Prudence sucked in a breath. "Sherman's march to the sea. I read about it in the papers."

Devlin smiled wryly. "Yes, well, I *lived* it. Never have

I seen such destruction. And by a man who claimed to be a man of God."

Prudence turned and began walking again. Devlin followed. There had been such agony in Devlin's face, Prudence was unsure of how to comfort him.

"Have you ever considered, Devlin," she suggested, "how much longer the war may have lasted if General Sherman hadn't done what he did? How many more people might have died?"

Devlin did not look at her. "If there's a God, a loving God, then why should there be wars in the first place?"

"Would you have God treat us as marionettes? Pull our strings to make us dance?" She glanced at him slyly. "Somehow, I cannot see you being a puppet, Devlin. You don't seem the type. You're far too much your own master."

"I know what you are saying," he told her. "I have heard the same said before. Still, there is too much evil in the world. I haven't turned from God, Prudence. I am merely struggling to understand."

"Some things we will never understand, not until that day when we stand in God's presence. God didn't create the evil, Devlin," she remonstrated softly. "Evil has always existed, the same as good. Darkness and light. Good and evil. Two sides of the same coin."

They reached Devlin's house where the carriage awaited. Devlin handed Prudence up and stood looking at her for a long time. She began to squirm under his perusal.

"You would make a fine preacher," he told her gently.

She shook her head. "I didn't mean to preach. You have told me often that you think I don't give myself enough credit. Perhaps you are the same. Maybe you should try to give yourself, and God, a little more credit."

"Maybe I should."

For the next several weeks, Prudence went with Devlin on Saturdays to watch "her boys," as she fondly called them, play baseball.

When Gaylord Fyfe discovered their secret, he immediately became involved. The giant's boundless energy and loving touch soon had the boys following him with open adoration. He was second only to Devlin, whom the boys tried to emulate as often as possible. Although Terence often came with them, the boys hung back from offering him the friendship they so readily gave to both Devlin and Gaylord. Terence did not seem to mind.

Before long, Constance expressed a desire to attend their impromptu baseball games. Amazed that her sister would deign to do something so improper, it took Devlin to point out to her the possible reason for her sister's interest.

"So, Constance," he teased, "you seem to have your eye on the other team's coach."

Surprised, Prudence turned to her sister and saw the color steal into her sister's cheeks.

"Are you jealous, Devlin?" Constance teased back.

Devlin only grinned before joining his team as their

turn arrived to be out in the field.

Prudence eyed her sister angrily. "Are you trying to make Devlin jealous?"

Constance gave her the look she reserved for servants and suitors who had found her disfavor. "Mind your own business, Prudence."

Exasperated, Prudence dropped down on the quilt next to her sister. "If you're not careful, you'll lose Devlin."

Constance sighed. "Oh, honestly, Pru, you are so naive."

Was Constance then so sure of Devlin that she would flirt with another man even in his presence? She hated the thought of Devlin being hurt. He had been more than kind to her, and she had convinced herself that the feelings she felt for him were the platonic feelings one had for a brother.

Remembering the kisses they had shared, she pushed other feelings deep down into the recesses of her being. If only she were sure of her sister, but then no one understood Constance.

The next Saturday Jessica joined them. Shaking her head, Prudence began to wonder what was happening to her family. Expecting an argument from Jessica when she learned of Terence's feelings about women and sports, Prudence was pleasantly surprised when it did not occur. Instead, Jessica seemed to be making an obvious effort to hold her tongue in check.

Constance managed to tease all three men at the same time, flitting from one to the other. Prudence had to admit, her sister had a way with men.

❧

The times Devlin came to pick Prudence up for their journey to the deaf school, she would try to draw from him the extent of his feelings for her sister. Devlin, though, was adept at outmaneuvering her.

"What are you asking me, Prudence?"

Stuttering, Prudence studied the reins gripped so effortlessly in Devlin's hands. "I. . .I was just wondering . . .I mean. . ."

He grinned and adroitly changed the subject. "Tell me about this Visible Speech. How can deaf persons learn to talk when they can't hear any sound?"

Happy to let the subject of her sister drop, Prudence told him about the code of symbols created by a man named Melville Bell that indicated the position of the throat, tongue, and lips in making sounds.

"The children can feel the vibration of the throat and the way the breath is exhaled to make each sound. Then they try to copy it. Mrs. Fuller is trying to see if she can get Mr. Bell to come and instruct her teachers better on how to use the charts. He has a son, a Mr. Alexander Graham Bell, who is living in Ontario, Canada. Both men are extremely interested in speech and are trying to make such a thing possible for the deaf. I admire them greatly."

He regarded her quizzically. "That's obvious. Your voice is very warm when you speak of them. Have you ever met them?"

"No, but I hope to someday."

He turned away from her. "You have a generous

heart, Prudence. And a lot of love."

Not knowing how to answer, Prudence remained silent.

After Devlin dropped her off, he reminded her that he would return at 4:00. However, when 4:00 rolled around and Devlin did not show, Prudence grew worried, for it was not like Devlin to forget her. Surely he would have sent word if he could not come.

No sooner had the thought materialized when the maid let a boy into the room where Prudence was cleaning up supplies. "This gentleman's here to see you, miss," the maid said.

Thinking he was from Devlin, Prudence smiled. "Thank you, Bridget."

The boy looked to be no more than fourteen. He quickly doffed his cap, twisting it in his hands. "Excuse me, miss. Mr. Drake done sent me to tell you that he's been delayed. He says to stay put and he'll be along to get you shortly."

First angry, then curious, Prudence asked him, "What's the delay?"

"One of Mr. Drake's warehouses be on fire, miss. Mr. Drake stayed to help."

"Thank you for telling me," she told him absently, wondering if Devlin was in any danger. Surely he would not do something so foolish as to risk his own life. Should she wait? It was not very far to walk and the daylight hours were much longer now that it was summer. Regardless of what Devlin had told her, she still felt she would be safe walking the streets in broad daylight.

As the boy turned to leave, she made a decision. "Tell Mr. Drake not to bother coming to pick me up. I'll walk." She felt a little tremor of fear run through her as she delivered this message. What would Devlin do? Surely he would not tell her father if she disobeyed him just this once.

Pressing her lips together, she gave herself a resounding lecture on allowing someone to so rule her thoughts and actions. She had things to do, and her parents would grow worried if she did not return soon. She had no idea how long Devlin would be. She waited as long as she dared then, chastising herself severely, she decided it was time to leave.

Letting herself out of the brownstone, Prudence walked quickly toward home. She was just passing an alley when she noticed movement within. Suddenly frightened, she would have hurried past, but a small sound caught her attention.

Crossing to the entrance, Prudence saw three large boys laughing at something they held on a string. A small yelp told Prudence what that small something was.

Forgetting to be afraid, Prudence marched into the alley, her hands on her hips, her hazel eyes flashing. "Just what do you think you're doing?"

Startled, the boys turned her way. They were momentarily frightened until they realized she was alone.

Suddenly, one boy grinned slyly as the other two fanned out to surround her. Prudence was filled with dread, knowing that she was helpless against the three.

"Well, would ya just look at her? Reckon the fancy

lady has any money in that purse she be carrying, Jed?"

The one named Jed grinned back at his partner in crime. "Reckon she just might."

Hearing a soft whine, Prudence turned her attention to the small pup lying helplessly, his throat choked by the cord tied round his neck. If she did not do something soon, the pup would die.

"Here," she told the apparent leader, shoving her purse at him, "take it and leave."

He grabbed the purse from her hand, dumping its contents on the ground. Quickly, he scooped up the bank notes and change that fell in the dirt. "Wow! The lady must be rich, guys."

Prudence tried to push past him to reach the dog, but he grabbed her arm roughly. "Not so fast, my lady."

Trying to twist out of his hands, Prudence begged him. "Please, let me help the dog."

The boy grinned a nasty grin. "Hey guys, we have a bleedin' heart here. Why'nt ya help us, lady, instead?"

Prudence could feel the others closing in and her dread grew. Glaring at him, Prudence demanded as firmly as she could, "Let me go!"

"Hey, Jed. She ain't half bad-lookin'."

The other boy snickered. "What you plannin' on doin', Tommy? Take her home to Mom?"

All three laughed. "That ain't such a bad idea, Jed. Maybe if we keep her for a spell someone will start to miss her. Know what I mean?"

The third boy's eyes went slowly over Prudence from head to foot. "Maybe we could have some fun in the meantime, huh?"

Prudence could feel the trembling that seized her limbs. Trying to get hold of her fast-fading courage, she jerked her arm free. "I said, let me go!"

"I'd do what the lady suggests, if I were you," a voice behind them said.

Startled, the boys turned to face the entrance to the alley and there Devlin stood, legs outstretched and fists on his hips. Though his face was in shadow, Prudence could see the gleam of his eyes.

Bravado ebbing fast, the three boys moved to different locations as they tried to figure a way out of the alley and past the man with the feral gleam in his eyes.

Jed pulled a knife from his boot and lunged forward. Devlin jumped back and to the side, grabbing the boy's coat and flinging him past him to the street beyond. Landing facedown in the dirt, the boy quickly struggled to his feet. Glaring at Devlin, he turned and quickly disappeared from sight.

Motioning with his hands, Devlin encouraged the other two to try, but both boys ran past him and followed their comrade. Devlin, still itching for a fight, turned his attention to Prudence, who was kneeling in the dirt, trying to untie the cord from the puppy's neck.

He knelt beside her, angrily shoving her hands away so that he could deal with the knot himself. He made short work of it.

Prudence lifted the pup into her arms, tears in her eyes as the poor little thing struggled for breath. "How could anyone be so cruel?"

Helping her to her feet, Devlin ushered her to the waiting carriage. The tick in his cheek warned Prudence to remain quiet, for Devlin was in a towering rage.

They had not gone far when Prudence ventured, "You won't tell Papa, will you?"

The tick intensified. "I warned you," he told her softly.

"Devlin—"

"What if I hadn't arrived when I did?" he bit out savagely. "What then?"

"But you did," she answered him quietly.

"Never again, Pru. Never will I take a chance of that happening again."

Chapter Eight

True to his word, Devlin ensconced himself with Prudence's father as soon as they arrived at her home. Prudence paced up and down as she waited for her father's verdict. She hadn't long to wait. Her father glowered at her from across his office; Devlin sat grim-faced in the chair beside the desk.

"Prudence, I have always considered myself a fair man. What have you to say about this whole thing?"

"Papa," she pleaded, throwing Devlin an angry glance and wondering just what he had told her father. "I didn't really disobey. You never told me I *couldn't* go to the deaf school."

Her father's lips twitched ever so slightly. "I was never given the opportunity, now was I?"

Sighing, Prudence dropped into the chair across from him. "I'm sure it's not as bad as Mr. Drake has made it out to be."

"Indeed. Then please explain." At her father's encouragement, Devlin gave Prudence a warning glance that she failed to heed. Launching into a description of her afternoon's account, Prudence hastened to make light of the incident. She was unaware of her father's growing anger until he interrupted her forcefully.

"Are you telling me you were attacked this afternoon?" her father asked.

Puzzled, Prudence's eyes flew to Devlin, who was staring at the ceiling.

Mr. Hilliard's anger turned on the young man. "And you knew of this and didn't tell me, Devlin?"

Devlin's eyes fixed steadily on the older man. "I didn't want to tell such things without Prudence being present to verify what I was saying."

Snorting, Mr. Hilliard turned back to his daughter. "Never again. Do you understand me?"

"But, Papa—"

"Mr. Hilliard, perhaps this could be worked out," Devlin offered.

Prudence glared angrily back at Devlin. "You stay out of this. You have caused me nothing but trouble with your overbearing, bossy ways. I hope I never see you again, and if I do, I will take great pleasure in pretending you don't exist!" So saying, she flounced out of the room.

Watching her exit, Devlin cleared his throat and turned his pale face to her father. "If I might speak to you a moment longer?" he asked.

❦

Devlin was not at church the following Sunday. Prudence squirmed in her seat as they sang a new song that was passing around the brotherhood. The song was called "Angry Words," and its words convicted her, especially the second verse.

"Love is much too pure and holy,
Friendship is too sacred far,
For a moment's reckless folly
Thus to desolate and mar."

Devlin had been a good friend to her, and she had destroyed that friendship with her own angry words. He had only been trying to protect her.

"Love one another, thus saith the Savior,
Children obey the Father's blest command."

Before the melancholy song was finished, she knew she would have to apologize—and the sooner, the better.

When Prudence arrived home, Constance informed the family that she would be out until that evening. Thinking she was meeting Devlin, no one said anything about it being the Sabbath Day. Her parents, though, gave her disapproving frowns.

Prudence hoped to see Devlin to apologize, but Constance ran out to meet the carriage when it arrived, and they drove off too quickly for Prudence to do so. Disconsolately, Prudence retired to her own room, throwing herself across her bed. If only she had had the time to apologize.

Getting up, Prudence quickly crossed to her wardrobe and pulled a small box from the bottom. This was her keepsake box, and it held the few mementos she held most dear. Pushing aside the other items in the box, she pulled out the valentine she had received almost four months ago. It still gave her heart a little thrill when she read the verse: *Her eyes like stars.* What a beautiful, romantic thought.

Frowning, she searched her mind for an elusive memory. Eyes widening, she remembered something Devlin had said to her. He had once told her that her eyes shone like starlight.

He had laughed, and so had she, for it was shortly after he had started to court Constance that he had said it, and in such a way that Prudence had felt he was complimenting a child.

Could the card have come from Devlin, and if so, why? There were times she had noticed him pensively watching her, and her heart had thundered in response, but other than those two unforgettable times, he had never kissed her, had never shown her even the slightest romantic interest. He had treated her gently and protectively, true, but she had attributed that to his own gallant nature.

Of course it was not proper to do so but, nevertheless, Prudence had yearned for him to kiss her. She stopped in wonder. Yes, she had wanted Devlin to take her in his arms and kiss her even when she thought he had belonged to her sister. Shocked, she realized she was in love with Devlin!

Sighing, she dropped to the chair at her dressing table. If only he could return her love. But what about Constance? If only Constance could love someone else and Devlin could love her. She snorted. And if only pigs could fly.

❧

When everyone gathered for supper that evening, Constance was still missing and Mr. Hilliard was growing angry at the delay of his meal.

"Let's eat," he told them. "I'll deal with that young woman when she finds her way home."

But two hours later, she still was not home and anger turned to worry. Mr. Hilliard had left the house some time earlier for a business appointment and had as yet not returned. Prudence paced the parlor until finally her mother suggested she might like to go to her own room. Prudence knew her own agitation was not helping her mother, so she agreed.

At 8:00, Prudence was about to suggest sending word to their father when Jessica entered her room, a sheet of paper clutched in her hands. Her face was as white as the paper.

"Here, read this," she told Prudence, thrusting the paper into her hands. "I found it in Constance's bedroom on her dressing table. It's addressed to you."

The color drained from Prudence's face as she read the note. "It can't be! Whatever would make her do such a thing?" Prudence dropped to her bed, her jelly-like legs refusing to hold her. "Why would she run away to get married? Father likes Devlin."

"What do we do?" Jessica wanted to know.

Prudence thought a moment before rising to her feet. Lines of determination settled across her face. "I'm going to try to stop them. Have Sims bring the carriage around. It's time I made a call on Mr. Devlin Drake."

Devlin stared into the fire, thinking about Prudence. He had never seen her so angry, but then he had never been so angry himself. Not since the war had he felt such a desire to kill someone. He was not sure what would have happened had the three boys who accosted Prudence not fled.

He had been able to explain the situation to her father, but it had taken a lot of persuasion to convince the older man to allow Prudence to continue her work at the school for the deaf.

Deciding to give Prudence time to herself, he had refrained from going to church, though the desire to be with her had been strong.

He finally admitted it to himself: He was in love with Prudence Hilliard. How had it happened? When had it happened? He supposed he should not be surprised. Hadn't he bristled whenever anyone had slighted her? Even his own cousin, Terence, had almost felt his wrath.

She was so beautiful. He was astounded that others could not see it for themselves. In her presence, the sun seemed a little brighter, the air a little sweeter.

He smiled wryly to himself. Boy, he had it bad.

When his doorbell rang at half past eight, he frowned, wondering who would be calling at this late hour. He opened the door and stared in astonishment at the object of his imagination, as though his own mind had conjured her up.

"Prudence! What are you doing here?" He glanced

past her shoulder to see if her father was with her. He scowled at her. "Are you alone?"

"I have to talk to you."

Eyebrows rising, he stepped back to let her pass. She turned to face him, the lights from the hall shining softly on her brown curls.

"Since you are still here, and it is almost time to retire for the night," she blushed, but went on determinedly, "I assume Constance is not with you."

Closing the door, he frowned at her. "Constance? What are you talking about?"

Prudence handed him her sister's note. "Jessica found this in Constance's room. She is missing."

Devlin read the note, his face going blank. "It's not me she's referring to," he told her absently. He looked down at her. "Wait here while I change my clothes and we'll go see Gaylord Fyfe."

"Gaylord knows nothing about it," she told him.

One eyebrow flew upward. "How do you know?"

"I've just come from there. I thought perhaps he was performing the ceremony, but he hasn't seen Constance since church this morning."

Brushing a hand across his face, Devlin tried to think of what to do. Suddenly, he went very still.

"What is it?" Prudence demanded. "What do you know?"

"Wait here," he told her, disappearing upstairs. He was back in a moment, a sheet of paper gripped tightly in his hand. Silently, he handed it to Prudence.

She took the paper and read it. For a minute, she

thought she was going to faint. "It can't be!"

Devlin grabbed her as she swayed, helping her to a chair in his den. He seated her near the fire, rubbing her hands briskly. Her face was whiter than he had ever seen it.

Prudence shook her head. "I just can't believe it! Terence and Constance!"

"Prudence, I'll take you home. Then I'll see if I can find them before—"

He did not finish but quickly left the room only to return moments later ready to leave. He helped Prudence into her own carriage, climbing in beside her and instructing the driver to return home. Devlin held her close, trying to soothe her trembling, and Prudence allowed herself to relax slightly. Whatever happened, Devlin was still here. Selfishly, she was glad.

When they reached the house, they found it in total confusion. Prudence's father had returned home only to find two of his daughters missing. He had been on the verge of searching for them himself when Prudence walked in the door. He angrily berated Prudence until she showed him Constance's letter.

Sinking to the settee, he buried his head in his hands. "I can't believe it. Why would she do such a thing?" Prudence, watching Jessica, had a pretty good idea.

Devlin handed him Terence's letter. "I think this will explain."

Prudence watched with sympathy as the message was read and Jessica's face went pale. Without a word, she flew from the room. Only Prudence had any idea how much Jessica had been affected. For the first time in her life, she had given her heart to a man, and he had rejected her.

"Shall I try to find them?" Devlin asked Mr. Hilliard.

He shook his head sadly. "No. She has been gone since early this morning. If they had this planned all along, they are probably halfway to England by now."

Mr. Hilliard helped his distraught wife to her feet and took her along to their bedroom.

Devlin watched them leave before he turned to Prudence. "I'm sorry," he said.

She shook her head but did not look at him. "You couldn't have known."

"True, but that's not what I'm apologizing for. I'm sorry for the other day when, in a moment of anger, I betrayed your trust."

She smiled at him, her eyes reflecting the amber light of the fire, making them seem more brown than green. "I am the one who should apologize."

He came to her then, placing his hands on her shoulders. "Prudence, I have something I need to tell you. Perhaps now is not a good time, but I can't wait any longer. I love you—" He was interrupted by a shrill laugh behind them. Dropping his hands, he quickly faced the open doorway.

Jessica stood there glowering at him, her angry eyes still shining with tears. "So now that your cousin has taken Constance away from you, you've decided to turn your attention to Prudence."

Flinching, Prudence moved away from his side. Devlin's face hardened. "I understand your feelings, Jessica, but don't try to make me the ogre. What happened had nothing to do with myself or Prudence."

"No?" She went to Prudence. "Can't you see how he's trying to use you? I told you men weren't to be trusted."

Prudence shook her head sadly. "No, Jess. You can't blame Devlin for what's happened. Even if Devlin had been jilted, do you think a man as handsome and wealthy as he is would need to console himself with someone like me?"

Angry at Prudence's disparagement of herself, Devlin turned to Jessica. "Jessica, why don't you ask yourself why Terence turned from you when he was so obviously smitten with you in the beginning? What could have turned him away? Maybe it had something to do with the fact that you constantly criticized him for being the man that he is."

"Devlin!" Prudence admonished.

"No, Pru. Jessica needs to see how her own actions have affected the result of this strange proceeding. Terence wanted a woman who could love him for what he is, as Constance obviously does. Not a woman who wanted him to be less than the man that he is."

Jessica glared angrily at him. "I think I hate you," she hissed between her teeth. She glared from one to the other before leaving them, tears streaming down her cheeks.

"Oh, Devlin. How could you? Can't you see she's hurting enough already?"

He smiled at her without humor. "Like the South."

Confused, she looked at him strangely. "What?"

He came to her then, folding her into his arms and tucking her head beneath his chin. She hesitated only a moment before relaxing against him and wrapping her own arms around his waist. "Do you remember how you said God didn't create the evil?" he asked.

He could feel her nod her head. "Well, Jessica helped me realize exactly what you were trying to say. She chose the path she wished to tread and she has to pay the consequences. No one but herself and her selfishness caused her pain. We all make our own decisions, foolish or not."

Placing his palms against her cheeks, he forced her to look at him. "Just like I decided long ago that I wanted a woman who was more than beautiful. I wanted a woman who loved God and lost little boys, who helped deaf children, and who took in stray puppies." His eyes darkened perceptibly. "My darling, could you, would you, take in another stray?"

She could only stare up at him in happiness, her eyes sparkling with her joy. "I knew in my heart it was you."

He raised an eyebrow in question.

"The valentine. It was you, wasn't it?" she asked.

For answer, he pulled her closer and kissed her with all the warmth he had longed to show her for some time now.

Prudence clung to him, returning his kisses with increasing ardor.

When Devlin pulled away, there was a fire in his eyes. "Your eyes are like stars, and they are only for me."

Prudence sighed as she gave her lips up to his kiss. It had been less than a year. The Italians were right, after all.

Darlene Mindrup
Darlene is a full-time homemaker and home-school teacher. A "radical feminist" turned "radical Christian," she lives in Arizona with her husband and two children. Darlene has also written several novels for Barbour Publishing's **Heartsong Presents** line, including *The Eagle and the Lamb, Edge of Destiny, The Rising Sun,* and *A Light Within.* She believes "romance is for everyone, not just the young and beautiful."

If you enjoyed *Spring's Memory,*
then read:

❦

Spring's Promise

A romantic collection of four
inspirational novellas including:

E-Love
Gloria Brandt

The Garden Plot
Rebecca Germany

Stormy Weather
Tracie Peterson

Bride To Be
Debra White Smith